BEYOND THIRTY
and
THE MAN-EATER

by Edgar Rice Burroughs

First Fiction House Edition June 2022

isbn 978-1-64720-586-7 (hardcover)
978-1-64720-585-0 (softcover)

Fiction House Press
www.FictionHousePress.com

BEYOND THIRTY
and
THE MAN-EATER

BEYOND THIRTY
and
THE MAN-EATER

by Edgar Rice Burroughs

SCIENCE-FICTION & FANTASY PUBLICATIONS

South Ozone Park 20, New York

1957

FIRST EDITION
Limited to 3,000 copies

CONTENTS

BEYOND THIRTY

EDGAR RICE BURROUGHS

A BIT OF HIS LIFE

Edgar Rice Burroughs was born in Chicago on September 1, 1875. His parents were fairly well to do and sent him to several private schools. The Harvard School in Chicago, Phillips-Exeter Academy in Andover, Massachusetts, and Michigan Military Academy at Orchard Lake, Michigan, helped to further his education and a liberal viewpoint shown in later life. He had a brief term of service in the U. S. Cavalry and was discharged as under age.

Burroughs married Emma Centennia Hulbert in 1900. Three children were the result of this marriage, John Coleman, Hulbert, and a daughter, Joan. The needs of this growing family prompted him to try several business ventures, mostly in Chicago, between the years 1900 and 1913, and failure ended all of them. Between ventures, he worked as a salesman and clerk; cowboy and storekeeper in Idaho; railroad policeman in Salt Lake City; gold miner in Oregon. One source stated that this last job was as a worker on a gold-dredge. For a while, he is said to have had an executive position with Sears-Roebuck.

By the time he was thirty-five, Burroughs was as complete a failure as you might find anywhere. As an outlet for this feeling of futility, he used to day-dream of fantastic adventures. While working for a patent medicine firm, he read the stories in some of the magazines that he brought home for checking advertisements. Most of them must have been pretty poor, and he decided that if publishers would pay for this material, he would try to put his dreams on paper.

All-Story Magazine published "Under the Moons of Mars" as a serial in the February to July, 1912 issues. The pseudonym he chose, Normal Bean, to show he was a down to earth person, was changed by either the publisher or printer to Norman Bean. Burroughs was piqued that his pun was spoiled and had no hesitation in using his own name for the next published story, the now world famous, "Tarzan of the Apes." Both were enthusiastically received by the readers and encouraged the production of further adventures on Mars and in the jungle.

A. C. McClurg of Chicago published his first book in 1914, "Tarzan of the Apes." "The Return of Tarzan" and "The Beasts of Tarzan" appeared in the two succeeding years. The first All-Story triumph, "Under the Moons of Mars" was also published, with a new title, "A Princess of Mars" in 1917. Until 1941, one or two of his books came out in each year.

Burroughs incorporated himself in 1923, and eight years later, in 1931, formed his own publishing company at Tarzana, California. This, of course, was named after his most famous character.

Burroughs was divorced in 1934 and remarried the following year to Florence Gilbert, or Dearholt. His second wife apparently had been married before and Gilbert seems to have been her maiden name. This marriage also ended in divorce in 1941.

A research library covered all of one wall in his Tarzana office, but Burroughs preferred an active outdoor life between writing each novel. He was in Hawaii in 1941 and witnessed the bombing of Pearl Harbor. Although sixty-six years old at the time, he managed to be accredited as a war correspondent to the Los Angeles Times and spent four years in Honolulu and the South Pacific during World War II. He was one of the oldest correspondents in the Pacific Theathre, if not the oldest.

Although he had a rugged constitution for his years, there is no doubt that this strenuous new life contributed to his final illness. He was invalided home and spent his final quiet years at Tarzana. He died on March 19, 1950, at the age of 74 years. A full and rewarding life.

Edgar Rice Burroughs was never known to entertain any delusions about the literary quality of his work since he maintained he wrote for money. On one occasion he remarked, "My writing helped me escape being broke and it helps the readers go off into another realm and share adventures they'd never have themselves." However, he seemed proud that in several cases his writing had been selected as outstanding examples of good literature. Over 35,000,000 copies of his books, in 56 languages, have been produced, so there seems a fair chance that his name will be remembered.

A report states that he left fifteen unpublished novels, but in a letter to me in 1949, Burroughs wrote, "I did start another TARZAN story after I returned from overseas; but I have never completed it, and the chances are that I never shall." These words were most prophetic for he passed away the following March after a series of heart attacks.

Bradford M. Day

CHAPTER I

Since earliest childhood I have been strangely fascinated by the mystery surrounding the history of the last days of twentieth century Europe. My interest is keenest, perhaps, not so much in relation to known facts as to speculation upon the unknowable of the two centuries that have rolled by since human intercourse between the Western and Eastern Hemispheres ceased -- the mystery of Europe's state following the termination of the Great War -- provided, of course, that the war had been terminated.

From out the meagerness of our censored histories we learned that for fifteen years after the cessation of diplomatic relations between the United States of North America and the belligerent nations of the Old World, news of more or less doubtful authenticity filtered, from time to time, into the Western Hemisphere from the Eastern.

Then came the fruition of that historic propaganda which is best described by its own slogan: "The East for the East -- the West for the West," and all further intercourse was stopped by statute.

Even prior to this, transoceanic commerce had practically ceased, owing to the perils and hazards of the mine-strewn waters of both the Atlantic and Pacific Oceans. Just when submarine activities ended we do not know; but the last vessel of this type sighted by a Pan-American merchantman was the huge Q 138, which discharged twenty-nine torpedoes at a Brazilian tank steamer off the Bermudas in the fall of

1922. A heavy sea and the excellent seamanship of the master of the Brazilian permitted the Pan-American to escape and report this last of a long series of outrages upon our commerce. God alone knows how many hundreds of our ancient ships fell prey to the roving steel sharks of blood-frenzied Europe. Countless were the vessels and men that passed over our eastern and western horizons never to return; but whether they met their fates before the belching tubes of submarines or among the aimlessly drifting mine fields, no man lived to tell.

And then came the great Pan-American Federation which linked the Western Hemisphere from pole to pole under a single flag, which joined the navies of the New World into the mightiest fighting force that ever sailed the seven seas -- the greatest argument for peace the world had ever known.

Since that day peace had reigned from the western shores of the Azores to the western shores of the Hawaiian Islands, nor has any man of either hemisphere dared cross 30W. or 175W. From 30 to 175 is ours -- from 30 to 175 is peace, prosperity and happiness.

Beyond was the great unknown. Even the geographies of of my boyhood showed nothing beyond. We were taught of nothing beyond. Speculation was discouraged. For two hundred years the Eastern Hemisphere had been wiped from the maps and histories of Pan-America. Its mention in fiction, even, was forbidden.

Our ships of peace patrol 30 and 175. What ships from beyond they have warned only the secret archives of government show; but, a naval officer myself, I have gathered from the traditions of the service that it has been fully two hundred years since smoke or sail has been sighted east of 30 or west of 175. The fate of the relinquished provinces which lay beyond the dead lines we couldonly speculate upon. That the military power which rose so suddenly in China after the fall of the republic, and which wrested Manchuria and Korea from Russia and Japan, and also absorbed the Phillippines is quite within the range of possibility.

It was the commander of a Chinese man-of-war who received a copy of the edict of 1921 from the hand of my illustrious ancestor, Admiral Turck, on 175, two hundred and six years ago, and from the yellowed pages of the admiral's diary I learned that the fate of the Phillippines were even then presaged by these Chinese naval officers.

Yes, for over two hundred years no man crossed 30 to 175 and lived to tell his story -- not until chance drew me across and back again, and public opinion, revolting at last against the drastic regulations of our long-dead forbears, demanded that my story be given to the world, and that the narrow interdict which commanded peace, prosperity, and happiness to halt at 30 and 175 be removed forever.

I am glad that it was given to me to be an instrument in the hands of Providence for the uplifting of benighted Europe, and the amelioration of the suffering, degradation, and abysmal ignorance in which I found her.

I shall not live to see the complete regeneration of the savage hordes of the Eastern Hemisphere -- that is a work which will require many generations, perhaps ages, so complete has been their reversion to savagery; but I know that the work has been started, and I am proud of the share in it which my generous countrymen have placed in my hands.

The government already possesses a complete official report of my adventures beyond 30. In the narrative I purpose telling my story in a less formal, and I hope, a more entertaining, style; though, being only a naval officer and without claim to the slightest literary ability, I shall most certainly fall far short of the possibilities which are inherent in my subject. That I have passed through the most wondrous adventures that have befallen a civilized man during the past two centuries encourages me in the belief that, however ill the telling, the facts themselves will command your interest to the final page.

Beyond thirty! Romance, adventure, strange peoples, fearsome beasts -- all the excitement and scurry of the lives of the twentieth century ancients that have been denied us in these dull days of peace and prosaic prosperity -- all, all lay beyond thirty, the invisible barrier between the stupid, commercial present and the carefree, barbarous past.

What boy has not sighed for the good old days of wars, revolutions, and riots: how I used to pore over the chronicles of those old days, those dear old days, when workmen went armed to their labors; when they fell upon one another with gun and bomb and dagger, and the streets ran red with blood! Ah, but those were the times when life was worth the living: when a man who went out by night knew not at which dark corner a "footpad" might leap upon and slay him; when wild beasts roamed the forest and the jungles, and there were savage men, and countries yet unexplored.

Now, in all the Western Hemisphere dwells no man who may not find a school house within walking distance of his home, or at least within flying distance. The wildest beast that roams our waste places lairs in the frozen north or the frozen south within a government reserve, where the curious may view him and feed him bread crusts from the hand with perfect impunity.

But beyond thirty! And I have gone there, and come back; and now you may go there, for no longer is it high treason, punishable by disgrace or death, to cross 30 or 175.

My name is Jefferson Turck. I am a lieutenant in the navy -- in the great Pan-American navy, the only navy which now exists in all the world.

I was born in Arizona, in the United States of North America, in the year of our Lord 2116. Therefore, I am twenty-one years old.

In early boyhood I tired of the teeming cities and overcrowded rural districts of Arizona. Every generation of Turcks for over two centuries has been represented in the navy. The navy called to me, as did the free, wide, unpeopled spaces of the mighty oceans. And so I joined the navy, coming up from the ranks, as we all must, learning our craft as we advance. My promotion was rapid, for my family seems to inherit naval lore. We are born officers, and I reserve to myself no special credit for an early advancement in the service.

At twenty I found myself a lieutenant in command of the

aero-submarine COLDWATER, of the SS-96 class. The COLDWATER was one of the first of the air and under-water craft which have been so greatly improved since its launching, and was possessed of innumerable weaknesses which, fortunately, have been eliminated in more recent vessels of similar type.

Even when I took command, she was fit only for the junk pile; but the world-old parsimony of government retained her in active service, and sent two hundred men to sea in her, with myself, a mere boy, in command of her, to patrol 30 from Iceland to the Azores.

Much of my service had been spent aboard the great merchantmen-of-war. These are the utility naval vessels that have transformed the navies of old, which burdened the peoples with taxes for their support, into the present day fleets of self-supporting ships that find ample time for target practice and gun drill while they bear freight and the mails from the continents to the far-scattered island of Pan-America.

This change in service was most welcome to me, especially as it brought with it coveted responsibilities of sole command, and I was prone to overlook the deficiencies of the COLDWATER in the natural pride I felt in my first ship.

The COLDWATER was fully equipped for two months patrolling -- the ordinary length of assignment to this service -- and a month had already passed, its monotony entirely unrelieved by sight of another craft, when the first of our misfortunes befell.

We had been riding out a storm at an altitude of about three thousand feet. All night we had hovered above the tossing billows of the moonlit clouds. The detonation of the thunder and the glare of lightning through an occasional rift in the vaporous wall proclaimed the continued fury of the tempest upon the surface of the sea; but we, far above it all, rode in comparative ease upon the upper gale. With the coming of dawn the clouds beneath us became a glorious sea of gold and silver, soft and beautiful; but they could not deceive us as to the blackness and the terrors of the storm-lashed ocean which they hid.

I was at breakfast when my chief engineer entered and saluted. His face was grave, and I thought he was even a trifle paler than usual.

"Well?" I asked.

He drew the back of his forefinger nervously across his brow in a gesture that was habitual with him in moments of mental stress.

"The gravitation–screen generators, sir," he said. "Number one went to the bad about an hour and a half ago. We have been working upon it steadily since; but I have to report, sir, that it is beyond repair."

"Number two will keep us supplied," I answered. "In the meantime we will send a wireless for relief."

"But that is the trouble, sir," he went on. "Number two has stopped. I knew it would come, sir. I made a report on these generators three years ago. I advised then that they both be scrapped. Their principle is entirely wrong. They're done for;" and, with a grim smile, "I shall at least have the satisfaction of knowing my report was accurate."

"Have we sufficient reserve screen to permit us to make land, or, at least, meet our relief halfway?" I asked.

"No, sir," he replied gravely; "we are sinking now."

"Have you anything further to report?" I asked.

"No, sir," he said.

"Very good," I replied; and, as I dismissed him, I rang for my wireless operator. When he appeared, I gave him a message to the secretary of the navy, to whom all vessels in service on 30 and 175 report direct. I explained our predicament, and stated that with what screening force remained I should continue in the air, making as rapid headway toward St. Johns as possible, and that when we were forced to take to the water I should continue in the same direction.

The accident occurred directly over 30 and about 52 N. The surface wind was blowing a tempest from the west. To attempt to ride out such a storm upon the surface seemed suicidal, for the COLDWATER was not designed for surface navigation except under fair weather conditions. Submerged, or in the air, she was tractable enough in any sort of weather when under control; but without her screen generators she was almost helpless, since she could not fly, and, if submerged, could not rise to the surface.

All these defects have been remedied in later models; but the knowledge did not help us any that day aboard the slowly settling COLDWATER, with an angry sea roaring beneath, a tempest raging out of the west, and 30 only a few knots astern.

To cross 30 or 175 has been, as you know, the direst calamity that could befall a naval commander. Court-martial and degradation follow swiftly, unless as is often the case, the unfortunate man takes his own life before this unjust and heartless regulation can hold him up to public scorn.

There has been in the past no excuse, no circumstance, that could palliate the offense.

"He was in command, and he took his ship across 30!" That was sufficient. It might not have been in any way his fault, as, in the case of the COLDWATER, it could not possibly have been justly charged to my account that the gravitation-screen generators were worthless; but well I knew that should chance have it that we were blown across 30 today -- as we might easily be before the terrific west wind that we could hear howling below us, the responsibility would fall upon my shoulders.

In a way, the regulation was a good one, for it certainly accomplished that for which it was intended. We all fought shy of 30 on the east and 175 on the west, and, though we had to skirt them pretty close, nothing but an act of God ever drew one of us across. You all are familiar with the naval tradition that a good officer could sense proximity to either line, and for my part, I am firmly convinced of the truth of this as I am that the compass finds the north without recourse to tedious processes of reasoning.

Old Admiral Sanchez was wont to maintain that he could smell 30, and the men of the first ship in which I sailed claimed that Coburn, the navigating officer, knew by name every wave along 30 from 60 N. to 60 S. However, I'd hate to vouch for this.

Well, to get back to my narrative; we kept on dropping slowly toward the surface the while we bucked the west wind, clawing away from 30 as fast as we could. I was on the bridge, and as we dropped from the brilliant sunlight into the dense vapor of clouds and on down through them to the wild, dark storm strata beneath, it seemed that my spirits dropped with the falling ship, and the buoyancy of hope ran low in sympathy.

The waves were running to tremendous heights, and the COLDWATER was not designed to meet such waves head on. Her elements were the blue ether, far above the raging storm, or the greater depths of ocean, which no storm could ruffle.

As I stood speculating upon our chances once we settled into the frightful Maelstrom beneath us and at the same time mentally computing the hours which must elapse before aid could reach us, the wireless operator clambered up the ladder to the bridge, and, disheveled and breathless, stood before me at salute. It needed by a glance at him to assure me that something was amiss.

"What now?" I asked.

"The wireless, sir!" he cried. "My God, sir, I cannot send."

"But the emergency outfit?" I asked.

"I have tried everything, sir. I have exhausted every resource. We cannot send," and he drew himself up and saluted again.

I dismissed him with a few kind words, for I knew that it was through no fault of his that the mechanism was antiquated and worthless, in common with the balance of the COLDWATER'S equipment. There was no finer operator in Pan-America than he.

The failure of the wireless did not appear as momentous to me as to him, which is not unnatural, since it is but human to feel that when our own little cog slips the entire universe must necessarily be put out of gear. I knew that if this storm was destined to blow us across 30, or send us to the bottom of the ocean, no help could reach us in time to prevent. I had ordered the message sent solely because regulations required it, and not with any particular hope that we could benefit by it in our present extremity.

I had little time to dwell upon the coincidence of the simultaneous failure of the wireless and the buoyancy generators, since very shortly after the COLDWATER had dropped so low over the waters that all my attention was necessarily centered upon the delicate business of settling upon the waves without breaking my ship's back. With our buoyancy generators in commission it would have been a simple thing to enter the water, since then it would have been but a trifling matter of a forty-five degree dive into the base of a huge wave. We should have cut into the water like a hot knife through butter, and been totally submerged with scarce a jar -- I have done it a thousand times -- but I did not dare submerge the COLDWATER for fear that it would remain submerged to the end of time -- a condition far from conductive to the longevity of commander or crew.

Most of my officers were older men than I. John Alvarez, my first officer, is twenty years my senior. He stood at my side on the bridge as the ship glided closer and closer to those stupendous waves. He watched my every move, but he was by far too fine an officer and gentleman to embarrass me by either comment or suggestion.

When I saw that we soon would touch, I ordered the ship brought around broadside to the wind, and there we hovered a moment until a huge wave reached up and seized us upon its crest, and then I gave the order that suddenly reversed the screening force, and let us into the ocean. Down into the trough we went, wallowing like the carcass of a dead whale, and then began the fight, with rudder and propellers, to force the COLDWATER back into the teeth of the gale and drive her on and on, farther and farther from relentless 30.

I think that we should have succeeded, even though the ship was wracked from stem to stern by the terrific buffetings she received, and though she were half submerged the greater part of the time, had no further accident befallen us.

We were making headway, though slowly, and it began to

look as though we were going to pull through. Alvarez never left my side, though I all but ordered him below for much-needed rest. My second officer, Porfirio Johnson, was also often on the bridge. He was a good officer, but a man for whom I had conceived a rather unreasoning aversion almost at the first moment of meeting him, an aversion which was not lessened by the knowledge which I subsequently gained that he looked upon my rapid promotion with jealousy. He was ten years my senior both in years and service, and I rather think he could never forget the fact that he had been an officer when I was a green apprentice.

As it became more and more apparent that the COLDWATER, under my seamanship, was weathering the tempest and giving promise of pulling through safely, I could have sworn that I perceived a shade of annoyance and disappointment growing upon his dark countenance. He left the bridge finally and went below. I do not know that he is directly responsible for what followed so shortly after; but I have always had my suspicions, and Alvarez is even more prone to place the blame upon him than I.

It was about six bells of the forenoon watch that Johnson returned to the bridge after an absence of some thirty minutes. He seemed nervous and ill at ease -- a fact which made little impression on me at the time, but which both Alvarez and I recalled subsequently.

Not three minutes after his reappearance at my side the COLDWATER suddenly commenced to lose headway. I seized the telephone at my elbow, pressing upon the button which would call the chief engineer to the instrument in the bowels of the ship, only to find him already at the receiver attempting to reach me.

"Numbers one, two, and five engines have broken down, sir," he called. "Shall we force the remaining three?"

"We can do nothing else," I bellowed into the transmitter.

"They won't stand the gaff, sir," he returned.

"Can you suggest a better plan?" I asked.

"No, sir," he replied.

"Then give them the gaff, lieutenant," I shouted back,

and hung up the receiver.

For twenty minutes the COLDWATER bucked the great seas with her three engines. I doubt if she advanced a foot; but it was enough to keep her nose in the wind, and, at least, we were not drifting toward 30.

Johnson and Alvarez were at my side when, without warning, the bow swung swiftly around and the ship fell into the trough of the sea.

"The other three have gone," I said, and I happened to be looking at Johnson as I spoke. Was it the shadow of a satisfied smile that crossed his thin lips? I do not know; but at least he did not weep.

"You always have been curious, sir, about the great unknown beyond 30," he said. "You are in a good way to have your curiosity satisfied." And then I could not mistake the slight sneer that curved his upper lip. There must have been a trace of disrespect in his tone or manner which escaped me, for Alvarez turned upon him like a flash.

"When Lieutenant Turck crosses 30," he said, "we shall all cross with him, and God help the officer or the man who reproaches him!"

"I shall not be a party to high treason," snapped Johnson. "The regulations are explicit, and if the COLDWATER crosses 30 it devolves upon you to place Lieutenant Turck under arrest and immediately exert every endeavor to bring the ship back into Pan-American waters."

"I shall not know," replied Alvarez, "that the COLDWATER passes 30; nor shall any other man aboard know it," and, with his words, he drew a revolver from his pocket, and before either I or Johnson could prevent it had put a bullet into every instrument upon the bridge, ruining them beyond repair.

And then he saluted me, and strode from the bridge, a martyr to loyalty and friendship, for, though no man might know that Lieutenant Jefferson Turck had taken his ship across 30, every man aboard would know that the first officer had committed a crime that was punishable by both degradation and death. Johnson turned and eyed me narrowly.

"Shall I place him under arrest?" he asked.

"You shall not," I replied. "Nor shall anyone else."

"You become a party to his crime!" he cried angrily.

"You may go below, Mr. Johnson," I said, "and attend to the work of unpacking the extra instruments and having them properly set upon the bridge."

He saluted, and left me, and for some time I stood, gazing out upon the angry waters, my mind filled with unhappy reflections upon the unjust fate that had overtaken me, and the sorrow and disgrace that I had unwittingly brought down upon my house.

I rejoiced that I should leave neither wife nor child to bear the burden of my shame throughout their lives.

As I thought upon my misfortune, I considered more clearly than ever before the unrighteousness of the regulation which was to prove my doom, and in the natural revolt against its injustice my anger rose, and there mounted within me a feeling which I imagine must have paralleled that spirit that once was prevalent among the ancients called anarchy.

For the first time in my life I found my sentiments arraying themselves against custom, tradition, and even government. The wave of rebellion swept over me in an instant, beginning with an heretical doubt as to the sanctity of the established order of things -- that fetish which has ruled Pan-Americans for two centuries, and which is based upon a blind faith in the infallibility of the prescience of the long-dead framers of the articles of Pan-American federation -- and ending in an adamantine determination to defend my honor and my life to the last ditch against the blind and senseless regulation which assumed the synonymity of misfortune and treason.

I would replace the destroyed instruments upon the bridge; every officer and man should know when we crossed 30. But then I should assert the spirit which dominated me, I should resist arrest, and insist upon bringing my ship back across the dead line, remaining at my post until we had reached New York. Then I should make a full report, and with it a demand upon public opinion that the dead lines be wiped forever from the seas.

I knew that I was right -- I knew that no more loyal officer wore the uniform of the navy -- I knew that I was a good officer and sailor, and I didn't propose submitting to degradation and discharge because a lot of old, preglacial fossils had declared over two hundred years before that no man should cross 30.

Even while these thoughts were passing through my mind I was busy with the details of my duties. I had seen to it that a sea anchor was rigged, and even now the men had completed their task, and the COLDWATER was swinging around rapidly, her nose pointing once more into the wind, and the frightful rolling consequent upon her wallowing in the trough was happily diminishing.

It was then that Johnson came hurrying to the bridge. One of his eyes was swollen and already darkening, and his lip was cut and bleeding. Without even the formality of a slaute, he burst upon me, white with fury.

"Lieutenant Alvarez attacked me!" he cried. "I demand that he be placed under arrest. I found him in the act of destroying the reserve instruments, and when I would have interfered to protect them he fell upon me and beat me. I demand that you arrest him!"

"You forget yourself, Mr. Johnson," I said. "You are not in command of the ship. I deplore the action of Lieutenant Alvarez, but I cannot expunge from my mind the loyalty and self-sacrificing friendship which has prompted him to his acts. Were I you, sir, I should profit by the example he has set. Further, Mr. Johnson, I intend retaining command of the ship, even though she crosses 30, and I shall demand implicit obedience from every officer and man aboard until I am properly relieved from duty by a superior officer in the port of New York."

"You mean to say that you will cross 30 without submitting to arrest?" he almost shouted.

"I do, sir," I replied: "and now you may go below, and when again you find it necessary to address me, you will please be so good as to bear in mind the fact that I am your commanding officer, and as such entitled to a salute."

He flushed, hesitated a moment, and then, saluting, turned upon his heel and left the bridge. Shortly after, Alvarez appeared. He was pale, and seemed to have aged ten years in the few brief minutes since I last had seen him. Saluting, he told me very simply what he had done, and asked that I place him under arrest.

I put my hand on his shoulder, and I guess that my voice trembled a trifle as, while reproving him for his act, I made it plain to him that my gratitude was no less potent a force than his loyalty to me. Then it was that I outlined to him my purpose to defy the regulation that had raised the dead lines, and to take my ship back to New York myself.

I did not ask him to share the responsibility with me. I merely stated that I should refuse to submit to arrest, and that I should demand of him and every other officer and man implicit obedience to my every command until we docked at home.

His face brightened at my words, and he assured me that I would find him as ready to acknowledge my command upon the wrong side of 30 as upon the right, an assurance which I hastened to tell him I did not need.

The storm continued to rage for three days, and as far as the wind scarce varied a point during all that time, I knew that we must be far beyond 30, drifting rapidly east by south. All this time it had been impossible to work upon the damaged engines or the gravity-screen generators; but we had a full set of instruments upon the bridge, for Alvarez, after discovering my intentions, had fetched the reserve instruments from his own cabin, where he had hidden them. Those which Johnson had seen him destroy had been a third set which only Alvarez had known were aboard the COLDWATER.

We waited impatiently for the sun, that we might determine our exact location, and upon the fourth day our vigil was rewarded a few minutes before noon.

Every officer and man aboard was tense with nervous excitement as we awaited the result of the reading. The crew had known almost as soon as I that we were doomed to cross

30, and I am inclined to believe that every man jack of them was tickled to death, for the spirits of adventure and romance still live in the hearts of men of the twenty-second century, even though there be little for them to feed upon between 30 and 175.

The men carried none of the burdens of responsibility -- they might cross 30 with impunity, and doubtless they would return to be heroes at home; but how different the home-coming of their commanding officer!

The wind had dropped to a steady blow, still from west by north, and the sea had gone down correspondingly. The crew, with the exception of those whose duties kept them below, were ranged on deck below the bridge. When our position was definitely fixed I personally announced it to the eager, waiting men.

"Men," I said, stepping forward to the handrail and looking down into their upturned, bronzed faces, "you are anxiously awaiting information as to the ship's position. It has been determined at latitude fifty degrees seven minutes north, longitude twenty degrees sixteen minutes west."

I paused and a buzz of animated comment ran through the massed men beneath me. "Beyond 30: but there will be no change in commanding officers, in routine or in discipline, until after we have docked again in New York."

As I ceased speaking and stepped back from the rail there was a roar of applause from the deck such as I never before had heard aboard a ship of peace. It recalled to my mind tales that I had read of the good old days when naval vessels were built to fight, when ships of peace had been man-of-war, and guns had flashed in other than futile target practice, and decks had run red with blood.

With the subsidence of the sea, we were able to go to work upon the damaged engines to some effect, and I also set men to examining the gravitation-screen generators with a view to putting them in working order should it prove not beyond our resources.

For two weeks we labored at the engines, which indisputably showed evidence of having been tampered with. I appointed a board to investigate and report upon the disaster; but it accomplished nothing other than to convince me that there were several officers upon it who were in full sympathy with Johnson, for, though no charges had been preferred against him, the board went out of its way specifically to exonerate him in its findings.

All this time we were drifting almost due east. The work upon the engines had progressed to such an extent that within a few hours we might expect to be able to proceed under our own power to the westward in the direction of Pan-American waters.

To relieve the monotony I had taken to fishing, and early that morning I had departed from the COLDWATER in one of the boats on such an excursion. A gentle west wind was blowing. The sea shimmered in the sunlight. A cloudless sky canopied us. With only a small compass to guide us, we bore toward the west for our sport, as I had made it a point never voluntarily to make an inch toward the east that I could avoid -- at least, they should not be able to charge me with a wilful violation of the dead lines regulation.

I had with me only the boat's ordinary complement of men -- three in all, and more than enough to handle any small power boat. I had not asked any of my officers to accompany me, as I wished to be alone, and very glad am I now that I had not. My only regret is that, in view of what befell us, it had been necessary to bring the three brave fellows who manned the boat.

Our fishing, which proved excellent, carried us so far to the west that we no longer could see the COLDWATER. The day wore on, until at last, about mid-afternoon, I gave the order to return to the ship.

We had proceeded but a short distance toward the east when one of the men gave an exclamation of excitement, at the same time pointing eastward. We all looked in the direction he had indicated, and there, a short distance above the horizon, we saw the outlines of the COLDWATER silhouetted against the sky.

"They've repaired the engines and the generators both,"

exclaimed one of the men.

It seemed impossible, but yet it had evidently been done. Only that morning, Lieutenant Johnson had told me that he feared that it would be impossible to repair the generators. I had put him in charge of this work, since he always had been accounted one of the best gravitation-screen men in the navy. He had invented several of the improvements that are incorporated in the later models of these generators, and I am convinced that he knows more concerning both the theory and the practice of screening gravitation than any living Pan-American.

At the sight of the COLDWATER once more under control, the three men burst into a glad cheer; but, for some reason for which I could not then account, I was strangely overcome by a premonition of personal misfortune. It was not that I now anticipated an early return to Pan-America and a board of inquiry, for I had rather looked forward to the fight that must follow my return. No, there was something else, something indefinable and vague that cast a strange gloom upon me as I saw my ship rising farther above the water and making straight in our direction.

I was not long in ascertaining a possible explanation of my depression, for, though we were plainly visible from the bridge of the aero-submarine and to the hundreds of men who swarmed her deck, the ship passed directly above us, not five hundred feet from the water, and sped directly westward.

We all shouted, and I fired my pistol to attract their attention, though I knew full well that all who cared to had observed us, but the ship moved steadily away, growing smaller and smaller to our view until at last she passed complete- out of sight.

CHAPTER II

What could it mean? I had left Alvarez in command. He was my most loyal subordinate. It was absolutely beyond the pale of possibility that Alvarez should desert me. No, there was some other explanation. Something occurred to place my second officer, Porfirio Johnson, in command -- I was sure of it; but why speculate? The futility of conjecture was only too palpable. The COLDWATER has abandoned us in mid ocean. Doubtless none of us would survive to know why.

The young man at the wheel of the power boat had turned her nose about as it became evident that the ship intended passing over us, and now he still held her in futile pursuit of the COLDWATER.

"Bring her about, Snider," I directed, "and hold her due east. We can't catch the COLDWATER, and we can't cross the Atlantic in this. Our only hope lies in making the nearest land, which, unless I am mistaken, is the Scilly Islands, off the southwest coast of England. Ever hear of England, Snider?"

"There's a part of the United States of North America that used to be known to the ancients as New England," he replied. "Is that where you mean, sir?"

"No, Snider," I replied. "The England I refer to was an island off the continent of Europe. It was the seat of a very powerful kingdom that flourished over two hundred years ago. A part of the United States of North America and all of the Federated States of Canada once belonged to this ancient

England."

"Europe," breathed one of the men, his voice tense with excitement. "My grandfather used to tell me stories of the world beyond 30. He had been a great student, and he had read much from forbidden books."

"In which I resemble your grandfather," I said, "for I, too, have read more even than naval officers are supposed to read, and, as you men know, we are permitted a greater latitude in the study of geography and history than men of other professions.

"Among the books and papers of Admiral Porter Turck, who lived two hundred years ago, and from whom I am descended, many volumes still exist, and are in my possession, which deal with the history and geography of ancient Europe. Usually I bring several of these books with me upon a cruise, and this time, among others, I have maps of Europe and her surrounding waters. I was studying them as we came away from the COLDWATER this morning, and luckily I have them with me."

"You are going to try to make Europe, sir?" asked Taylor, the young man who had last spoken.

"It is the nearest land," I replied. "I have always wanted to explore the forgotten lands of the Eastern Hemisphere. Here's our chance. To remain at sea is to perish. None of us ever will see home again. Let us make the best of it, and enjoy while we do live that which is forbidden the balance of our race -- the adventure and the mystery which lie beyond 30."

Taylor and Delcarte seized the spirit of my mood; but Snider, I think, was a trifle sceptical,

"It is treason, sir," I replied; "but there is no law which compels us to visit punishment upon ourselves. Could we return to Pan-America, I should be the first to insist that we face it; but we know that's not possible. Even if this craft would carry us so far, we haven't enough water or food for more than three days.

"We are doomed, Snider, to die far from home and without ever again looking upon the face of another fellow countryman than those who sit here now in this boat. Isn't that punishment sufficient for even the most exacting judge?"

Even Snider had to admit that it was.

"Very well, then, let us live while we live, and enjoy to the fullest whatever of adventure or pleasure each new day brings, since any day may be our last, and we shall be dead for a considerable while."

I could see that Snider was still fearful; but Taylor and Delcarte responded with a hearty, "Aye, aye, sir!"

They were of different mold. Both were sons of naval officers. They represented the aristocracy of birth, and they dared to think for themselves.

Snider was in the minority, and so we continued toward the east. Beyond 30, and separated from my ship, my authority ceased. I held leadership, if I was to hold it at all, by virtue of personal qualifications only; but I did not doubt my ability to remain the director of our destinies in so far as they were amenable to human agencies. I have always led. While my brain and brawn remain unimpaired I shall continue always to lead. Following is an art which Turcks do not easily learn.

It was not until the third day that we raised land, dead ahead, which I took, from my map, to be the isles of Scilly; but such a gale was blowing that I did not dare attempt to land, and so we passed to the north of them, skirted Land's End, and entered the English Channel.

I think that up to that moment I had never experienced such a thrill as passed through me when I realized that I was navigating those historic waters. The lifelong dreams that I never had dared hope to see fulfilled were at last a reality; but under what forlorn circumstances!

Never could I return to my native land. To the end of my days I must remain in exile. Yet even these thoughts failed to dampen my ardor.

My eyes scanned the waters. To the north I could see the rockbound coast of Cornwall. Mine were the first American eyes to rest upon it for more than two hundred years. In vain I searched for some sign of ancient commerce that, if history is to be believed, must have dotted the bosom of the Channel with white sails and blackened the heavens with the smoke of countless funnels; but as far as eye could reach the tossing waters of the Channel were empty and deserted.

Toward midnight the wind and sea abated, so that shortly after dawn I determined to make inshore in an attempt to effect a landing, for we were sadly in need of fresh water and food.

According to my observations, we were just off Ram Head, and it was my intention to enter Plymouth Bay and visit Plymouth. From my map it appeared that this city lay back from the coast a short distance; and there was another city given as Devonport, which appeared to lie at the mouth of the river Tamar.

However, I knew that it would make little difference which city we entered, as the English People were famed of old for their hospitality toward visiting mariners. As we approached the mouth of the bay I looked for the fishing craft which I expected to see emerging thus early in the day for their labors; but even after we rounded Ram Head and were well within the waters of the bay I saw no vessel, neither was there buoy nor light nor any other mark to show larger ships the channel, and I wondered much at this.

The coast was densely overgrown, nor was any building or sign of man apparent from the water. Up the bay and into the River Tamar we motored through a solitude as unbroken as that which rested upon the waters of the channel. For all we could see, there was no indication that man had ever set his foot upon this silent coast.

I was nonplused, and then, for the first time, there crept over me an intuition of the truth.

Here was no sign of war. As far as this portion of the Devon coast was concerned, that seemed to have been over for many years; but neither were there any people, yet I could not find it within myself to believe that I should find no inhabitants in England. Reasoning thus, I discovered that it was improbable that a state of war still existed, and that the people all had been drawn from this portion of England to some other, where they might better defend themselves against an invader.

But what of their ancient coast defenses? What was there here in Plymouth Bay to prevent an enemy landing in force and marching where they wished? Nothing. I could not believe that any enlightened military nation, such as the ancient English are reputed to have been, would have voluntarily so deserted an exposed coast and an excellent harbor to the mercies of an enemy.

I found myself becoming more and more deeply involved in quandary. The puzzle which confronted me I could not unravel. We had landed, and I now stood upon the spot where, according to my map, a large city should rear its spires and chimneys. There was nothing but rough, broken ground covered densely with weeds and brambles, and tall, rank, grass.

Had a city ever stood there, no sign of it remained. The roughness and unevenness of the ground suggested something of a great mass of debris hidden by the accumulation of centuries of undergrowth.

I drew the short cutlass with which both officers and men of the navy are, as you know, armed out of courtesy to the traditions and memories of the past, and with its point dug into the loam about the roots of the vegetation growing at my feet.

The blade entered the soil for a matter of seven inches, when it struck upon something stonelike. Digging about the obstacle, I presently loosened it, and when I had withdrawn it from its sepulcher I found the thing to be an ancient brick of clay, baked in an oven.

Delcarte we had left in charge of the boat; but Snider and Taylor were with me, and, following my example, each engaged in the fascinating sport of prospecting for antiques. Each of us uncovered a great number of these bricks, until we commenced to weary of the monotony of it, when Snider suddenly gave an exclamation of excitement, and, as I turned to look, he held up a human skull for my inspection.

I took it from him and examined it. Directly in the center

of the forehead was a small round hole. The gentleman had evidently come to his end defending his country from an invader.

Snider again held aloft another trophy of the search -- a metal spike and some tarnished and corroded metal ornaments. They had lain close beside the skull.

With the point of his cutlass Snider scraped the dirt and verdigris from the face of the larger ornament.

"An inscription," he said, and handed the thing to me.

They were the spike and ornaments of an ancient German helmet. Before long we had uncovered many other indications that a great battle had been fought upon the ground where we stood; but I was then and still am at loss to account for the presence of German soldiers upon the English coast so far from London, which history suggests would have been the natural goal of an invader.

I can only account for it by assuming that either England was temporarily conquered by the Teutons, or that an invasion of so vast proportions was undertaken that German troops were hurled upon the English coast in huge numbers and that landings were necessarily effected at many places simultaneously. Subsequent discoveries tend to strengthen this view.

We dug about for a short time with our cutlasses until I became convinced that a city had stood upon the spot at some time in the past, and that beneath our feet, crumbled and dead, lay ancient Devonport.

I could not repress a sigh at the thought of the havoc war had wrought in this part of England, at least. Farther east, nearer London, we should find things very different. There would be the civilization that two centuries must have wrought upon our English cousins as they had upon us. There would be mighty cities, cultivated fields, happy people. There we would be welcomed as long-lost brothers. There would we find a great nation anxious to learn of the world beyond their side of 30, as I had been anxious to learn of that which lay beyond our side of the dead line.

I turned back toward the boat.

"Come, men!" I said. "We will go up the river and fill our casks with fresh water, search for food and fuel, and then tomorrow be in readiness to push on toward the east. I am going to London."

CHAPTER 

Thé report of a gun blasted the silence of a dead Devonport with startling abruptness.

It came from the direction of the launch, and in an instant we three were running for the boat as fast as our legs would carry us. As we came in sight of it we saw Delcarte a hundred yards inland from the launch, leaning over something which lay upon the ground. As we called to him he waved his cap, and, stooping, lifted a small deer for our inspection.

I was about to congratulate him on his trophy when we were startled by a horrid, half-human, half-bestial scream a little ahead and to the right of us. It seemed to come from a clump of rank and tangled brush not far from where DelCarte stood. It was a horrid, fearsome sound, the like of which never had fallen upon my ears before.

We looked in the direction from which it came. The smile had died from Delcarte's lips. Even at the distance we were from him I saw his face go suddenly white, and he quickly threw his rifle to his shoulder. At the same moment the thing that had given tongue to the cry moved from the concealing brushwood far enough for us, too, to see it.

Both Taylor and Snider gave little gasps of astonishment and dismay.

"What is it, sir?" asked the latter.

The creature stood about the height of a tall man's waist at the shoulders, and was long and gaunt and sinuous, and with a tawny coat striped with black, and with white throat and belly. In conformation it was similar to a cat -- a huge cat, exaggerated colossal cat, with fiendish eyes and the most devilish cast of countenance, as it wrinkled its bristling snout and bared its great yellow fangs.

It was pacing, or rather, slinking, straight for Delcarte, who had now leveled his rifle upon it.

"What is it, sir?" mumbled Snider again, and then a half-forgotten picture from an old natural history sprang to my mind, and I recognized in the frightful beast the Felis tigris of ancient Asia, specimens of which had, in former centuries, been exhibited in the Western Hemisphere.

Snider and Taylor were armed with rifles and revolvers, while I carried only a revolver. Seizing Snider's rifle from his trembling hands, I called to Taylor to follow me, and together we ran forward, shouting, to attract the beast's attention from Delcarte until we should all be quite close enough to attack with the greatest assurance of success.

I cried to Delcarte not to fire until we reached his side, for I was fearful lest our small caliber, steel-jacketed bullets should, far from killing the beast, tend merely to enrage it still further. But he misunderstood me, thinking that I had ordered him to fire.

With the report of his rifle the tiger stopped short in apparent surprise, then turned and bit savagely at its shoulder for an instant, after which it wheeled again toward Delcarte, issuing the most terrific roars and screams, and launched itself, with incredible speed, toward the brave fellow, who now stood his ground pumping bullets from his automatic rifle as rapidly as the weapon would fire.

Taylor and I also opened up on the creature, and as it was broadside to us it offered a splendid target, though for all the impression we appeared to make upon the great cat we might as well have been launching soap bubbles at it.

Straight as a torpedo it rushed for Delcarte, and, as Taylor and I stumbled on through the tall grass toward our unfortunate comrade, we saw the tiger rear upon him and crush him to the earth.

Not a backward step had the noble Delcarte taken. Two

hundred years of peace had not sapped the red blood from his courageous line. He went down beneath that avalanche of bestial savagery still working his gun and with his face toward his antagonist. Even in the instant that I thought him dead I could not help but feel a thrill of pride that he was one of my men -- one of my class, a Pan-American gentleman of birth, and that he had demonstrated one of the principle contentions of the army-and-navy adherents -- that military training was necessary for the salvation of personal courage in the Pan-American race which for generations had had to face no dangers more grave than those incident to ordinary life in a highly civilized community, safeguarded by every means at the disposal of a perfectly organized and all-powerful government utilizing the best that advanced science could suggest.

As we ran toward Delcarte, both Taylor and I were struck by the fact that the beast upon him appeared not to be mauling him, but lay quiet and motionless upon its prey, and when we were quite close, and the muzzles of our guns were at the animal's head, I saw the explanation of this sudden cessation of hostilities -- Felis tigris was dead.

One of our bullets, or one of the last that Delcarte fired, had penetrated the heart, and the beast had died even as it sprawled forward crushing Delcarte to the ground.

A moment later, with our assistance, the man had scrambled from beneath the carcass of his would-be slayer, without a scratch to indicate how close to death he had been.

Delcarte's buoyancy was entirely unruffled. He came from under the tiger with a broad grin on his handsome face, nor could I perceive that a muscle trembled or that his voice showed the least indication of nervousness or excitement.

With the termination of the adventure, we began to speculate upon the explanation of the presence of this savage brute at large so great a distance from its native habitat. My readings had taught me that it was practically unknown outside of Asia, and that, so late as the twentieth century, at least, there had been no savage beasts outside captivity in England.

As we talked, Snider joined us, and I returned his rifle to

him. Taylor and Delcarte picked up the slain deer, and we all started down toward the launch, walking slowly. Delcarte wanted to fetch the tiger's skin; but I had to deny him permission, since we had no means to properly cure it.

Upon the beach, we skinned the deer and cut away as much meat as we thought we could dispose of, and as we were again embarking to continue up the river for fresh water and fuel, we were startled by a series of screams from the bushes a short distance away.

"Another Felis tigris," said Taylor

"Or a dozen of them," supplemented Delcarte, and, even as he spoke, there leaped into sight, one after another, eight of the beasts - full grown, magnificent specimens.

At sight of us, they came charging down like infuriated demons. I saw that three rifles would be no match for them; and so I gave the word to put out from shore, hoping that the "tiger," as the ancients called him, could not swim.

Sure enough, they all halted at the beach, pacing back and forth, uttering fiendish cries, and glaring at us in the most malevolent manner.

As we motored away, we presently heard the calls of similar animals far inland. They seemed to be answering the cries of their fellows at the water's edge, and from the wide distribution and great volume of the sound we came to the conclusion that enormous numbers of these beasts must roam the adjacent country.

"They have eaten up the inhabitants," murmured Snider, shuddering.

"I imagine you are right," I agreed, "for their extreme boldness and fearlessness in the presence of man would suggest either that man is entirely unknown to them, or that they are extremely familiar with him as their natural and most easily procured prey."

"But where did they come from?" asked Delcarte. "Could they have traveled here from Asia?"

I shook my head. The thing was a puzzle to me. I knew that it was practically beyond reason to imagine that tigers had crossed the mountain ranges and rivers and all the great continent of Europe to travel this far from their native lairs, and entirely impossible that they should have crossed the English Channel at all. Yet here they were, and in great numbers.

We continued up the Tamar several miles, filled our casks, and then landed to cook some of our deer steak, and have the first square meal that had fallen to our lot since the COLDWATER deserted us. But scarce had we built our fire and prepared the meat for cooking than Snider, whose eyes had been constantly roving about the landscape from the moment that we left the launch, touched me on the arm and pointed to a clump of bushes which grew a couple of hundred yards away.

Half concealed behind their screening foliage I saw the yellow and black of a big tiger, and, as I looked, the beast stalked majestically toward us. A moment later, he was followed by another and another, and it is needless to state that we beat a hasty retreat to the launch.

The country was apparently infested by these huge carnivora, for after three other attempts to land and cook our food we were forced to abandon the idea entirely, as each time we were driven off by hunting tigers.

It was also equally impossible to obtain the necessary ingredients for our chemical fuel, and, as we had very little left aboard, we determined to step our folding mast and proceed under sail, hoarding our fuel supply for use in emergencies.

I may say that it was with no regret that we bid adieu to Tigerland, as we rechristened ancient Devon, and, beating out into the Channel, turned the launch's nose southeast, to round Bolt Head and continue up the coast toward the Strait of Dover and the North Sea.

I was determined to reach London as soon as possible, that we might obtain fresh clothing, meet with cultured people, and learn from the lips of Englishmen the secret of the two centuries since the East had been divorced from the West.

Our first stopping place was the Isle of Wight. We entered the Solent about ten o'clock one morning, and I must confess that my heart sank as we came close to shore. No lighthouse was visible, though one was plainly indicated upon my map. Upon neither shore was sign of human habitation. We skirted the northern shore of the island in fruitless search for man, and then at last landed upon an eastern point, where Newport should have stood, but where only weeds and great trees and tangled wild wood rioted, and not a single man-made thing was visible to the eye.

Before landing, I had the men substitute soft bullets for the steel-jacketed projectiles with which their belts and magazines were filled. Thus equipped, we felt upon more even terms with the tigers; but there was no sign of the tigers, and I decided that they must be confined to the mainland.

After eating, we set out in search of fuel, leaving Taylor to guard the launch. For some reason I could not trust Snider alone. I knew that he looked with disapproval upon my plan to visit England, and I did not know but what at his first opportunity he might desert us, taking the launch with him, and attempt to return to Pan-America.

That he would be fool enough to venture it I did not doubt.

We had gone inland for a mile or more, and were passing through a park-like wood, when we came suddenly upon the first human beings we had seen since we sighted the English coast.

There were a score of men in the party. Hairy, half-naked men they were, resting in the shade of a great tree. At the first sight of us they sprang to their feet with wild yells, seizing long spears that had lain beside them as they rested.

For a matter of fifty yards they ran from us as rapidly as they could, and then they turned and surveyed us for a moment. Evidently emboldened by the scarcity of our numbers, they commenced to advance upon us, brandishing their spears and shouting horribly.

They were short and muscular of build, with long hair and beards tangled and matted with filth. Their heads, however, were shapely, and their eyes, though fierce and warlike, were intelligent.

Appreciation of these physical attributes came later, of course, when I had better opportunity to study the men at close range and under circumstances less fraught with danger and excitement. At the moment I saw, and with unmixed wonder, only a score of wild savages charging down upon us, where I had expected to find a community of civilized and enlightened people.

Each of us was armed with rifle, revolver, and cutlass, but as we stood shoulder to shoulder facing the wild men I was loath to give the command to fire upon them, inflicting death or suffering upon strangers with whom we had no quarrel, and so I attempted to restrain them for the moment that we might parley with them.

To this end I raised my left hand above my head with the palm toward them as the most natural gesture indicative of peaceful intentions which occurred to me. At the same time I called aloud to them that we were friends, though, from their appearance, there was nothing to indicate that they might understand Pan-American, or ancient English, which are of course practically identical.

At my gesture and words they ceased their shouting and came to a halt a few paces from us. Then, in deep tones, one who was in advance of the others and whom I took to be the chief or leader of the party replied in a tongue which while intelligible to us, was so distorted from the English language from which it evidently had sprung that it was with difficulty that we interpreted it.

"Who are you," he asked, "and from what country?"

I told him that we were from Pan-America, but he only shook his head and asked where that was. He had never heard of it, or of the Atlantic Ocean which I told him separated his country from mine.

"It has been two hundred years," I told him, "since a Pan-American visited England."

"England?" he asked. "What is England?"

"Why this is a part of England!" I exclaimed.

"This is Grubitten," he assured me. "I know nothing about England, and I have lived here all my life."

It was not until long after that the derivation of Grubitten occurred to me. Unquestionably it is a corruption of Great Britain, a name formerly given to the large island comprising England, Scotland and Wales. Subsequently we heard it pronounced Grabritin and Grubritten.

I then asked the fellow if he could direct us to Ryde or Newport; but again he shook his head, and said that he never had heard of such countries. And when I asked him if there were any cities in this country he did not know what I meant, never having heard the word cities.

I explained my meaning as best I could by stating that by city I referred to a place where many people lived together in houses.

"Oh," he exclaimed, "you mean a camp! Yes, there are two great camps here, East Camp and West Camp. We are from East Camp."

The use of the word camp to describe a collection of habitations naturally suggested war to me, and my next question was as to whether the war was over, and who had been victorious.

"No," he replied to this question. "The war is not yet over; but it soon will be, and it will end, as it always does, with the Westenders running away -- we, the Eastenders, are always victorious."

"No," I said, seeing that he referred to the petty tribal wars of his little island, "I mean the Great War, the war with Germany. Is it ended -- and who was victorious?"

He shook his head impatiently.

"I never heard," he said, "of any of these strange countries of which you speak."

It seemed incredible, and yet it was true. These people living at the very seat of the Great War knew nothing of it, though but two centuries had passed since, to our knowledge, it had been running in the height of its titanic frightfulness all about them, and to us upon the far side of the Atlantic still was a subject of keen interest.

Here was a lifelong inhabitant of the Isle of Wight who never had heard of either Germany or England! I turned to him quite suddenly with a new question.

"What people live upon the mainland?" I asked, and pointed in the direction of the Hants coast.

"No one lives there," he replied.

"Long ago, it is said, my people dwelt across the waters upon that other land; but the wild beasts devoured them in such numbers that finally they were driven here, paddling across upon logs and driftwood, nor has any dared return since, because of the frightful creatures which dwell in that horrid country."

"Do no other peoples ever come to your country in ships?" I asked.

He never heard the word ship before, and did not know its meaning; but he assured me that until we came he had thought that there were no other peoples in the world other than the Grubittens, who consist of the Eastenders and the Westenders of the ancient Isle of Wight.

Assured that we were inclined to friendliness, our new acquaintances led us to their village, or, as they call it, camp. There we found a thousand people, perhaps, dwelling in rude shelters, and living upon the fruits of the chase and such sea food as is obtainable close to shore, for they had no boats, nor any knowledge of such things.

Their weapons were most primitive, consisting of rude spears tipped with pieces of metal pounded roughly into shape. They had no literature, no religion, and recognized no law other than the law of might. They produce fire by striking a bit of flint and steel together, but for the most part they ate their food raw. Marriage is unknown among them, and while they have the word, mother, they did not know what I meant by "father". The males fight for the favor of the females. They practice infanticide, and kill the aged and the physically unfit.

The family consists of the mother and the children, the men dwelling sometimes in one hut and sometimes in another. Owing to their bloody duels, they are always numerically inferior to the women, so there is shelter for them all.

We spent several hours in the village, where we were objects of the greatest curiosity. The inhabitants examined our clothing and all our belongings, and asked innumerable questions concerning the strange country from which we had come and the manner of our coming.

I questioned many of them concerning past historical events; but they knew nothing beyond the narrow limits of their island and the savage, primitive life they led there. London they had never heard of, and they assured me that I would find no human beings upon the mainland.

Much saddened by what I had seen, I took my departure from them, and the three of us made our way back to the launch, accompanied by about five hundred men, women, girls, and boys.

As we sailed away, after procuring the necessary ingredients of our chemical fuel, the Grubittens lined the shore in silent wonder at the strange sight of our dainty craft dancing over the sparkling waters, and watched us until we were lost to their sight.

CHAPTER IV

It was during the morning of July 6, 2137, that we entered the mouth of the Thames -- to the best of my knowledge the first Western keel to cut those historic waters for two hundred and twenty-one years!

But where were the tugs and the lighters and the barges, the lightships and the buoys, and all those countless attributes which went to make up the myriad life of the ancient Thames?

Gone! All gone! Only silence and desolation reigned where once the commerce of the world had centered.

I could not help but compare this once great waterway with the waters about our New York, or Rio, or San Diego, or Valparisso. They had become what they are today during the two centuries of the profound peace which we of the navy have been prone to deplore. And what, during this same period, had shorn the waters of the Thames of their pristine grandeur?

Militarist that I am, I could find but a single word of explanation -- war!

I bowed my head and turned my eyes downward from the lonely and depressing sight, and in a silence which none of us seemed willing to break, we proceeded up the deserted river.

We had reached a point which, from my map, I imagined must have been about the former site of Erith, when I discovered a small band of antelope a short distance inland. As we were now entirely out of meat once more, and as I had given up all expectations of finding a city upon the site of ancient London, I determined to land and bag a couple of the animals.

Assured that they would be timid and easily frightened, I decided to stalk them alone, telling the men to wait at the boat until I called to them to come and carry the carcasses back to the shore.

Crawling carefully through the vegetation, making use of such trees and bushes as afforded shelter, I came at last almost within easy range of my quarry, when the antlered head of the buck went suddenly into the air, and then, as though in accordance with a prearranged signal, the whole band moved slowly off, farther inland.

As their pace was leisurely, I determined to follow them until I came again within range, as I was sure that they would stop and feed in a short time.

They must have led me a mile or more at least before they again halted and commenced to browse upon the rank, luxuriant grasses. All the time that I had followed them I had kept both eyes and ears alert for sign or sound that would indicate the presence of Felis tigris; but so far not the slightest indication of the beast had been apparent.

As I crept closer to the antelope, sure this time of a good shot at a large buck, I suddenly saw something that caused me to forget all about my prey in wonderment.

It was the figure of an immense grey-black creature, rearing its colossal shoulders twelve or fourteen feet above the ground. Never in my life had I seen such a beast, nor did I at first recognize it, so different in appearance is the live reality from the stuffed, unnatural specimens preserved to us in our museums.

But presently I guessed the identity of the mighty creature as Elphas africanus, or, as the ancient commonly described it, African elephant.

The antelope, although in plain view of the huge beast, paid not the slightest attention to it, and I was so wrapped up in watching the mighty pachyderm that I quite forgot to shoot at the buck and presently, and in quite a startling manner, it became impossible to do so.

The elephant was browsing upon the young and tender shoots of some low bushes, waving his great ears and switching his short tail. The antelope, scarce twenty paces from him, continued their feeding, when suddenly, from close beside the latter, there came a most terrifying roar, and I saw a great, tawny body shoot from the concealing verdure beyond the antelope full upon the back of a small buck.

Instantly the scene changed from one of quiet and peace to indescribable chaos. The startled and terrified buck uttered cries of agony. His fellows broke and leaped off in all directions. The elephant raised his trunk, and, trumpeting loudly, lumbered off through the wood, crushing down small trees and trampling bushes in his mad flight.

Growling horribly, a huge lion stood across the body of his prey -- such a creature as no Pan-American of the twenty-second century had ever beheld until my eyes rested upon this lordly specimen of "the king of beasts." But what a different creature was this fierce-eyed demon, palpitating with life and vigor, glossy of coat, alert, growling, magnificent, from the dingy, motheaten replicas beneath their glass cases in the stuffy halls of our public museums.

I had never hoped or expected to see a living lion, tiger, or elephant -- using the common terms that were familiar to the ancients, since they seem to me less unwieldy than those now in general use among us -- and so it was with sentiments not unmixed with awe that I stood gazing at this regal beast as, above the carcass of his kill, he roared out his challenge to the world.

So enthralled was I by the spectacle that I quite forgot myself, and the better to view him, the great lion, I had risen to my feet and stood, not fifty paces from him, in full view.

For a moment he did not see me, his attention being directed toward the retreating elephant, and I had ample time to feast my eyes upon his splendid proportions, his great head, and his thick black mane.

Ah, what thoughts passed through my mind in those brief

moments as I stood there in rapt fascination! I had come to find a wondrous civilization, and instead I found a wild-beast monarch of the realm where English kings had ruled. A lion reigned, undisturbed, within a few miles of the seat of one of the greatest governments the world has ever known, his domain a howling wilderness, where yesterday fell the shadows of the largest city in the world.

It was appalling; but my reflections upon this depressing subject were doomed to sudden extinction -- the lion had discovered me.

For an instant he stood silent and motionless as one of the mangy effigies at home; but only for an instant. Then, with a most ferocious roar, and without the slightest hesitancy or warning, he charged upon me.

He forsook the prey already dead beneath him for the pleasures of the delectable tidbit, man. From the remorselessness with which the great carnivora of modern England hunted man, I am constrained to believe that, whatever their appetites in times past, they have cultivated a gruesome taste for human flesh.

As I threw my rifle to my shoulder, I thanked God, the ancient God of my ancestors, that I had replaced the hard-jacketed bullets in my weapon with soft-nosed projectiles, for though this was my first experience with Felis leo, I knew the moment that I faced that charge that even my wonderfully perfected firearm would be as futile as a peashooter unless I chanced to place my first bullet in a vital spot.

Unless you had seen it you could not believe credible the speed of a charging lion. Apparently the animal is not built for speed, nor can he maintain it for long; but for a matter of forty or fifty yards there is, I believe, no animal on earth that can overtake him.

Like a bolt he bore down upon me; but, fortunately for me, I did not lose my head. I guessed that no bullet would kill him instantly. I doubted that I could pierce his skull. There was hope, though, in finding his heart through his exposed chest, or, better yet, of breaking his shoulder or foreleg, and bringing him up long enough to pump more bullets into him and finish him.

I covered his left shoulder and pulled the trigger as he was almost upon me. It stopped him. With a terrific howl of pain and rage, the brute rolled over and over upon the ground almost to my feet. As he came I pumped two more bullets into him, and as he struggled to rise, clawing viciously at me, I put a bullet in his spine.

That finished him, and I am free to admit that I was mighty glad of it. There was a great tree close behind me, and, stepping within its shade, I leaned against it, wiping the perspiration from my face, for the day was hot, and the exertion and excitement left me exhausted.

I stood there, resting, for a moment, preparatory to turning and retracing my steps to the launch, when, without warning, something whizzed through space straight toward me. There was a dull thud of impact as it struck the tree, and as I dodged to one side and turned to look at the thing I saw a heavy spear imbedded in the wood not three inches from where my head had been.

The thing had come from a little to one side of me, and, without waiting to investigate at the instant, I leaped behind the tree, and, circling it, peered around the other side to get a sight of my would-be murderer.

This time I was pitted against men -- the spear told me that all too plainly -- but so long as they didn't take me unawares or from behind I had little fear of them.

Cautiously I edged about the far side of the trees until I could obtain a view of the spot from which the spear must have come, and when I did I saw the head of a man just emerging from behind a bush.

The fellow was quite similar in type to those I had seen upon the Isle of Wight. He was hairy and unkempt, and as he finally stepped into view I saw that he was garbed in the same primitive fashion.

He stood for a moment gazing about in search of me, and then he advanced. As he did so a number of others, precisely like him, stepped from the concealing verdure of nearby bushes and followed in his wake. Keeping the tree between them and me, I ran back a short distance until I found a clump of underbrush that would effectually conceal me, for I wished to discover the strength of the party and its armament before attempting to parley with it.

The useless destruction of any of these poor creatures was the farthest idea from my mind. I should have liked to have spoken with them; but I did not care to risk having to use my high-powered rifle upon them other than in the last extremity.

Once in my new place of concealment, I watched them as they approached the tree. There were about thirty men in the party and one woman -- a girl whose hands seemed to be bound behind her and who was being pulled along by two of the men.

They came forward warily, peering cautiously into every bush and halting often. At the body of the lion, they paused, and I could see from their gesticulations and the higher pitch of their voices that they were much excited over my kill.

But presently they resumed their search for me, and as they advanced I became suddenly aware of the unnecessary brutality with which the girl's guards were treating her. She stumbled once, not far from my place of concealment, and after the balance of the party had passed me. As she did so one of the men at her side jerked her roughly to her feet and struck her across the mouth with his fist.

Instantly my blood boiled, and forgetting every consideration of caution, I leaped from my concealment, and, springing to the man's side, felled him with a blow.

So unexpected had been my act that it found him and his fellow unprepared; but instantly the latter drew the knife that protruded from his belt and lunged viciously at me, at the same time giving voice to a wild cry of alarm.

The girl shrank back at sight of me, her eyes wide in astonishment, and then my antagonist was upon me. I parried his first blow with my forearm, at the same time delivering a powerful blow to his jaw that sent him reeling back; but he was at me again in an instant, though in the brief interim I had time to draw my revolver.

I saw his companion crawling slowly to his feet, and the others of the party racing down upon me. There was no time to argue now, other than with the weapons we wore, and so, as the fellow lunged at me again with the wicked-looking knife, I covered his heart and pulled the trigger.

Without a sound, he slipped to the earth, and then I turned the weapon upon the other guard, who was now about to attack me. He, too, collapsed, and I was alone with the astonished girl.

The balance of the party was some twenty paces from us, but coming rapidly. I seized her arm and drew her after me behind a nearby tree, for I had seen that with both their comrades down the party were preparing to launch their spears.

With the girl safe behind the tree, I stepped out in sight of the advancing foe, shouting to them that I was no enemy, and that they should halt and listen to me; but for answer they only yelled in derision and launched a couple of spears at me, both of which missed.

I saw then that I must fight, yet still I hated to slay them, and it was only as a final resort that I dropped two of them with my rifle, bringing the others to a temporary halt. Again I appealed to them to desist; but they only mistook my solicitude for them for fear, and, with shouts of rage and derision, leaped forward once again to overwhelm me.

It was now quite evident that I must punish them severely, or, myself, die and relinquish the girl once more to her captors. Neither of these things had I the slightest notion of doing, and so I again stepped from behind the tree, and, with all the care and deliberation of target practice, I commenced picking off the foremost of my assailants.

One by one the wild men dropped, yet on came the others, fierce and vengeful, until, only a few remaining, these seemed to realize the futility of combating my modern weapon with their primitive spears, and, still howling wrathfully, withdrew toward the west.

Now, for the first time, I had an opportunity to turn my attention toward the girl, who had stood, silent and motionless, behind me as I pumped death into my enemies and hers from my automatic rifle.

She was of medium height, well formed, and with fine, clear-cut features. Her forehead was high, and her eyes both intelligent and beautiful. Exposure to the sun had browned a smooth and velvety skin to a shade which seemed to enhance rather than mar an altogether lovely picture of youthful femininity.

A trace of apprehension marked her expression -- I cannot call it fear since I have learned to know her -- and astonishment was still apparent in her eyes. She stood quite erect, her hands still bound behind her, and met my gaze with level, proud return.

"What language do you speak?" I asked. "Do you understand mine?"

"Yes," she replied; "it is similar to my own -- I am Grabritin. What are you?"

"I am a Pan-American," I answered. She shook her head. "What is that?"

I pointed toward the west. "Far away, across the ocean."

Her expression altered a trifle. A slight frown contracted her brow. The expression of apprehension deepened.

"Take off your cap," she said, and when, to humor her strange request, I did as she bid, she appeared relieved. Then she edged to one side and leaned over seemingly to peer behind me. I turned quickly to see what she discovered, but finding nothing, wheeled about to see that her expression was once more altered.

"You are not from there?" and she pointed toward the east. It was a half question. "You are not from across the water there?"

"No," I assured her, "I am from Pan-America, far away to the west. Have you ever heard of Pan-America?"

She shook her head in negation. "I do not care where you are from," she explained, "if you are not from there, and I am sure you are not, for the men from there have horns and tails."

It was with difficulty that I restrained a smile.

"Who are the men from there?" I asked.

"They are bad men," she replied. "Some of my people do not believe that there are such creatures; but we have a legend -- a very old, old legend, that once the men from there came across to Grabritin. They came upon the water, and under the water, and even in the air. They came in great numbers, so that they rolled across the land like a great gray fog. They brought with them thunder and lightning and smoke that killed, and they fell upon us and slew our people by the thousands and the hundreds of thousands; but at last we drove them back to the water's edge, back into the sea, where many were drowned. Some escaped, and these our people followed -- men, women, and even children, we followed them back. That is all. The legend says our people never returned. Maybe they were all killed. Maybe they still are there. But this, also, is in the legend, that as we drove the men back across the water they swore that they would return, and that when they left our shores they would leave no human being alive behind them. I was afraid that you were from there."

"By what name were these men called?" I asked.

"We call them only the 'men from there,' " she replied, pointing toward the east. "I have never heard that they had another name."

In the light of what I knew of ancient history, it was not difficult for me to guess the nationality of those she described simply as "the men from over there". But what utter and appalling devastation the Great War must have wrought to have erased not only every sign of civilization from the face of this great land; but even the name of the enemy from the knowledge and language of the people.

I could only account for it on the hypothesis that the country had been entirely depopulated except for a few scattered and forgotten children, who, in some marvelous manner, had been preserved by Providence to repopulate the land. These children had, doubtless, been too young to retain in their memories to transmit to their children any but the vaguest suggestion of the cataclysm which had overwhelmed their parents.

Professor Cortoran, since my return to Pan-America, has suggested another theory which is not entirely without claim to serious consideration. He points out that it is quite beyond the pale of human instinct to desert little children as my theory suggests the ancient English must have done. He is more inclined to believe that the expulsion of the foe from England was synchronous with widespread victories by the allies upon the continent, and that the people of England merely emigrated from their ruined cities and their devastated, blood-drenched fields to the mainland, in the hope of finding in the domain of the conquered enemy cities and farms which should replace those they had lost.

The learned professor assumes that while a long-continued war had strengthened rather than weakened the instinct of paternal devotion, it had also dulled other humanitarian instincts, and raised to the first magnitude the law of the survival of the fittest, with the result that when the exodus took place the strong, the intelligent, and the cunning, together with their offspring, crossed the waters of the Channel or the North Sea to the continent, leaving in unhappy England only the helpless inmates of asylums for the feeble-minded and insane.

My objection to this, that the present inhabitants of England are mentally fit, and could therefore, not have descended from an ancestry of undiluted lunacy he brushes aside with the assertion that insanity is not necessarily hereditary, and that even though it was, in many cases, a return to natural conditions from the state of high civilization which is thought to have induced mental disease in the ancient world would, after several generations, have thoroughly expunged every trace of the affliction from the brains and nerves of the descendants of the original maniacs.

Personally, I do not place much stock in Professor Cortoran's theory, though I admit that I am prejudiced. Naturally one does not care to believe that the object of his greatest affection is descended from a gibbering idiot and a raving maniac.

But I am forgetting the continuity of my narrative -- a

continuity which I desire to maintain, though I fear that I shall often be led astray, so numerous and varied are the bypaths of speculation which lead from the present day story of the Grabritins into the mysterious past of their forbears.

As I stood talking with the girl I presently recollected that she still was bound, and with a word of apology I drew my knife and cut the rawhide thongs which confined her wrists at her back.

She thanked me, and with such a sweet smile that I should have been amply repaid by it for a much more arduous service.

"And now," I said, "let me accompany you to your home and see you safely again under the protection of your friends."

"No," she said, with a hint of alarm in her voice; "you must not come with me -- Buckingham will kill you."

Buckingham. The name was famous in ancient English history. Its survival, with many other illustrious names, is one of the strongest arguments in refutal of Professor Cortoran's theory; yet it opens no new doors to the past, and, on the whole, rather adds to than dissipates the mystery.

"And who is Buckingham," I asked, "and why should he wish to kill me?"

"He would think that you had stolen me," she replied, "and as he wishes me for himself, he will kill any other whom he thinks desires me. He killed Wettin a few days ago. My mother told me once that Wettin was my father. He was king. Now Buckingham is king."

Here, evidently, were a people slightly superior to those of the Isle of Wight. These must have at least the rudiments of civilized government since they recognized one among them as ruler, with the title king. Also, they retained the word father. The girl's pronunciation, while far from identical with ours, was much closer than the tortured dialect of the Eastenders of the Isle of Wight. The longer I talked with her the more hopeful I became of finding here, among her people, some records, or traditions, which might assist in clearing up the historic enigma of the past two centuries. I asked her if we were far from the city of London; but she did not know what I meant. When I tried to explain, describing mighty buildings of stone and brick, broad avenues, parks, palaces, and countless people she but shook her head sadly.

"There is no such place near by," she said. "Only the Camp of the Lions has places of stone where the beasts lair; but there are no people in the Camp of the Lions. Who would dare go there!" And she shuddered.

"The Camp of the Lions," I repeated. "And where is that, and what?"

"It is there," she said, pointing up the river toward the west. "I have seen it from a great distance, but I have never been there. We are much afraid of the lions, for this is their country, and they are angry that man has come to live here.

"Far away there," and she pointed toward the southwest, "is the land of tigers, which is even worse than this, the land of the lions, for the tigers are more numerous than the lions and hungrier for human flesh. There were tigers here long ago, but both the lions and the men set upon them and drove them off."

"Where did these savage beasts come from?" I asked.

"Oh," she replied, "they have been here always -- it is their country."

"Do they not kill and eat your people?" I asked.

"Often, when we meet them by accident, and we are too few to slay them, or when one goes too close to their camp; but seldom do they hunt us, for they find what food they need among the deer and wild cattle, and, too, we make them gifts, for are we not intruders in their country? Really we live upon good terms with them, though I should not care to meet one were there not many spears in my party."

"I should like to visit this Camp of the Lions," I said.

"Oh, no, you must not!" cried the girl. "That would be terrible. They would eat you." For a moment, then, she seemed lost in thought; but presently she turned upon me with: "You must go now, for any minute Buckingham may come in search of me. Long since should they have learned that I am gone from the camp -- they watch over me very closely -- and they will set out after me. Go! I shall wait here until they come in search of me."

"No," I told her. "I'll not leave you alone in a land infested by lions and other wild beasts. If you won't let me go as far as your camp with you, then I'll wait here until they come in search of you."

"Please go!" she begged. "You have saved me, and I would save you: but nothing will save you if Buckingham gets his hands on you. He is a bad man. He wishes to have me for his woman so that he may be king. He would kill anyone who befriended me, for fear that I might become another's."

"Didn't you say that Buckingham is already the king?" I asked.

"He is. He took my mother for his woman after he had killed Wettin; but my mother will die soon -- she is very old -- and then the man to whom I belong will become king."

Finally, after much questioning, I got the thing through my head. It appears that the line of descent is through the women. A man is merely head of his wife's family -- that is all. If she chances to be the oldest female member of the "royal" house, he is king. Very naively the girl explained that there was seldom any doubt as to who a child's mother was.

This accounted for the girl's importance in the community and for Buckingham's anxiety to claim her, though she told me that she did not wish to become his woman, for he was a bad man and would make a bad king. But he was powerful and there was no other man who dared dispute his wishes.

"Why not come with me," I suggested, "if you do not wish to become Buckingham's?"

"Where would you take me?" she asked.

Where, indeed! I had not thought of that; but before I could reply to her question she shook her head and said "No, I cannot leave my people. I must stay and do my best even if Buckingham gets me; but you must go at once. Do not wait until it is too late. The lions have had no offering for a long time, and Buckingham would seize upon the first stranger as a gift to them."

I did not perfectly understand what she meant, and was about to ask her when a heavy body leaped upon me from behind, and great arms encircled my neck. I struggled to free myself and turn upon my antagonist, but in another instant I was overwhelmed by a half dozen powerful, half-naked men, while a score of others surrounded me, a couple of whom seized the girl.

I fought as best I could for my liberty and for hers, but the weight of numbers was too great, though I had the satisfaction at least of giving them a good fight.

When they had overpowered me, and I stood, my hands bound behind me, at the girl's side, she gazed commiseratingly at me.

"It is too bad that you did not do as I bid you," she said, "for now it has happened just as I feared -- Buckingham has you."

"Which is Buckingham?" I asked.

"I am Buckingham," growled a burly, unwashed brute, swaggering truculently before me. "And who are you who would have stolen my woman?"

The girl spoke up then and tried to explain that I had not stolen her; but on the contrary I had saved her from the men from the "Elephant Country" who were carrying her away.

Buckingham only sneered at her explanation, and a moment later gave the command that started us all off toward the west. We marched for a matter of an hour or so, coming at last to a collection of rude huts, fashioned from branches of trees covered with skins and grasses and sometimes plastered with mud. All about the camp they had erected a wall of saplings pointed at the tops and fire hardened.

This palisade was a protection against both man and beasts, and within it dwelt upward of two thousand persons, the shelters being built very close together, and sometimes partially underground, like deep trenches, with the poles and hides above merely as protection from the sun and rain.

The older part of the camp consisted almost wholly of trenches, as though this had been the original form of dwellings which was slowly giving way to the drier and airier surface domiciles. In these trench habitations I saw a survival of the military trenches which formed so famous a part of the operations of the warring nations during the twentieth century.

The women wore a single light deerskin about their hips, for it was summer, and quite warm. The men, too, were clothed in a single garment, usually the pelt of some beast of prey. The hair of both men and women was confined by a rawhide thong passing about the forehead and tied behind. In this leathern band was stuck feathers, flowers, or the tails of small mammals. All wore necklaces of the teeth or claws of wild beasts, and there were numerous metal wristlets and anklets among them.

They wore, in fact, every indication of a most primitive people -- a race which had not yet risen to the heights of agriculture or even the possession of domestic animals. They were hunters -- the lowest plane in the evolution of the human race of which science takes cognizance.

And yet as I looked at their well shaped heads, their handsome features, and their intelligent eyes, it was difficult to believe that I was not among my own. It was only when I took into consideration their mode of living, their scant apparel, the lack of every least luxury among them, that I was forced to admit that they were, in truth, but ignorant savages.

Buckingham had relieved me of my weapons, though he had not the slightest idea of their purpose or uses, and when we reached the camp he exhibited both me and my arms with every indication of pride in this great capture.

The inhabitants flocked around me, examining my clothing, and exclaiming in wonderment at each new discovery of button, buckle, pocket, and flap. It seemed incredible that such a thing could be, almost within a stone's throw of the spot where but a brief two centuries before had stood the greatest city of the world.

They bound me to a small tree that grew in the middle of one of their crooked streets; but the girl they released as soon as we had entered the enclosure. The people greeted her with every mark of respect as she hastened to a large hut near the center of the camp.

Presently she returned with a fine looking, white-haired woman, who proved to be her mother. The older woman carried herself with a regal dignity that seemed quite remarkable in a place of such primitive squalor.

The people fell aside as she approached, making a wide way for her and her daughter. When they had come near and stopped before me the older woman addressed me.

"My daughter has told me," she said, "of the manner in which you rescued her from the men of the elephant country. If Wettin lived you would be well treated; but Buckingham has taken me now, and is king. You can hope for nothing from such a beast as Buckingham."

The fact that Buckingham stood within a pace of us and was an interested listener appeared not to temper her expressions in the slightest.

"Buckingham is a pig," she continued. "He is a coward. He came upon Wettin from behind and ran his spear through him. He will not be king for long. Some one will make a face at him, and he will run away and jump into the river."

The people began to titter and clap their hands. Buckingham became red in the face. It was evident that he was far from popular.

"If he dared," went on the old lady, "he would kill me now; but he does not dare. He is too great a coward. If I could help you I should gladly do so; but I am only queen -- the vehicle that has helped carry down, unsullied, the royal blood from the days when Grabritin was a mighty country."

The old queen's words had a noticeable effect upon the mob of curious savages which surrounded me. The moment they discovered that the old queen was friendly to me and that I had rescued her daughter they commenced to accord me a more friendly interest, and I heard many words spoken in my behalf, and demands were made that I not be harmed.

But now Buckingham interfered. He had no intention of being robbed of his prey. Blustering and storming, he ordered the people back to their huts, at the same time directing two of his warriors to confine me in a dugout in one of the trenches close to his own shelter.

Here they threw me upon the ground, binding my ankles together and trussing them up to my wrists behind. There they left me, lying upon my stomach -- a most uncomfortable and strained position, to which was added the pain where the cords cut into my flesh.

Just a few days ago my mind had been filled with the anticipation of the friendly welcome I should find among the cultured Englishmen of London. Today I should be sitting in the place of honor at the banquet board of one of London's most exclusive clubs, feted and lionized.

The actuality! Here I lay, bound hand and foot, doubtless almost upon the very site of a part of ancient London, yet all about me was a primeval wilderness, and I was a captive of half-naked wild men.

I wondered what had become of Delcarte and Taylor and Snider. Would they search for me? They could never find me, I feared, yet if they did, what could they accomplish against this horde of savage warriors?

Would that I could warn them. I thought of the girl -- doubtless she could get word to them; but how was I to communicate with her? Would she come to see me before I was killed? It seemed incredible that she should not make some slight attempt to befriend me; yet, as I recalled, she had made no effort to speak with me after we had reached the village -- she had hastened to her mother the moment she had been liberated. Though she had returned with the old queen, she had not spoken to me, even then. I began to have my doubts.

Finally I came to the conclusion that I was absolutely friendless except for the old queen. For some unaccountable reason my rage against the girl for her ingratitude rose to colossal proportions.

For a long time I waited for some one to come to my prison whom I might ask to bear word to the queen; but I seemed to have been forgotten. The strained position in which I lay became unbearable. I wriggled and twisted until I managed to turn myself partially upon my side, where I lay half facing the entrance to the dugout.

Presently my attention was attracted by the shadow of something moving in the trench without, and a moment later the figure of a child appeared, creeping upon all fours, as, wide-eyed, and prompted by childish curiosity, a little girl crawled to the entrance of my hut and peered cautiously and fearfully in.

I did not speak at first for fear of frightening the little one away; but when I was satisfied that her eyes had become sufficiently accustomed to the subdued light of the interior, I smiled.

Instantly the expression of fear faded from her eyes to be replaced with an answering smile.

"Who are you little girl?" I asked.

"My name is Mary," she replied. "I am Victory's sister."

"And who is Victory?"

"You do not know who Victory is?" she asked, in astonishment.

I shook my head in negation.

"You saved her from the elephant country people, and yet you say you do not know her!" she exclaimed.

"Oh, so she is Victory, and you are her sister! I have not heard her name before -- that is why I did not know whom you meant," I explained. Here was just the messenger for me. Fate was becoming more kind.

"Will you do something for me, Mary?" I asked.

"If I can."

"Go to your mother, the queen, and ask her to come to me," I said. "I have a favor to ask."

She said that she would, and with a parting smile she left me.

For what seemed many hours I awaited her return, chafing with impatience. The afternoon wore on and night came, and yet no one came near me. My captors brought me neither food or water. I was suffering considerable pain where the rawhide thongs cut into my swollen flesh. I thought that they had either forgotten me, or that it was their intention to leave me here to die of starvation.

Once I heard a great uproar in the village. Men were shouting -- women were screaming and moaning. After a time this subsided, and again there was a long interval of silence.

Half the night must have been spent when I heard a sound in the trench near the hut -- it resembled muffled sobs. Presently a figure appeared, silhouetted against the lesser darkness beyond the doorway. It crept inside the hut.

"Are you here?" whispered a childlike voice.

It was Mary! She had returned. The thongs no longer hurt me -- the pangs of hunger and thirst disappeared. I realized that it had been loneliness from which I suffered most.

"Mary!" I exclaimed. "You are a good girl. You have come back, after all -- I had commenced to think that you would not. Did you give my message to the queen? Will she come? Where is she?"

The child's sobs increased, and she flung herself upon the dirt floor of the hut, apparently overcome by grief.

"What is it?" I asked. "Why do you cry?"

"The queen, my mother, will not come to you," she said, between sobs. "She is dead. Buckingham has killed her. Now he will take Victory, for Victory is queen. He kept us fastened up in our shelter, for fear that Victory would escape him; but I dug a hole beneath the back wall and got out. I came to you, because you saved Victory once before, and I thought that you might save her again, and me, also. Tell me that you will."

"I am bound and helpless, Mary," I replied. "Otherwise I would do what I could to save you and your sister."

"I will set you free!" cried the girl, creeping to my side. "I will set you free, and then you may come and slay Buckingham."

"Gladly!" I assented.

"We must hurry," she went on, as she fumbled with the hard knots in the stiffened rawhide, "for Buckingham will be after you soon. He must make an offering to the lions at dawn before he can take Victory -- the taking of a queen requires a human offering!"

"And I am to be the offering?" I asked.

"Yes," she said, tugging at a knot. "Buckingham has been wanting a sacrifice ever since he killed Wettin, that he might slay my mother and take Victory."

The thought was horrible, not solely because of the hideous fate to which I was condemned; but from the contemplation it engendered of the sad decadence of a once enlightened race. To these depths of ignorance, brutality, and superstition had the vaunted civilization of twentieth-century England been plunged, and by what? War! I felt the structure of our time-honored militaristic arguments crumbling about me.

Mary labored with the thongs that confined me. They proved refractory -- defying her tender, childish fingers. She assured me, however, that she would release me, if "they" did not come too soon.

But, alas, they came. We heard them coming down the trench, and I bade Mary hide in a corner, lest she be discovered and punished. There was naught else she could do, and so she crawled away into the Stygian blackness behind me.

Presently two warriors entered. The leader exhibited a unique method of discovering my whereabouts in the darkness. He advanced slowly, kicking out viciously before him. Finally he kicked me in the face --then he knew where I was.

A moment later I had been jerked roughly to my feet. One of the fellows stopped and severed the bonds that held my ankles. I could scarcely stand alone. The two pulled and hauled me through the low doorway and along the trench. A party of forty or fifty warriors were awaiting us at the brink of the excavation some hundred yards from the hut.

Hands were lowered to us, and we were dragged to the surface. Then commenced a long march. We stumbled through the underbrush wet with dew, our way lighted by a score of torchbearers who surrounded us; but the torches were not to light the way -- that was but incidental. They were carried to keep off the huge carnivora that moaned and coughed and roared about us.

The noises were hideous. The whole country seemed alive

with lions. Yellow-green eyes blazed wickedly at us from out the surrounding darkness. My escort carried long, heavy spears. These they kept ever pointed toward the beast of prey, and I learned from snatches of the conversation I overheard that occasionally there might be a lion who would brave even the terrors of fire to leap in upon human prey -- it was for such that the spears were always couched.

But nothing of the sort occurred during this hideous death march, and with the first pale heralding of dawn we reached our goal -- an open place in the midst of a tangled wildwood. Here rose in crumbling grandeur the first evidences I had seen of the ancient civilization which once had graced fair Albion -- a single, time-worn arch of masonry.

"The entrance to the Camp of the Lions!" murmured one of the party in a voice husky with awe.

Here the party knelt, while Buckingham recited a weird, prayer-like chant. It was rather long, and I recall only a portion of it, which ran, if my memory serves me, somewhat as follows:

"Lord of Grabritin, we
Fall on our knees to thee,
This gift to bring.
Greatest of kings art thou!
To thee we humbly bow!
Peace to our camp allow.
God save thee, king!

Then the party rose, and dragging me to the crumbling arch, made me fast to a huge, corroded, copper ring which was dangling from an eyebolt imbedded in the masonry.

None of them, not even Buckingham, seemed to feel any personal animosity toward me. They were naturally rough and brutal, as primitive men are supposed to have been since the dawn of humanity; but they did not go out of their way to maltreat me.

With the coming of dawn the number of lions about us seemed to have greatly diminished -- at least they made less noise -- and as Buckingham and his party disappeared into the woods, leaving me alone to my terrible fate, I could hear the grumblings and growlings of the beasts diminishing with the sound of the chant, which the party still continued. It appeared that the lions had failed to note that I had been left for their breakfast, and had followed off after their worshippers instead.

But I knew the reprieve would be but for a short time, and though I had no wish to die, I must confess that I rather wished the ordeal over and the peace of oblivion upon me.

The voices of the men and the lions receded in the distance, until finally quiet reigned about me., broken only by the sweet voices of birds and the sighing of the summer wind in the trees.

It seemed impossible to believe that in this peaceful woodland setting the frightful thing was to occur which must come with the passing of the next lion who chanced within sight or smell of the crumbling arch.

I strove to tear myself loose from my bonds; but succeeded only in tightening them about my arms. Then I remained passive for a long time, letting the scenes of my lifetime pass in review before my mind's eye.

I tried to imagine the astonishment, incredulity, and horror with which my family and friends would be overwhelmed if, for an instant, space could be annihilated and they could see me at the gates of London.

The gates of London! Where was the multitude hurrying to the marts of trade after a night of pleasure or rest? Where was the clang of tramcar gongs, the screech of motor horns, the vast murmur of a dense throng?

Where were they? And as I asked the question a lone, gaunt lion strode from the tangled jungle upon the far side of the clearing. Majestically and noiselessly upon his padded feet the king of beasts moved slowly toward the gates of London and toward me.

Was I afraid? I fear that I was almost afraid. I know that I thought that fear was coming to me, and so I straightened up and squared my shoulders and looked the lion straight in the eyes -- and waited.

It is not a nice way to die -- alone, with one's hands fast bound, beneath the fangs and talons of a beast of prey. No, it is not a nice way to die, nor a pretty way.

The lion was halfway across the clearing when I heard a slight sound behind me. The great cat stopped in his tracks. He lashed his tail against his sides now, instead of simply twitching its tip, and his low moan became a thunderous roar.

As I craned my neck to catch a glimpse of the thing that had aroused the fury of the beast before me, it sprang through the arched gateway and was at my side -- with parted lips and heaving bosom and disheveled hair -- a bronzed and lovely vision to eyes that had never harbored hope of rescue.

It was Victory, and in her arms she clutched my rifle and revolver. A long knife was in the doeskin belt that supported the doeskin skirt tightly about her lithe limbs. She dropped my weapons at my feet, and, snatching the knife from its resting place, severed the bonds that held me. I was free, and the lion was preparing to charge.

"Run!" I cried to the girl, as I bent and seized my rifle; but she only stood there at my side, her bared blade ready in her hand.

The lion was bounding toward us now in prodigous leaps. I raised the rifle and fired. It was a lucky shot, for I had no time to aim carefully, and when the beast crumpled and rolled, lifeless, to the ground, I went upon my knees and gave thanks to the God of my ancestors.

And, still upon my knees, I turned, and taking the girl's hand in mine, I kissed it. She smiled at that, and laid her other hand upon my head.

"You have strange customs in your country," she said.

I could not but smile at that when I thought how strange it would seem to my countrymen could they but see me kneeling there on the site of London, kissing the hand of England's queen.

"And now," I said, as I rose, "you must return to the safety of your camp. I will go with you until you are near enough to continue alone in safety -- then I shall try to return to my comrades."

"I will not return to the camp," she replied.

"But what shall you do?" I asked.

"I do not know -- only I shall never go back while Buckingham lives. I should rather die than go back to him. Mary came to me, after they had taken you from the camp, and told me. I found your strange weapons and followed with them. It took me a little longer, for often I had to hide in the trees that the lions might not get me; but I came in time, and now you are free to go back to your friends."

"And leave you here?" I exclaimed.

She nodded, but I could see through all her brave front that she was frightened at the thought. I could not leave her, of course; but what in the world I was to do, cumbered with the care of a young woman, and a queen at that, I was at a loss to know. I pointed out that phase of it to her; but she only shrugged her shapely shoulders and pointed to her knife.

It was evident that she felt entirely competent to protect herself.

As we stood there we heard the sound of voices. They were coming from the forest through which we had passed when we had come from camp.

"They are searching for me," said the girl. "Where shall we hide?"

I didn't relish hiding; but when I thought of the innumerable dangers which surrounded us and the comparatively small amount of ammunition that I had with me, I hesitated to provoke a battle with Buckingham and his warriors when, by flight, I could avoid them and preserve my cartridges against emergencies which could not be escaped.

"Would they follow us there?" I asked, pointing through the archway into the Camp of the Lions.

"Never," she replied, "for, in the first place, they would know that we would not dare go there, and in the second they themselves would not dare."

"Then we shall take refuge in the Camp of the Lions," I said.

She shuddered and drew closer to me.

"You dare?" she asked.

"Why not?" I returned. "We shall be safe from Buckingham, and you have seen, for the second time in two days, that lions are harmless before my weapons. Then, too, I can find my friends easiest in this direction, for the River Thames runs through this place you call the Camp of the Lions, and it is farther down the Thames that my friends are awaiting me. Do you not dare come with me?"

"I dare follow wherever you lead," she answered simply.

And so I turned and passed beneath the great arch into the city of London.

CHAPTER V

As we entered deeper into what had once been the city, the evidences of man's past occupancy became more frequent. For a mile from the arch there was only a riot of weeds and undergrowth and trees covering small mounds and little hillocks that, I was sure, were formed of the ruins of stately buildings of the dead past.

But presently we came upon a district where shattered walls still raised their crumbling tops in sad silence above the grass-grown sepulchers of their fallen fellows. Softened and mellowed by ancient ivy stood these sentinels of sorrow, their scarred faces still revealing the rents and gashes of shrapnel and of bomb.

Contrary to our expectations, we found little indication that lions in any great numbers laired in this part of ancient London. Well-worn pathways, molded by padded paws, led through the cavernous windows or doorways of a few of the ruins we passed, and once we saw the savage face of a great, black-maned lion scowling down upon us from a shattered stone balcony.

We followed down the bank of the Thames after we came upon it. I was anxious to look with my own eyes upon the famous bridge, and I guessed, too, that the river would lead me into that part of London where stood Westminster Abbey and the Tower.

Realizing that the section through which we had been passing was doubtless outlying, and therefore not so built up with large structures as the more centrally located part of the old town, I felt sure that farther down the river I should find the ruins larger. The bridge would be there in part, at least, and so would remain the walls of many of the great edifices of the past. There would be no such complete ruin of large structures as I had seen among the smaller buildings.

But when I had come to that part of the city which I judged to have contained the relics I sought I found havoc that had been wrought there even greater than elsewhere.

At one point upon the bosom of the Thames there rises a few feet above the water a single, disintegrating mound of masonry. Opposite it, upon either bank of the river, are tumbled piles of ruins overgrown with vegetation.

These, I am forced to believe, are all that remain of London Bridge, for nowhere else along the river is there any other slightest sign of pier or abutment.

Rounding the base of a large pile of grass-covered debris, we came suddenly upon the best preserved ruin we had yet discovered. The entire lower story and a part of the second story of what must once have been a splendid public building rose from a great knoll of shrubbery and trees, while ivy, thick and luxuriant, clambered upward to the summit of the broken walls.

In many places the gray stone was still exposed, its smoothly chiseled face pitted with the scars of battle. The massive portal yawned, somber and sorrowful, before us, giving a glimpse of marble halls within.

The temptation to enter was too great. I wished to explore the interior of this one remaining monument of civilization now dead beyond recall. Through this same portal, within these very marble halls, had Gray and Chamberlin and Kitchener and Shaw, perhaps, come and gone with the other great ones of the past.

I took Victory's hand in mine.

"Come!" I said. "I do not know the name by which this great pile was known, nor the purposes it fulfilled. It may have been the palace of your sires, Victory. From some great throne within your forebears may have directed the destinies of half the world. Come!"

I must confess to a feeling of awe as we entered the rotunda of the great building. Pieces of massive furniture of another day still stood where man had placed them centuries ago. They were littered with dust and broken stone and plaster; but, otherwise, so perfect was their preservation I could hardly believe that two centuries had rolled by since human eyes were last set upon them.

Through one great room after another we wandered, hand in hand, while Victory asked many questions and for the first time I began to realize something of the magnificence and power of the race from whose loins she had sprung.

Splendid tapestries, now mildewed and rotting, hung upon the walls. There were mural paintings, too, depicting great historic events of the past. For the first time Victory saw the likeness of a horse, and she was much affected by a huge oil which depicted some ancient cavalry charge against a battery of field guns.

In other pictures there were steamships, battleships, submarines, and quaint looking railway trains -- all small and antiquated in appearance to me, but wonderful to Victory. She told me that she would like to remain for the rest of her life where she could look at those pictures daily.

From room to room we passed until presently we emerged into a mighty chamber, dark and gloomy, for its high and narrow windows were choked and clogged by ivy. Along one paneled wall we groped, our eyes slowly becoming accustomed to the darkness. A rank and pungent odor pervaded the atmosphere.

We had made our way about half the distance across one end of the great apartment when a low growl from the far end brought us to a startled halt.

Straining my eyes through the gloom, I made out a raised dais at the extreme opposite end of the hall. Upon the dais stood two great chairs, highbacked and with great arms.

The throne of England! But what were those strange forms about it?

Victory gave my hand a quick, excited little squeeze.

"The lions!" she whispered.

Yes, lions indeed! Sprawled about the dais were a dozen huge forms, while upon the seat of one of the thrones a small cub lay curled in slumber.

As we stood there for a moment, spellbound by the sight of those fearsome creatures occupying the very thrones of the sovereigns of England, the low growl was repeated, and a great male rose slowly to his feet.

His devilish eyes bored straight through the semidarkness toward us. He had discovered the interloper. What right had man within this palace of the beasts? Again he opened his giant jaws, and this time there rumbled forth a warning roar.

Instantly eight or ten of the other beasts leaped to their feet. Already the great fellow who had spied us was advancing slowly in our direction. I held my rifle ready; but how futile it appeared in the face of this savage horde.

The foremost beast broke into a slow trot, and at his heels came the others. All were roaring now, and the din of their great voices reverberating through the halls and corridors of the palace formed the most frightful chorus of thunderous savagery imaginable to the mind of man.

And then the leader charged, and upon the hideous pandemonium broke the sharp crack of my rifle, once, twice, thrice. Three lions rolled, struggling and biting, to the floor. Victory seized my arm, with a quick: "This way! Here is a door," and a moment later we were in a tiny antechamber at the foot of a narrow stone staircase.

Up this we backed, Victory just behind me, as the first of the remaining lions leaped from the throne room and sprang for the stairs. Again I fired; but others of the ferocious beasts leaped over their fallen fellows and pursued us.

The stairs were very narrow -- that was all that saved us -- for as I backed slowly upward, but a single lion could attack me at a time, and the carcasses of those I slew impeded the rushes of the others.

At last we reached the top. There was a long corridor from which opened many doorways. One, directly behind us, was tight closed. If we could open it and pass into the chamber behind we might find a respite from attack.

The remaining lions were roaring horribly. I saw one sneaking very slowly up the stairs toward us.

"Try that door," I called to Victory. "See if it will open."

She ran up to it and pushed.

"Turn the knob!" I cried, seeing that she did not know how to open a door; but neither did she know what I meant by knob.

I put a bullet in the spine of the approaching lion and leaped to Victory's side. The door resisted my first efforts to swing it inward. Rusted hinges and swollen wood held it tightly closed; but at last it gave, and just as another lion mounted to the top of the stairway it swung in, and I pushed Victory across the threshold.

Then I turned to meet the renewed attack of the savage foe. One lion fell in his tracks, another stumbled to my very feet, and then I leaped within and slammed the portal to.

A quick glance showed me that this was the only door to the small apartment in which we had found sanctuary, and, with a sigh of relief, I leaned for a moment against the panels of the stout barrier that separated us from the ramping demons without.

Across the room, between two windows, stood a flat-topped desk. A little pile of white and brown lay upon it close to the opposite edge. After a moment of rest I crossed the room to investigate. The white was the bleached human bones -- the skull, collar bones, arms, and a few of the upper ribs of a man. The brown was the dust of a decayed military cap and blouse. In a chair before the desk were other bones, while more still strewed the floor beneath the desk and about the chair. A man had died sitting there with his face buried in his arms -- two hundred years ago.

Beneath the desk were a pair of spurred military boots, green and rotten with decay. In them were the leg bones of a man. Among the tiny bones of the hands was an ancient fountain pen, as good, apparently, as the day it was made, and a metal covered memoranda book, closed over the bones of an index finger.

It was a gruesome sight -- a pitiful sight -- this lone inhabitant of mighty London.

I picked up the metal covered memoranda book. Its pages were rotten and stuck together. Only here and there was a sentence or a part of a sentence legible. The first that I could read was near the middle of the little volume:

"His majesty left for Tunbridge Wells today, he . . . jesty was stricken . . . terday. God give she does not die . . . am military governor of Lon . . "

And farther on:

"It is awful . . . hundred deaths today . . . . worse than the bombardm . . . "

Nearer the end I picked out the following:

"I promised his maj . . . . e will find me here when he ret . . . . alone."

The most legible passage was on the next page:

"Thank God we drove them out. There is not a single. . . man on British soil today; but at what awful cost. I tried to persuade Sir Phillip to urge the people to remain; but they are mad with fear of the Death, and rage at our enemies. He tells me that the coast cities are packed . . . waiting to be taken across. What will become of England, with none left to rebuild her shattered cities!"

And the last entry:

" . . . . alone. Only the wild beasts . . . A lion is roaring now beneath the palace windows. I think the people feared the beasts even more than they did the Death. But they are gone, all gone, and to what? How much better conditions will they find on the continent? All gone -- only I remain. I promised his majesty, and when he returns he will find that I was true to my trust; for I shall be awaiting him. God save the King!"

That was all. This brave and forever nameless officer died nobly at his post -- true to his country and his king. It was the Death, no doubt, that took him.

Some of the entries had been dated. From the few legible letters and figures which remained I judge the end came some time in August, 1937; but of that I am not at all certain.

The diary has cleared up at least one mystery that had puzzled me not a little, and now I am surprised that I had not guessed its solution myself -- the presence of African and Asiatic beasts in England.

Acclimated by years of confinement in the zoological gardens, they were fitted to resume in England the wild existence for which nature had intended them, and once free, had evidently bred prolifically, in marked contrast to the captive exotics of twentieth century Pan-America, which had gradually become fewer until extinction occurred some time during the twenty-first century.

The Palace, if such it was, lay not far from the banks of the Thames. The room in which we were imprisoned overlooked the river, and I determined to attempt to escape in this direction.

To descend through the palace was out of the question; but outside we could discover no lions. The stems of the ivy which clambered upward past the window of the room were as large around as my arm. I knew that they would support our weight, and as we could gain nothing by remaining longer in the palace, I decided to descend by way of the ivy and follow along down the river in the direction of the launch.

Naturally I was much handicapped by the presence of the girl; but I could not abandon her, though I had no idea what I should do with her after rejoining my companions. That she would prove a burden and an embarrassment I was certain, but she had made it equally plain to me that she would never return to her people to mate with Buckingham.

I owed my life to her, and, all other considerations aside, that was sufficient demand upon my gratitude and my honor to necessitate my suffering every inconvenience in her service. Too, she was queen of England; but, by far the most potent argument in her favor, she was a woman in distress -- and a young and very beautiful one.

And so, though I wished a thousand times that she was back in her camp, I never let her guess it; but did all that lay within my power to serve and protect her. I thank God now that I did so.

With the lions still padding back and forth beyond the closed door, Victory and I crossed the room to one of the windows. I had outlined my plan to her, and she had assured me that she could descend the ivy without assistance. In fact she smiled a trifle at my question.

Swinging myself outward, I began the descent, and had come to within a few feet of the ground, being just opposite a narrow window, when I was startled by a savage growl almost in my ear, and then a great taloned paw darted from the aperture to seize me, and I saw the snarling face of a lion within the embrasure.

Releasing my hold upon the ivy, I dropped the remaining distance to the ground, saved from laceration only because the lion's paw struck the thick stem of ivy.

The creature was making a frightful racket now, leaping back and forth from the floor to the broad window ledge, tearing at the masonry with his claws in vain attempts to reach me; but the opening was too narrow, and the masonry too solid.

Victory had commenced the descent, but I called to her to stop just above the window, and, as the lion reappeared, growling and snarling, I put a . 33 bullet in his face, and at the same moment Victory slipped quickly past him, dropping into my upraised arms that were awaiting her.

The roaring of the beasts that had discovered us, together with the report of my rifle, had set the balance of the fierce inmates of the palace into the most frightful uproar I have ever heard.

I feared that it would not be long before intelligence or instinct would draw them from the interiors and set them upon our trail, the river, nor had we much more than reached it when a lion bounded around the corner of the edifice we had just quitted and stood looking about as though in search of us.

Following, came others, while Victory and I crouched in hiding behind a clump of bushes close to the bank of the river. The beasts sniffed about the ground for a while, but they did not chance to go near the spot where we had stood beneath the window that had given us escape.

Presently a black-maned male raised his head, and, with cocked ears and glaring eyes, gazed straight at the bush behind which we lay. I could have sworn that he had discovered us, and when he took a few short and stately steps in our direction I raised my rifle and covered him; but after a long, tense moment he looked away, and turned to glare in another direction.

I breathed a sigh of relief, and so did Victory -- I could feel her body quiver as she lay pressed close to me, our cheeks almost touching as we both peered through the same small opening in the foliage.

I turned to give her a reassuring smile as the lion indicated that he had not seen us, and as I did so she, too, turned her face toward mine, for the same purpose, doubtless. Anyway, as our heads turned simultaneously, our lips brushed together. A startled expression came into Victory's eyes as she drew back in evident confusion.

As for me, the strangest sensation that I have ever experienced claimed me for an instant. A peculiar, tingling thrill ran through my veins, and my head swam. I could not account for it.

Naturally, being a naval officer and consequently in the best society of the federation, I have seen much of women. With others, I have laughed at the assertions of the savants that modern man is a cold and passionless creation in comparison with the males of former ages -- in a word, that love, as the one grand passion, had ceased to exist.

I do not know, now, but that they were more nearly right than we have guessed, at least in so far as modern civilized woman is concerned. I have kissed many women -- young and beautiful and middle aged and old, and many that I had no business kissing -- but never before had I experienced that remarkable and altogether delightful thrill that followed the accidental brushing of my lips against the lips of Victory.

The occurrence interested me, and I was tempted to experiment further; but when I would have essayed it another new and entirely unaccountable force restrained me -- for the first time in my life I felt embarrassment in the presence of a woman..

What further might have developed I cannot say, for at that moment a perfect she-devil of a lioness, with keener eyes than her lord and master, discovered us. She came trotting toward our place of concealment, growling and baring her yellow fangs.

I waited for an instant, hoping that I might be mistaken, and that she would turn off in some other direction; but no -- she increased her trot to a gallop, and then I fired at her; but the bullet, though it struck her full in the breast, didn't stop her.

Screaming with pain and rage, the creature fairly flew toward us. Behind her came other lions. Our case looked hopeless. We were upon the brink of the river. There seemed no avenue of escape, and I knew that even my modern automatic rifle was inadequate in the face of so many of these fierce beasts.

To remain where we were would have been suicidal. We were both standing now, Victory keeping her place bravely at my side, when I reached the only decision open to me.

Seizing the girl's hand, I turned, just as the lioness crashed into the opposite side of the bushes, and, dragging Victory after me, leaped over the edge of the bank into the river.

I did not know that lions are not fond of water, nor did I know if Victory could swim; but death, immediate and terrible, stared us in the face if we remained, and so I took the chance.

At this point the current ran close to the shore, so that we were immediately in deep water, and, to my intense satisfaction, Victory struck out with a strong, overhand stroke and set all my fears on her account at rest.

But my relief was short-lived. That lioness, as I have said before, was a veritable devil. She stood for a moment glaring at us, then like a shot she sprang into the river and swam swiftly after us.

Victory was a length ahead of me.

"Swim for the other shore!" I called to her.

I was much impeded by my rifle, having to swim with one hand while I clung to my precious weapon with the other. The girl had seen the lioness take to the water, and she had also seen that I was swimming much more slowly than she, and what did she do? She started to drop back to my side.

"Go on!" I cried. "Make for the other shore, and then follow down until you find my friends. Tell them that I sent you, and with orders that they are to protect you. Go on! Go on!"

But she only waited until we were again swimming side by side, and I saw that she had drawn her long knife, and was holding it between her teeth.

"Do as I tell you!" I said to her sharply; but she shook her head.

The lioness was overhauling us rapidly. She was swimming silently, her chin just touching the water; but blood was streaming from between her lips. It was evident that her lungs were pierced.

She was almost upon me. I saw that in a moment she would take me under her forepaws, or seize me in those great jaws. I felt that my time had come; but I meant to die fighting, and so I turned, and, treading water, raised my rifle above my head and awaited her.

Victory, animated by a bravery no less ferocious than that of the dumb beast assailing us, swam straight for me. It all happened so swiftly that I cannot recall the details of the kaleidoscopic action which ensued. I knew that I rose high out of the water, and, with clubbed rifle, dealt the animal a terrific blow upon the skull; that I saw Victory, her long blade flashing in her hand, close, striking, upon the beast; that a great paw fell upon my shoulder, and that I was swept beneath the surface of the water like a straw before the prow of a freighter.

Still clinging to my rifle, I rose again, to see the lioness struggling in her death throes but an arm's length from me. Scarcely had I risen than the beast turned upon her side, struggled frantically for an instant, and then sank.

CHAPTER VI

Victory was nowhere in sight. Alone, I floated upon the bosom of the Thames. In that brief instant I believe that I suffered more mental anguish than I have crowded into all the balance of my life before or since. A few hours before, I had been wishing that I might be rid of her, and now that she was gone I would have given my life to have her back again.

Wearily I turned to swim about the spot where she had disappeared, hoping that she might rise once at least, and I would be given the opportunity to save her; and, as I turned, the water boiled before my face and her head shot up before me. I was on the point of striking out to seize her, when a happy smile illumined her features.

"You are not dead!" she cried. "I have been searching the bottom for you. I was sure that the blow she gave you must have disabled you," and she glanced about for the lioness.

"She has gone?" she asked.

"Dead," I replied.

"The blow you struck her with the thing you call rifle stunned her," she explained, "and then I swam in close enough to get my knife into her heart."

Ah, such a girl! I could not but wonder what one of our own Pan-American women would have done under like circumstances; but then, of course, they have not been trained by stern necessity to cope with the emergencies and dangers of savage primeval life.

Along the bank we had just quitted a score of lions paced

to and fro, growling menacingly. We could not return, and we struck out for the opposite shore. I am a strong swimmer, and had no doubt as to my ability to cross the river; but I was not so sure about Victory, so I swam close behind her, to be ready to give her assistance should she need it.

She did not, however, reaching the opposite bank as fresh, apparently, as when she entered the water. Victory is a wonder. Each day that we were together brought new proofs of it. Nor was it her courage or vitality only which amazed me. She had a head on those shapely shoulders of hers, and dignity! My, but she could be regal when she chose!

She told me that the lions were fewer upon this side of the river; but that there were many wolves, running in great packs later in the year. Now they were north somewhere, and we should have little to fear from them, though we might meet with a few.

My first concern was to take my weapons apart and dry them, which was rather difficult in the face of the fact that every rag about me was drenched; but finally, thanks to the sun and much rubbing, I succeeded, though I had no oil to lubricate them.

We ate some wild berries and roots that Victory found, and then we set off again down the river, keeping an eye open for game on one side and the launch on the other, for I thought that Delcarte, who would be the natural leader during my absence, might run up the Thames in search of me.

The balance of that day we sought in vain for game or for the launch, and when night came we lay down, our stomachs empty, to sleep beneath the stars. We were entirely unprotected from attack from wild beasts, and for this reason I remained awake most of the night, on guard; but nothing approached us, though I could hear the lions roaring across the river, and once I thought I heard the howl of a beast to the north of us -- it might have been a wolf.

Altogether, it was a most unpleasant night, and I determined then that if we were forced to sleep out again that I should provide some sort of shelter which would protect us from attack while we slept.

Toward morning I dozed, and the sun was well up when Victory aroused me by gently shaking my shoulder.

"Antelope!" she whispered in my ear; and, as I raised my head, she pointed upriver. Crawling to my knees, I looked in the direction she indicated, to see a buck standing upon a little knol some two hundred yards from us. There was good cover between the animal and me, and so, though I might have hit him at two hundred yards, I preferred to crawl closer to him and make sure of the meat we both so craved.

I had covered about fifty yards of the distance, and the beast was still feeding peacefully, so I thought that I would make even surer of a hit by going ahead another fifty yards, when the animal suddenly raised his head and looked away upriver. His whole attitude proclaimed that he was startled by something beyond him that I could not see.

Realizing that he might break and run and that I should then probably miss him entirely, I raised my rifle to my shoulder; but even as I did so the animal leaped into the air, and simultaneously there was a sound of a shot from beyond the knoll.

For an instant I was dumbfounded. Had the report come from downriver, I should have instantly thought that one of my own men had fired; but coming from upriver it puzzled me considerably. Who could there be with firearms in primitive England other than we of the COLDWATER?

Victory was directly behind me, and I motioned for her to lie down, as I did, behind the bush from which I had been upon the point of firing at the antelope. We could see that the buck was quite dead, and from our hiding place we waited to discover the identity of his slayer when the latter should approach and claim his kill.

We had not long to wait, and when I saw the head and shoulders of a man appear above the crest of the knoll, I sprang to my feet, with a heartfelt cry of joy, for it was Delcarte.

At the sound of my voice, Delcarte half raised his rifle in readiness for the attack of an enemy; but a moment later he recognized me, and was coming rapidly to meet us. Behind him was Snider. They both were astounded to see me upon the north bank of the river, and much more so at the sight of my companion.

Then I introduced them to Victory, and told them that she was queen of England. They thought, at first, that I was joking; but when I had recounted my adventures and they realized that I was in earnest they believed me.

They told me that they had followed me inshore when I had not returned from the hunt; that they had met the men of the elephant country, and had had a short and one-sided battle with the fellows, and that afterward they had returned to the launch with a prisoner, from whom they had learned that I had probably been captured by the men of the lion country.

With the prisoner as a guide they had set off upriver in search of me, but had been much delayed by motor trouble, and had finally camped after dark a half mile above the spot where Victory and I had spent the night -- they must have passed us in the dark, and why I did not hear the sound of the propeller I do not know, unless it passed me at a time when the lions were making an unusually ear-splitting din upon the opposite side.

Taking the antelope with us, we all returned to the launch, where we found Taylor as delighted to see me alive again as Delcarte had been. I cannot say truthfully that Snider evinced much enthusiasm at my rescue.

Taylor had found the ingredients for chemical fuel, and the distilling of them had, with the motor trouble, accounted for their delay in setting out after me.

The prisoner that Delcarte and Snider had taken was a powerful young fellow, from the elephant country. Notwithstanding the fact that they had all assured him to the contrary, he still could not believe that we would not kill him.

He assured us that his name was Thirty-Six, and, as he could not count above ten, I am sure that he had no conception of the correct meaning of the word, and that it may have been handed down to him either from the military number of an ancestor who had served in the English ranks during the Great War, or that originally it was the number of some famous regiment with which a forbear fought.

Now that we were reunited, we held a council to determine what course we should pursue in the immediate future. Snider was still for setting out to sea and returning to Pan-America, but the better judgement of Delcarte and Taylor ridiculed the suggestion -- we should not have lived a fortnight.

To remain in England, constantly menaced by wild beasts and men equally as wild, seemed about as bad. I suggested that we cross the channel and ascertain if we could not discover a more enlightened and civilized people upon the continent. I was sure that some trace of the ancient culture and greatness of Europe must remain. Germany, probably, would be much as it was during the twentieth century, for, in common with most Pan-Americans, I was positive that Germany had been victorious in the Great War.

But Snider demurred at the suggestion. He said that it was bad enough to have come this far -- he did not want to make it worse by going to the continent. The outcome of it was that I finally lost my patience, and told him that from then on he would do what I thought best -- that I purposed to assume command of the party, and that they might all consider themselves under my orders, as much so as though we were still aboard the COLDWATER and in Pan-American waters.

Delcarte and Taylor immediately assured me that they had not for an instant assumed anything different, and that they were as ready to follow and obey me here as they would be upon the other side of 30.

Snider said nothing; but he wore a sullen scowl, and I wished then, as I had before and as I did to a much greater extent later, that fate had not decreed that he should have chanced to be a member of the launch's party upon that memorable day when last we quitted the COLDWATER.

Victory, who was given a voice in our councils, was all for going to the continent, or anywhere else, in fact, where she might see new sights and experience new adventures.

"Afterward we can come back to Grabritin," she said,

"and if Buckingham is not dead and we can catch him away from his men and kill him, then I can return to my people, and we can all live in peace and happiness."

She spoke of killing Buckingham with no greater concern than one might evince in the contemplated destruction of a sheep; yet she was neither cruel nor vindicative. In fact, Victory is a very sweet and womanly woman; but human life is of small account beyond 30 -- a legacy from the bloody days when thousands of men perished in the trenches between the rising and the setting of a sun; when they laid them lengthwise in these same trenches and sprinkled dirt over them; when the Germans corded their corpses like wood and set fire to them; when women and children and old men were butchered; and great passenger ships torpedoed without warning.

Thirty-six, finally assured that we did not intend slaying him, was as keen to accompany us as was Victory.

The crossing to the continent was uneventful; its monotony being relieved, however, by the childish delight of Victory and Thirty-six in the novel experience of riding safely upon the bosom of the water, and of being so far from land.

With the possible exception of Snider, the little party appeared in the best of spirits, laughing and joking, or interestedly discussing the possibilities which the future held for us, what we should find upon the continent, and whether the inhabitants would be civilized or barbarian peoples.

Victory asked me to explain the difference between the two, and when I had tried to do so as clearly as possible, she broke into a gay little laugh.

"Oh," she cried, "then I am a barbarian!"

I could not but laugh, too, as I admitted that she was, indeed, a barbarian. She was not offended, taking the matter as a huge joke; but some time thereafter she sat in silence, apparently deep in thought. Finally she looked up at me, her strong white teeth gleaming behind her smiling lips.

"Should you take that thing you call 'razor' " she said, "and cut the hair from the face of Thirty-six, and exchange garments with him, you would be the barbarian and Thirty-six the civilized man. There is no other difference between you, except your weapons. Cloth you in a wolfskin, give you a knife and a spear, and set you down in the woods of Grabritin -- of what service would your civilization be to you?"

Delcarte and Taylor smiled at her reply, but Thirty-six and Snider laughed uproariously. I was not surprised at Thirty-six, but I thought that Snider laughed louder than the occasion warranted. As a matter of fact, Snider, it seemed to me, was taking advantage of every opportunity, however slight, to show insubordination, and I determined then that at the first real breach of discipline I should take action that would remind Snider, ever after, that I was still his commanding officer.

I could not help but notice that his eyes were much upon Victory, and I did not like it, for I knew the type of man he was; but as it would not be necessary ever to leave the girl alone with him I felt no apprehension for her safety.

After the incident of the discussion of barbarians I thought that Victory's manner toward me changed perceptibly. She held aloof from me, and when Snider took his turn at the wheel, sat beside him, upon the pretext that she wished to learn how to steer the launch. I wondered if she had guessed the man's antipathy for me, and was seeking his company solely for the purpose of piquing me.

Snider was, too, taking full advantage of his opportunity. Often he leaned toward the girl to whisper in her ear, and he laughed much, which was unusual with Snider.

Of course, it was nothing at all to me; yet, for some unaccountable reason, the sight of the two of them sitting there so close to one another and seeming to be enjoying each other's society to such a degree irritated me tremendously, and put me in such a bad humor that I took no pleasure whatsoever in the last few hours of the crossing.

We aimed to land near the site of ancient Ostend; but when we neared the coast we discovered no indication of any human habitations whatever, let alone a city. After we had landed, we found the same howling wilderness about us that we had discovered on the British Isle -- there was no slightest indication that civilized man had ever set a foot upon that portion of the continent of Europe.

Although I had feared as much, since our experience in England, I could not but own to a feeling of marked disappointment, and to the gravest fears of the future, which induced a mental depression that was in no way dissipated by the continued familiarity between Victory and Snider.

I was angry with myself that I permitted that matter to affect me as it had. I did not wish to admit to myself that I was angry with this uncultured little savage -- that it made the slightest difference to me what she did, or what she did not do -- or that I could so lower myself as to feel personal enmity toward a common sailor; and yet, to be honest, I was doing both.

Finding nothing to detain us about the spot where Ostend once had stood, we set out up the coast in search of the mouth of the River Rhine, which I purposed ascending in search of civilized man. It was my intention to explore the Rhine as far up as the launch would take us. If we found no civilization there we would return to the North Sea, continue up the coast to the Elbe, and follow that river and the canals of Berlin. Here, at least, I was sure that we should find what we sought; and, if not, then all Europe had reverted to barbarism.

The weather remained fine, and we made excellent progress, but everywhere along the Rhine we met with the same disappointment -- no sign of civilized man; in fact, no sign of man at all.

I was not enjoying the exploration of modern Europe as I had anticipated -- I was unhappy. Victory seemed changed, too. I had enjoyed her company at first; but since the trip across the Channel I had held aloof from her.

Her chin was in the air most of the time, and yet I rather think that she regretted her friendliness with Snider, for I noticed that she avoided him entirely. He, on the contrary, emboldened by her former friendliness, sought every opportunity to be near her. I should have liked nothing better than a reasonably good excuse to punch his head; yet, paradoxically, I was ashamed of myself for harboring him any ill will. I realized that there was something the matter with me; but I did not know what it was.

Matters remained thus for several days, and we continued our journey up the Rhine. At Cologne, I had hoped to find some reassuring indications; but there was no Cologne, and as there had been no other cities along the river up to that point, the devastation was infinitely greater than time alone could have wrought. Great guns, bombs, and mines must have leveled every building that man had raised, and then nature, unhindered, had covered the ghastly evidence of human depravity with her beauteous mantle of verdure. Splendid trees reared their stately tops where splendid cathedrals once had reared their domes, and sweet wild flowers blossomed in simple serenity in soil that once was drenched with human blood.

Nature had reclaimed what man had once stolen from her and defiled. A herd of zebras grazed where once the German kaiser may have reviewed his troops. An antelope rested peacefully in a bed of daisies where, perhaps, two hundred years ago a big gun belched its terror-laden messages of death, of hate, of destruction against the works of man and God alike.

We were in need of fresh meat, yet I hesitated to shatter the quiet and peaceful serenity of the view with the crack of a rifle and the death of one of those beautiful creatures before us. But it must be done -- we must eat. I left the work to Delcarte, however, and in a moment we had two antelope and the landscape to ourselves.

After eating, we boarded the launch and continued up the river. For two days we passed through a primeval wilderness, unrelieved. In the afternoon of the second day we landed upon the west bank of the river, and, leaving Snider and Thirty-six to guard Victory and the launch, Delcarte, Taylor, and I set out after game.

We tramped away from the river for upwards of an hour before discovering anything, and then only a small red deer, which Taylor brought down with a neat shot of two hundred yards. It was getting too late to proceed farther, so we rigged a sling, and the two men carried the deer back toward the launch while I walked a hundred yards ahead, in the hope of bagging something further for our larder.

We had covered about half the distance to the river, when I suddenly came face to face with a man. He was primitive and uncouth in appearance as the Grabritins -- a shaggy, unkempt savage, clothed in a shirt of skin cured with the head on, the latter surmounting his own head to form a bonnet, and giving to him a most fearful and ferocious aspect.

The fellow was armed with a long spear and a club, the latter dangling down his back from a leathern thong about his neck. His feet were incased in hide sandals.

At sight of me, he halted for an instant, then turned and dove into the forest, and, though I called reassuringly to him in English he did not return nor did I again see him.

The sight of the wild man raised my hopes once more that elsewhere we might find men in higher state of civilization -- it was the society of civilized man that I craved -- and so, with a lighter heart, I continued on toward the river and the launch.

I was still some distance ahead of Delcarte and Taylor when I came in sight of the Rhine again; but I came to the water's edge before I noticed that anything was amiss with the party we had left there a few hours before.

My first intimation of disaster was the absence of the launch from its former moorings; and then, a moment later, I discovered the body of a man lying upon the bank. Running toward it, I saw that it was Thirty-six, and as I stopped and raised the Grabritin's head in my arms I heard a faint moan break from his lips. He was not dead; but that he was badly injured was all too evident.

Delcarte and Taylor came up a moment later, and the three of us worked over the fellow, hoping to revive him that he might tell us what had happened, and what had become of the others. My first thought was prompted by the sight I had recently had of the savage native. The little party had evidently been surprised, and in the attack Thirty-six had been wounded and the others taken prisoners. The thought was almost like a physical blow in the face -- it stunned me. Victory in the hands of these abysmal brutes! It was frightful. I almost shook poor Thirty-six in my efforts to revive him.

I explained my theory to the others, and then Delcarte shattered it by a single movement of a hand -- he drew aside the lion's skin that covered half of the Grabritin's breast, revealing a neat, round hole in Thirty-six's chest -- a hole that could have been made by no other weapon than a rifle.

"Snider!" I exclaimed. Delcarte nodded. At about the same time the eyelids of the wounded man fluttered, and raised. He looked up at us, and very slowly the light of consciousness returned to his eyes.

"What happened, Thirty-six?" I asked him.

He tried to reply, but the effort caused him to cough, bringing about a hemorrhage of the lungs and again he fell back exhausted. For several long minutes he lay as one dead, then in an almost inaudible whisper he spoke.

"Snider --." He paused, tried to speak again, raised a hand, and pointed downriver. "They -- went -- back," and then he shuddered convulsively and died.

None of us voiced his belief; but I think they were all alike: Victory and Snider had stolen the launch, and deserted us.

CHAPTER VII

We stood there, grouped about the body of the dead Grabritin, looking futilely down the river to where it made an abrupt curve to the west a quarter of a mile below us, and was lost to sight, as though we expected to see the truant returning to us with our precious launch -- the thing that meant life or death to us in this unfriendly, savage world.

I felt, rather than saw, Taylor turn his eyes slowly toward my profile, and, as mine swung to meet them, the expression upon his face recalled me to my duty and responsibility as an officer.

The utter hopelessness that was reflected in his face must have been the counterpart of what I myself felt; but in that brief instant I determined to hide my own misgivings that I might bolster up the courage of the others.

"We are lost!" was written as plainly upon Taylor's face as though his features were the printed words upon an open book. He was thinking of the launch, and of the launch alone. Was I? I tried to think that I was; but a greater grief than the loss of the launch could have engendered in me filled my heart -- a sullen, gnawing misery which I tried to deny -- which I refused to admit -- but which persisted in obsessing me until my heart rose and filled my throat, and I could not speak when I would have uttered words of reassurance to my companions.

And then rage came to my relief -- rage against the vile traitor who had deserted three of his fellow countrymen in so frightful a position. I tried to feel an equal rage against the woman; but somehow I could not, and kept searching for excuses for her -- her youth, her inexperience, her savagery.

My rising anger swept away my temporary helplessness. I smiled, and told Taylor not to look so glum.

"We will follow them," I said, "and the chances are that we shall overtake them. They will not travel as rapidly as Snider probably hopes. He will be forced to halt for fuel and for food, and the launch must follow the windings of the river; we can take short cuts while they are traversing the detour. I have my map -- thank God! I always carry it upon my person -- and with that and the compass we will have an advantage over them."

My words seemed to cheer them both, and they were for starting off at once in pursuit. There was no reason why we should delay, and we set forth down the river. As we tramped along, we discussed a question that was uppermost in the mind of each -- what we should do with Snider when we had captured him, for with the action of pursuit had come the optimistic conviction that we should succeed. As a matter of fact, we had to succeed. The very thought of remaining in this utter wilderness for the rest of our lives was impossible.

We arrived at nothing very definite in the matter of Snider's punishment, since Taylor was for shooting him, Delcarte insisting upon that he should be hanged, while I, although fully conscious of the gravity of his offense, could not bring myself to giving the death penalty.

I fell to wondering what charm Victory had found in such a man as Snider, and why I insisted upon finding excuses for her and trying to defend her indefensible act. She was nothing to me. Aside from the natural gratitude I felt for her since she had saved my life, I owed her nothing. She was a half-naked little savage -- I a gentleman, and an officer in the world's greatest navy. There could be no close bonds of interest between us.

This line of reflection I discovered to be as distressing as the former; but, though I tried to turn my mind to other things, it persisted in returning to the vision of an oval face, sun-tanned; of smiling lips, revealing white and even teeth; of brave eyes that harbored no shadow of guile; and of a tumbling mass of wavy hair that crowned the lovliest picture on which my eyes had ever rested.

Every time this vision presented itself I felt myself turn cold with rage and hate against Snider. I could forgive the launch; but if he had wronged her he should die -- he should die at my own hands; in this I was determined.

For two days we followed the river northward, cutting off where we could, but confined for the most part to the game trails that paralleled the stream. One afternoon, we cut across a narrow neck of land that saved us many miles, where the river wound to the west and back again.

Here we decided to halt, for we had had a hard day of it, and, if the truth were known, I think that we had all given up hope of overtaking the launch other than by the merest accident.

We had shot a deer just before our halt, and, as Taylor and Delcarte were preparing it, I walked down to the water to fill our canteens. I had just finished, and was straightening up, when something floating around a bend above me caught my eye. For a moment I could not believe the testimony of my own senses. It was a boat.

I shouted to Delcarte and Taylor, who came running to my side.

"The launch!" cried Delcarte; and, indeed, it was the launch, floating downriver from above us. Where had it been? How had we passed it? And how were we to reach it now, should Snider and the girl discover us?

"It's drifting," said Taylor. "I see no one in it."

I was stripping off my clothes, and Delcarte soon followed my example. I told Taylor to remain on shore with the clothing and rifles. He might also serve us better there, since it would give him an opportunity to take a shot at Snider should the man discover us and show himself.

With powerful strokes we swam out in the path of the oncoming launch. Being a stronger swimmer than Delcarte, I soon was far in the lead, reaching the center of the channel just as the launch bore down upon me. It was drifting broadside on. I seized the gunwale and raised myself quickly, so that my chin topped the side. I expected a blow the moment that I came within the view of the occupants; but no blow fell.

Snider lay upon his back in the bottom of the boat alone. Even before I had clambered in and stooped above him I knew that he was dead. Without examining him further, I ran forward to the control board and pressed the starting button. To my relief, the mechanism responded -- the launch was uninjured. Coming about, I picked up Delcarte. He was astounded at the sight that met his eyes, and immediately fell to examining Snider's body for signs of life or an explanation of the manner in which he met his death.

The fellow had been dead for hours -- he was cold and still; but Delcarte's search was not without results, for above Snider's heart was a wound, a slit about an inch in length -- such a slit as a sharp knife would make, and in the dead fingers of one hand was clutched a strand of long brown hair -- Victory's hair was brown.

They say that dead men tell no tales; but Snider told the story of his end as clearly as though the dead lips had parted and poured forth the truth. The beast had attacked the girl, and she had defended her honor.

We buried Snider beside the Rhine, and no stone marks his last resting place. Beasts do not require headstones.

Then we set out in the launch, turning her nose upstream. When I had told Delcarte and Taylor that I intended searching for the girl, neither had demurred.

"We had her wrong in our thoughts," said Delcarte, "and the least that we can do in expiation is to find and rescue her."

We called her name aloud every few minutes as we motored up the river; but, though we returned all the way to our former camping place, we did not find her. I then decided to retrace our journey, letting Taylor handle the launch, while Delcarte and I, upon opposite sides of the river , searched for some sign of the spot where Victory had landed.

We found nothing until we had reached a point a few miles

above the spot where I had first seen the launch drifting down toward us, and there I discovered the remnants of a recent camp fire.

That Victory carried flint and steel I was aware, and that it was she who built the fire I was positive; but which way had she gone since she stopped here?

Would she go on down the river, that she might thus bring herself nearer her own Grabritin, or would she have sought to search for us upstream, where she had seen us last?

I had hailed Taylor, and sent him across the river to take in Delcarte, that the two might join me and discuss my discovery and our future plans.

While waiting for them, I stood looking out over the river, my back toward the woods that stretched away to the east behind me. Delcarte was just stepping into the launch upon the opposite side of the stream, when, without the least warning, I was violently seized by both arms and about the waist -- three or four men were upon me at once; my rifle was snatched from my hands and my revolver from my belt.

I struggled for an instant; but finding my efforts of no avail, I ceased them, and turned my head to have a look at my assailants. At the same time several others of them walked around in front of me, and, to my astonishment, I found myself looking upon uniformed soldiery, armed with rifles, revolvers, and sabers, but with faces as black as coal.

CHAPTER VIII

Delcarte and Taylor were now in midstream, coming toward us, and I called to them to keep aloof until I knew whether the intentions of my captors were friendly or otherwise. My good men wanted to come on and annihilate the blacks; but there were upward of a hundred of the latter, all well armed, and so I commanded Delcarte to keep out of harm's way, and stay where he was till I needed him.

A young officer called and beckoned to them; but they refused to come, and so he gave orders that resulted in my hands being secured at my back, after which the company marched away, straight toward the east.

I noticed that the men wore spurs, which seemed strange to me; but when, late in the afternoon, we arrived at their encampment, I discovered that my captors were cavalrymen.

In the center of a plain stood a log fort, with blockhouses at each of its four corners. As we approached, I saw a herd of cavalry horses grazing under guard outside the walls of the post. They were small, stocky horses; but the telltale saddle galls proclaimed their calling. The flag flying from a tall staff inside the palisade was one which I had never before seen or heard of.

We marched directly into the compound, where the company was dismissed, with the exception of a guard of four privates, who escorted me in the wake of the young officer. The latter led us across a small parade ground, where a battery of light field guns was parked, and toward a log building, in front of which rose the flagstaff.

I was escorted within the building into the presence of an old negro, a fine looking man, with a dignified and military bearing. He was a colonel, I was to learn later, and to him I owe the very humane treatment that was accorded me while I remained his prisoner.

He listened to the report of his junior, and then turned to question me; but with no better results than the former had accomplished. Then he summoned an orderly, and gave some instructions. The soldier saluted, and left the room, returning in about five minutes with a hairy old white man -- just such a savage, primeval-looking fellow as I had discovered in the woods the day that Snider had disappeared with the launch.

The colonel evidently expected to use the fellow as interpreter; but when the savage addressed me it was in a language as foreign to me as was that of the blacks. At last the old officer gave it up, and, shaking his head, gave instructions for my removal.

From his office I was led to a guardhouse, in which I found about fifty half-naked whites, clad in the skins of wild beasts. I tried to converse with them, but not one of them could understand Pan-American, nor could I make head or tail of their jargon.

For over a month I remained a prisoner there, working from morning until night at odd jobs about the headquarters building of the commanding officer. The other prisoners worked harder than I did, and I owe my better treatment solely to the kindliness and discrimination of the old colonel.

What had become of Victory, of Delcarte, of Taylor I could not know; nor did it seem likely that I should ever learn. I was most depressed; but I whiled away my time in performing the duties given me to the best of my ability and attempting to learn the language of my captors.

Who they were or where they came from was a mystery to me. That they were the outpost of some powerful black nation seemed likely, yet where the seat of that nation lay I could not guess.

They looked upon the whites as their inferiors, and treated us accordingly. They had a literature of their own, and many of the men, even the common soldiers, were omnivorous readers. Every two weeks a dust-covered trooper would trot his jaded mount into the post and deliver a bulging sack of mail at headquarters. The next day he would be away again upon a fresh horse toward the south, carrying the soldiers' letters to friends in that far off land of mystery from whence they all had come.

Troops, sometimes mounted and sometimes afoot, left the post daily for what I assumed to be patrol duty. I judged the little force of a thousand men were detailed here to maintain the authority of a distant government in a conquered country. Later, I learned that my surmise was correct, and this was but one of a great chain of similar posts that dotted the new frontier of the black nation into whose hands I had fallen.

Slowly I learned their tongue, so that I could understand what was said before me, and make myself understood. I had seen from the first that I was being treated as a slave -- that all whites that fell into the hands of the blacks were thus treated.

Almost daily new prisoners were brought in, and about three weeks after I was brought in to the post a troop of cavalry came from the south to relieve one of the troops stationed there. There was great jubilation in the encampment after the arrival of the newcomers, old friendships were renewed and new ones made; but the happiest men were those of the troop that was to be relieved.

The next morning they started away, and as they were forced upon the parade ground we prisoners were marched from our quarters and lined up before them. A couple of long chains were brought, with rings in the links every few feet. At first I could not guess the purpose of these chains; but I was soon to learn.

A couple of soldiers snapped the first ring around the neck of a powerful white slave, and one by one the rest of us were herded to our places, and the work of shackling us neck to neck commenced.

The colonel stood watching the procedure. Presently his eyes fell upon me, and he spoke to a young officer at his side. The latter stepped toward me and motioned me to follow him. I did so, and was led back to the colonel.

By this time I could understand a few words of their strange language, and when the colonel asked me if I would prefer to remain at the post as his body servant, I signified my willingness as emphatically as possible, for I had seen enough of the brutality of the common soldiers toward their white slaves to have no desire to start out upon a march of unknown length, chained by the neck, and driven on by the great whips that a score of the soldiers carried to accelerate the speed of their charges.

About three hundred prisoners who had been housed in six prisons at the post marched out of the gates that morning, toward what fate and what future I could not guess. Neither had the poor devils themselves more than the most vague conception of what lay in store for them, except that they were going elsewhere to continue in the slavery that they had known since their capture by their black conquerors -- a slavery that was to continue until death released them.

My position was altered at the post. From working about the headquarters office, I was transferred to the colonel's living quarters. I had greater freedom, and no longer slept in one of the prisons, but had a little room to myself off the kitchen of the colonel's log house.

My master was always kind to me, and under him I rapidly learned the language of my captors, and much concerning them that had been a mystery to me before. His name was Abu Belik. He was a colonel in the cavalry of Abysinns, a country of which I do not remember ever hearing, but which Colonel Belik assured me is the oldest civilized country in the world.

Colonel Belik was born in Adis Abeba, the capital of the empire, and until recently had been in command of the emperor's palace guard. Jealousy and the ambition and intrigue of another officer had lost him the favor of his emperor, and he had been detailed to this frontier post as a mark of his sovereign's displeasure.

Some fifty years before, the young emperor, Menelek XIV, was ambitious. He knew that a great world lay across the waters far to the north of his capitol. Once he had crossed the desert and looked out upon the blue sea that was the norther boundary of his dominions.

There lay another world to conquer. Menelek busied himself with the building of a great fleet, though his people were not a maritime race. His army crossed into Europe. It met with little resistance, and for fifty years his soldiers had been pushing his boundaries farther and farther toward the north.

"The yellow men from the east and north are contesting our rights here now," said the colonel; "but we shall win -- we shall conquer the world, carrying Christianity to all the benighted heathen of Europe, and Asia as well."

"You are a Christian people?" I asked.

He looked at me in surprise, nodding his head affirmatively.

"I am a Christian," I said. "My people are the most powerful on earth."

He smiled, and shook his head indulgently, as a father to a child who sets up his childish judgment against that of his elders.

Then I set out to prove my point. I told him of our cities, of our army, of our great navy. He came right back at me asking for figures, and when he was done I had to admit that only in our navy were we numerically superior.

Menelek XIV is the undisputed ruler of all the continent of Africa; of all of ancient Europe except the British Isles, Scandinavia, and eastern Russia; and has large possessions and prosperous colonies in what once were Arabia and Turkey in Asia.

He has a standing army of ten million men, and his people possess slaves -- white slaves -- to the number of ten or fifteen million.

Colonel Belik was much surprised, however, upon his

part, to learn of the great nation which lay across the ocean, and when he found that I was a naval officer, he was inclined to accord me even greater consideration than formerly. It was difficult for him to believe my assertion that there were but few blacks in my country, and that these occupied a lower social plane than the whites.

Just the reverse is true in Colonel Belik's land. He considered whites inferior beings, creatures of a lower order, and assuring me that even the few white freemen of Abyssinia were never accorded anything approximating a position of social equality with the blacks. They live in the poorer districts of the cities, in little white colonies, and a black who marries a white is socially ostracized.

The arms and ammunition of the Abyssinians are greatly inferior to ours, yet they are tremendously effective against the ill-armed barbarians of Europe. Their rifles are of a type similar to the magazine rifles of twentieth century Pan-America, but carrying only five cartridges in the magazine, in addition to the one in the chamber. They are of extraordinary length, even those of the cavalry; are scientifically rifled, and of extreme accuracy.

The Abyssinians themselves are a fine looking race of black men -- tall, muscular, with fine teeth, and regular features, which incline distinctly toward Semitic mold -- I refer to the full-blooded natives of Abyssinia. They are the patricians -- the aristocracy. The army is officered almost exclusively by them. Among the soldiery a lower type of negro predominates, with thicker lips and broader, flatter noses. These men are recruited, so the colonel told me, from among the conquered tribes of Africa. They are good soldiers -- brave and loyal. They can read and write, and they are endowed with a self-confidence and pride which, from my readings of the words of ancient African explorers, must have been wanting in their earliest progenitors. On the whole, it is apparent that the black race has thrived far better in the past two centuries under men of its own color than it had under the domination of whites during all previous history.

I had been a prisoner at the little frontier post for over a month, when orders came to Colonel Belik to hasten to the eastern frontier with the major portion of his command, leaving only one troop to garrison the fort. As his body servant, I accompanied him mounted upon a fiery little Abyssinian pony.

We marched rapidly for ten days through the heart of the ancient German empire, halting when night found us in proximity to water. Often we passed small posts similar to that at which the colonel's regiment had been quartered, finding in each instance that only a single company or troop remained for defence, the balance having been withdrawn toward the northeast, in the same direction in which we were moving.

Naturally, the colonel had not confided to me the nature of his orders; but the rapidity of our march and the fact that all available troops were being hastened toward the northeast assured me that a matter of vital importance to the dominion of Menelek XIV in that part of Europe was threatening or had already broken.

I could not believe that a simple rising of the savage tribes of whites would necessitate the mobilizing of such a force as we presently met with converging from the south into our trail. There were large bodies of cavalry and infantry, endless streams of artillery wagons and guns, and countless horse-drawn covered vehicles laden with camp equipage, munitions, and provisions.

Here, for the first time, I saw camels, great caravans of them, bearing all sorts of heavy burdens, and miles upon miles of elephants doing similar service. It was a scene of wondrous and barbaric splendor, for the men and beasts from the south were gaily caparisoned in rich colors, in marked contrast to the gray uniformed forces of the frontier, with which I had been familiar.

The rumor reached us that Menelek himself was coming, and the pitch of excitement to which this announcement raised the troops was little short of miraculous -- at least, to one of my race and nationality whose rulers for centuries had been but ordinary men, holding office at the will of the people for a few brief years.

As I witnessed it, I could not but speculate upon the moral effect upon his troops of a sovereign's presence in the midst of battle. All else being equal in war between the troops of a republic and an empire, could not this exhilerated mental state, amounting almost to hysteria on the part of the imperial troops, weigh heavily against the soldiers of a president? I wonder.

But if the emperor chanced to be absent! What then? Again I wonder.

On the eleventh day we reached our destination -- a walled frontier city of about twenty thousand. We passed some lakes, and crossed some old canals before entering the gates. Within, beside the frame buildings, were many built of ancient brick and well-cut stone. These, I was told, were of material taken from the ruins of the ancient city which, once, had stood upon the site of the present town.

The name of the town, translated from the Abyssinian, is New Gondar. It stands, I am convinced, upon the ruins of ancient Berlin, the one time capitol of the old German empire; but except for the old building material used in the new town there is no sign of the former city.

The day after we arrived, the town was gaily decorated with flags, streamers, gorgeous rugs, and banners, for the rumor had proved true -- the emperor was coming.

Colonel Belik had accorded me the greatest liberty, permitting me to go where I pleased, after my few duties had been performed. As a result of his kindness, I spent much time wandering about New Gondar, talking with the inhabitants, and exploring this city of black men.

As I had been given a semi-military uniform which bore insignia indicating that I was an officer's body servant, even the blacks treated me with a species of respect, though I could see by their manner that I was really as the dirt beneath their feet. They answered my questions civilly enough; but they would not enter into conversation with me. It was from her slaves that I learned the gossip of the city.

Troops were pouring in from the west and south, and

pouring out toward the east. I asked an old slave who was sweeping the dirt into little piles in the gutters of the street where the soldiers were going. He looked at me in surprise.

"Why, to fight the yellow men, of course," he said. "They have crossed the border, and are marching toward New Gondar."

"Who will win?" I asked.

He shrugged his shoulders. "Who knows?" he said. "I hope it will be the yellow men; but Menelek is powerful -- it will take many yellow men to defeat him."

Crowds were gathering along the sidewalks to view the emperor's entry into the city. I took my place among them, although I hate crowds, and I am glad that I did, for I witnessed such a spectacle of barbaric splendor as no other Pan-American has ever looked upon.

Down the broad main thoroughfare, which may once have been the historic Unter den Linden, came a brilliant cortege. At the head rode a regiment of red-coated hussars -- enormous men, black as night. There were troops of riflemen mounted on camels. The emperor rode in a golden howdah upon the back of a huge elephant so covered with rich hangings and embellished with scintillating gems that scarce more than the beast's eyes and feet were visible.

Menelek was a rather gross looking man, well past middle age, but he carried himself with an air of dignity befitting one descended in unbroken line from the Prophet -- as is his claim.

His eyes were bright but crafty, and his features denoted both sensuality and cruelness. In his youth he may have been a rather fine looking black, but when I saw him his appearance was revolting -- to me,at least.

Following the emperor came regiment after regiment from the various branches of the service, among them batteries of field guns mounted on elephants.

In the center of the troops following the imperial elephant marched a great caravan of slaves. The old street sweeper at my elbow told me that these were the gifts brought in from the far outlying districts by the commanding officers of the frontier posts. The amjority of them were women, destined, I was told, for the harems of the emperor and his favorites. It made my old companion clench his fists to see those poor white women marching past to their horrid fates, and, though I shared his sentiments, I was as powerless to alter their destinies as he.

For a week the troops kept pouring in and out of New Gondar -- in always from the south and west; but always toward the east. Each new contingent brought its gifts to the emperor. From the south they brought rugs and ornaments and jewels; from the west, slaves; for the commanding officers of the western frontier posts had naught else to bring.

From the number of women they brought, I judged that they knew the weakness of their imperial master.

And then soldiers commenced coming in from the east, but not with the gay assurance of those who came from the south and west -- no, these others came in covered wagons, blood-soaked and suffering. They came at first in little parties of eight or ten, and then they came in fifties, in hundreds, and one day a thousand maimed and dying men were carted into New Gondar.

It was then that Menelek XIV became uneasy. For fifty years his armies had conquered wherever they had marched. At first he had led them in person, lately his presence within a hundred miles of the battle line had been sufficient for large engagements -- for minor ones only the knowledge that they were fighting for the glory of their sovereign was necessary to win victories.

One morning, New Gondar was awakened by the booming of cannon. It was the first intimation that the townspeople had received that the enemy was forcing the imperial troops back upon the city. Dust covered couriers galloped in from the front. Fresh troops hastened from the city, and about noon Menelek rode out surrounded by his staff.

For three days thereafter we could hear the cannonading and the spitting of the small arms, for the battle line was scarce two leagues from New Gondar. The city was filled with wounded. Just outside, soldiers were engaged in throwing up earthworks. It was evident to the least enlightened that Menelek expected further reverses.

And then the imperial troops fell back upon these new defenses; or, rather, they were forced back by the enemy. Shells commenced to fall within the city. Menelek returned and took up his headquarters in the stone building that was called the palace. That night came a lull in the hostilities -- a truce had been arranged.

Colonel Belik summoned me about seven o'clock to dress him for a function at the palace. In the midst of death and defeat the emperor was about to give a great banquet to his officers. I was to accompany my master and wait upon him -- I, Jefferson Turck, lieutenant in the Pan-American navy!

In the privacy of the colonel's quarters I had become accustomed to my menial duties, lightened as they were by the natural kindliness of my master; but the thought of appearing in public as a common slave revolted every fine instinct within me. Yet there was nothing for it but to obey.

I cannot, even now, bring myself to a narration of the humiliation which I experienced that night as I stood behind my black master in silent servility, now pouring his wine, now cutting up his meats for him, now fanning him with a large, plumed fan of feathers.

As fond as I had grown of him, I could have thrust a knife into him, so keenly did I feel the affront that had been put upon me. But at last the long banquet was concluded. The tables were removed. The emperor ascended a dais at one end of the room and seated himself upon a throne, and the entertainment commenced. It was only what ancient history might have led me to expect -- musicians, dancing girls, jugglers, and the like.

Near midnight, the master of ceremonies announced that the slave women who had been presented to the emperor since his arrival in New Gondar would be exhibited, that the royal host would select such as he wished, after which he would present the balance of them to his guests. Ah, what royal generosity!

A small door at one side of the room opened, and the

poor creatures filed in and were ranged in a long line before the throne. Their backs were toward me. I saw only an occasional profile as now and then a bolder spirit among them turned to survey the apartment and the gorgeous assemblage of officers in their brilliant dress uniforms. They were profiles of young girls, and pretty; but horror was indelibly stamped upon them all. I shuddered as I contemplated their sad fate, and turned my eyes away.

I heard the master of ceremonies command them to prostrate themselves before the emperor, and the sounds as they went upon their knees before him, touching their foreheads to the floor. Then came the official's voice again, in sharp and peremptory command.

"Down, slave!" he cried. "Make obeisance to your sovereign!"

I looked up, attracted by the tone of the man's voice, to see a single, straight, slim figure standing erect in the center of the line of prostrate girls, her arms folded across her breast and little chin in the air. Her back was toward me -- I could not see her face, though I should like to see the countenance of this savage young lioness, standing there defiant among that herd of terrified sheep.

"Down! Down!" shouted the master of ceremonies, taking a step toward her and half drawing his sword.

My blood boiled. To stand there, inactive, while a negro struck down that brave girl of my own race! Instinctively I took a forward step to place myself in the man's path; but at the same instant Menelek raised his hand in a gesture that halted the officer. The emperor seemed interested, but in no way angered at the girl's attitude.

"Let us inquire," he said in a smooth, pleasant voice, "why this young woman refuses to do homage to her sovereign," and he put the question himself directly to her.

She answered him in Abyssinian, but brokenly and with an accent that betrayed how recently she had acquired her slight knowledge of the tongue.

"I go on my knees to no one," she said. "I have no sovereign. I myself am sovereign in my own country."

Menelek, at her words, leaned back in his throne and laughed uproariously. Following his example, which seemed always the correct procedure, the assembled guests vied with one another in an effort to laugh more noisily than the emperor.

The girl but tilted her chin a bit higher in the air -- even her back proclaimed her utter contempt for her captors. Finally Menelek restored quiet by the simple expedient of a frown, whereupon each loyal guest exchanged his mirthful mien for an emulative scowl.

"And who," asked Menelek, "are you, and by what name is your country called?"

"I am Victory, Queen of Grabritin," replied the girl so quickly and so unexpectedly that I gasped in astonishment.

CHAPTER IX

Victory! She was here, a slave to these black conquerors. Once more I started toward her; but better judgment held me back -- I could do nothing to help her other than by stealth. Could I even accomplish aught by this means? I did not know. It seemed beyond the pale of possibility, and yet I should try.

"And you will not bend the knee to me?" continued Menelek, after she had spoken. Victory shook her head in a most decided negation.

"You shall be my first choice, then," said the emperor. "I like your spirit, for the breaking of it will add to my pleasure in you, and never fear but that it shall be broken -- this very night. Take her to my apartments," and he motioned to an officer at his side.

I was surprised to see Victory follow the man off in apparent quiet submission. I tried to follow, that I might be near her against some opportunity to speak with her or assist in her escape; but, after I had followed them from the throne room, through several other apartments, and down a long corridor, I found my further progress barred by a soldier who stood guard before a doorway through which the officer conducted Victory.

Almost immediately the officer reappeared and started back in the direction of the throne room. I had been hiding in a doorway after the guard had turned me back, having taken refuge there while his back was turned, and, as the officer approached me, I withdrew into the room beyond, which was in darkness. There I remained for a long time, watching the sentry before the door of the room in which Victory was a prisoner, and awaiting some favorable circumstance which would give me entry to her.

I have not attempted to fully describe my sensations at the moment I recognized Victory, because, I can assure you, they were entirely indescribable. I should never have imagined that the sight of any human being could affect me as had this unexpected discovery of Victory in the same room in which I was, while I had thought of her for weeks either as dead, or at best hundreds of miles to the west, and as irretrievably lost to me as though she were, in truth, dead.

I was filled with a strange, mad impulse to be near her. It was not enough merely to assist her, or protect her -- I desired to touch her -- to take her in my arms. I was astounded at myself. Another thing puzzled me -- it was my incomprehensible feeling of elation since I had again seen her. With a fate worse than death staring her in the face, and with the knowledge that I should probably die defending her within the hour, I was still happier than I had been for weeks -- and all because I had seen again for a few brief minutes the figure of a little heathen maiden. I couldn't account for it, and it angered me; I had never before felt any such sensations in the presence of a woman, and I had made love to some very beautiful ones in my time.

It seemed ages that I stood in the shadow of that doorway, in the ill-lit corridor of the palace of Menelek XIV. A sickly gas jet cast a sad pallor upon the black face of the sentry. The fellow seemed rooted to the spot. Evidently he would never leave, or turn his back again.

I had been in hiding but a short time when I heard the sound of distant cannon. The truce had ended, and the battle had been resumed. Very shortly thereafter the earth shook to the explosion of a shell within the city, and from time to time thereafter other shells burst at no great distance from the palace. The yellow men were bombarding New Gondar again.

Presently officers and slaves commenced to traverse the

corridor on matters pertaining to their duties, and then came the emperor, scowling and wrathful. He was followed by a few personal attendants, whom he dismissed at the doorway to his apartments -- the same doorway through which Victory had been taken. I chafed to follow him; but the corridor was filled with people. At last they betook themselves to their own apartments, which lay upon either side of the corridor.

An officer and a slave entered the very room in which I hid, forcing me to flatten myself to one side in the darkness until they had passed. Then the slave made a light, and I knew that I must find another hiding place.

Stepping boldly into the corridor, I saw that it was now empty save for the single sentry before the emperor's door. He glanced up as I emerged from the room, the occupants of which had not seen me. I walked straight toward the soldier, my mind made up in an instant. I tried to simulate an expression of cringing servility, and I must have succeeded, for I entirely threw the man off his guard, so that he permitted me to approach within reach of his rifle before stopping me. Then it was too late -- for him.

Without a word or a warning, I snatched the piece from his grasp, and, at the same time, struck him a terrific blow between the eyes with my clenched fist. He staggered back in surprise, too dumbfounded even to cry out, and then I clubbed his rifle and felled him with a single mighty blow.

A moment later, I had burst into the room beyond. It was empty!

I gazed about, mad with disappointment. Two doors opened from this to other rooms. I ran to the nearer and listened. Yes, voices were coming from beyond and one was a woman's, level and cold and filled with scorn. There was no terror in it. It was Victory's.

I turned the knob and pushed the door inward just in time to see Menelek seize the girl and drag her toward the far end of the apartment. At the same instant there was a deafening roar just outside the palace -- a shell had struck much nearer than any of its predecessors. The noise of it drowned my rapid rush across the room.

But in her struggles, Victory turned Menelek about so that he saw me. She was striking him in the face with her clenched fist, and now he was choking her.

At sight of me, he gave voice to a roar of anger.

"What means this, slave?" he cried. "Out of here! Out of here! Quick, before I kill you!"

But for answer I rushed upon him, striking him with the butt of the rifle. He staggered back, dropping Victory to the floor, and then he cried aloud for the guard, and came at me. Again and again I struck him; but his thick skull might have been armor plate, for all the damage I did it.

He tried to close with me, seizing the rifle, but I was stronger than he, and, wrenching the weapon from his grasp, tossed it aside and made for his throat with my bare hands. I had not dared fire the weapon for fear that its report would bring the larger guard stationed at the farther end of the corridor.

We struggled about the room, striking one another, knocking over furniture, and rolling upon the floor. Menelek was a powerful man, and he was fighting for his life. Continually he kept calling for the guard, until I succeeded in getting a grip upon his throat; but it was too late. His cries had been heard, and suddenly the door burst open, and a score of armed guardsmen rushed into the apartment.

Victory seized the rifle from the floor and leaped between me and them. I had the black emperor upon his back, and both my hands were at his throat, choking the life from him.

The rest happened in the fraction of a second. There was a rending crash above us, then a deafening explosion within the chamber. Smoke and powder fumes filled the room. Half stunned, I rose from the lifeless body of my antagonist just in time to see Victory stagger to her feet and turn toward me. Slowly the smoke cleared to reveal the shattered remnants of the guard. A shell had fallen through the palace roof and exploded just in the rear of the detachment of guardsmen who were coming to the rescue of their emperor. Why neither Victory nor I were struck is a miracle. The room was a wreck. A great, jagged hole was torn in the ceiling, and the wall toward the corridor had been blown entirely out.

As I rose, Victory had risen, too, and started toward me; but when she saw that I was uninjured she stopped, and stood there in the center of the demolished apartment looking at me. Her expression was inscrutable -- I could not guess whether she was glad to see me, or not.

"Victory!" I cried. "Thank God that you are safe!" And I approached her, a greater gladness in my heart than I had felt since the moment that I knew the COLDWATER must be swept beyond 30.

There was no answering gladness in her eyes. Instead, she stamped her little foot in anger.

"Why did it have to be you who saved me!" she exclaimed. "I hate you!"

"Hate me?" I asked. "Why should you hate me, Victory? I do not hate you. I -- I -- ." What was I about to say? I was very close to her as a great light broke over me. Why had I never realized it before? The truth accounted for a great many hitherto inexplicable moods that had claimed me from time to time since first I had seen Victory.

"Why should I hate you?" she repeated. "Because Snider told me -- he told me that you had promised me to him; but he did not get me. I killed him, as I should like to kill you!"

"Snider lied!" I cried; and then I seized her and held her in my arms, and made her listen to me, though she struggled and fought like a young lioness. "I love you, Victory. You must know that I love you -- that I have always loved you, and that I never could have made so base a promise."

She ceased her struggles, just a trifle; but still tried to push me from her. "You called me a barbarian!" she said.

Ah, so that was it! That still rankled. I crushed her to me.

"You could not love a barbarian," she went on; but she had ceased to struggle.

"But I do love a barbarian, Victory!" I cried; "the dearest barbarian in the world."

She raised her eyes to mine, and then her smooth, brown arms encircled my neck and drew my lips down to hers.

"I love you -- I have loved you always!" she said, and then she buried her face upon my shoulder and sobbed. "I have been so unhappy," she said; "but I could not die while I thought that you might live."

As we stood there, momentarily forgetful of all else than our new found happiness, the ferocity of the bombardment increased until scarce thirty seconds elapsed between the shells that rained about the palace.

To remain long would be to invite certain death. We could not escape the way that we had entered the apartment, for not only was the corridor now choked with debris, but beyond the corridor there were doubtless many members of the emperor's household who would stop us.

Upon the opposite side of the room was another door, and toward this I led the way. It opened into a third apartment with windows overlooking an inner court. From one of these windows I surveyed the courtyard. Apparently it was empty, and the rooms upon the opposite side were unlighted.

Assisting Victory to the open, I followed, and together we crossed the court, discovering upon the opposite side a number of wide, wooden doors set in the wall of the palace, with small windows between. As we stood close behind one of the doors, listening, a horse within neighed.

"The stables!" I whispered; and, a moment later, had pushed back a door and entered. From the city about us we could hear the din of great commotion, and quite close the sounds of battle -- the crack of thousands of rifles, the yells of the soldiers, the hoarse commands of officers, and the blare of bugles.

The bombardment had ceased as suddenly as it had commenced. I judged that the enemy was storming the city, for the sounds we heard were the sounds of hand-to-hand combat.

Within the stables I groped about until I had found saddles and bridles for two horses; but afterward, in the darkness, I could find but a single mount. The doors of the opposite side, leading to the street, were open, and we could see great multitudes of men, women, and children fleeing toward the west. Soldiers, afoot and mounted, were joining the mad exodus.

Now and then a camel or an elephant would pass bearing some officer or dignitary to safety. It was evident that the city would fall at any moment -- a fact which was amply proclaimed by the terror-stricken haste of the fear-mad mob.

Horse, camel, and elephant trod helpless women and children beneath their feet. A common soldier dragged a general from his mount, and, leaping to the animal's back, fled down the packed street toward the west. A woman seized a gun and brained a court dignitary, whose horse had trampled her child to death. Shrieks, curses, commands, supplications filled the air. It was a frightful scene -- one that will be burned upon my memory forever.

I had saddled and bridled the single horse which had evidently been overlooked by the royal household in its flight, and, standing a little back in the shadow of the stable's interior, Victory and I watched the surging throng without.

To have entered it would have been to have courted greater danger than we were already in. We decided to wait until the stress of blacks thinned, and for more than an hour we stood there while the sounds of battle raged upon the eastern side of the city and the population flew toward the west. More and more numerous became the uniformed soldiers among the fleeing throng, until, toward the last, the street was packed with them. It was no orderly retreat; but a rout, complete and terrible.

The fighting was steadily approaching us now, until the crack of rifles sounded in the very street upon which we were looking. And then came a handful of brave men -- a little rear guard backing slowly toward the west, working their smoking rifles in feverish haste as they fired volley after volley at the foe we could not see.

But these were pressed back and back until the first line of the enemy came opposite our shelter. They were men of medium height, with olive complexions and almond eyes. In them I recognized the descendants of the ancient Chinese race.

They were well uniformed and superbly armed, and they fought bravely and under perfect discipline. So rapt was I in the exciting events transpiring in the street that I did not hear the approach of a body of men from behind. It was a party of the conquerors who had entered the palace and were searching it.

They came upon us so unexpectedly that we were prisoners before we realized what had happened. That night we were held under a strong guard just outside the eastern wall of the city, and the next morning were started upon a long march toward the east.

Our captors were not unkind to us, and treated the women prisoners with respect. We marched for many days -- so many that I lost count of them -- and at last we came to another city -- a Chinese city this time -- which stands upon the site of ancient Moscow.

It is only a small frontier city; but it is well built and well kept. Here a large military force is maintained, and here also, is a terminus of the railroad that crosses modern China to the Pacific.

There was every evidence of a high civilization in all that we saw within the city, which, in connection with the humane treatment that had been accorded all prisoners upon the long and tiresome march, encouraged me to hope that I might appeal to some high officer here for the treatment which my rank and birth merited.

We could converse with our captors only through the medium of interpreters who spoke both Chinese and Abyssinian; but there were many of these, and shortly after we reached the city I persuaded one of them to carry a verbal message to the officer who had commanded the troops during the return from New Gondar, asking that I might be given a hearing by some high official.

The reply to my request was a summons to appear before the officer to whom I had addressed my appeal. A sergeant came for me along with the interpreter, and I managed to obtain his permission to let Victory accompany me -- I had never left her alone with the prisoners since we had been captured.

To my delight I found that the officer into whose presence

we were conducted spoke Abyssinian fluently. He was astounded when I told him that I was a Pan-American. Unlike all others whom I had spoken with since my arrival in Europe, he was well acquainted with ancient history -- was familiar with twentieth century conditions in Pan-America, and after putting a half dozen questions to me was satisfied that I spoke the truth.

When I told him that Victory was Queen of England he showed little surprise, telling me that in their recent explorations in ancient Russia they had found many decendants of the old nobility and royalty.

He immediately set aside a comfortable house for us, furnished us with servants and with money, and in other ways showed us every attention and kindness.

He told me that he would telegraph his emperor at once, and the result was that we were presently commanded to repair to Peking and present ourselves before the ruler.

We made the journey in a comfortable railway carriage, through a country which, as we traveled farther toward the east, showed increasing evidence of prosperity and wealth.

At the imperial court we were received with great kindness, the emperor being most inquisitive about the state of modern Pan-America. He told me that while he personally deplored the existence of the strict regulations which had raised a barrier between the east and the west, he had felt, as had his predecessors, that recognition of the wishes of the great Pan-American federation would be most conducive to the continued peace of the world.

His empire includes all of Asia, and the islands of the Pacific as far east as 175W. The empire of Japan no longer exists, having been conquered and absorbed by China over a hundred years ago. The Philippines are well administered, and constitute one of the most progressive colonies of the Chinese empire.

The emperor told me that the building of this great empire and the spreading of enlightenment among its diversified and savage peoples had required all the best efforts of nearly two hundred years. Upon his accession to the throne he had found the labor well nigh perfected and had turned his attention to the reclamation of Europe.

His ambition is to wrest it from the hands of the blacks, and then to attempt the work of elevating its fallen peoples to the high estate from which the Great War precipitated them.

I asked him who was victorious in that war; and he shook his head sadly as he replied:

"Pan-America, perhaps, and China, with the blacks of Abyssinia," he said. "Those who did not fight were the only ones to reap any of the rewards that are supposed to belong to victory. The combatants reaped naught but annihilation. You have seen -- better than any man you must realize that there was no victory for any nation embroiled in that frightful war."

"When did it end?" I asked him.

Again he shook his head. "It has not ended yet. There has never been a formal peace declared in Europe -- after a while there were none left to make peace, and the rude tribes which sprang from the survivors continued to fight among themselves because they knew no better condition of society. War razed the works of man -- war and pestilence razed man. God give that there shall never be such another war!"

You all know how Porfirio Johnson returned to Pan-America with John Alvarez in chains; how Alvarez's trial raised a popular demonstration that the government could not ignore. His eloquent appeal -- not for himself, but for me -- is historic, as are its results. You know how a fleet was sent across the Atlantic to search for me, how the restrictions against crossing 30 to 175 were removed forever, and how the officers were brought to Peking, arriving upon the very day that Victory and I were married at the imperial court.

My return to Pan-America was very different from anything I could possibly have imagined a year before. Instead of being received as a traitor to my country, I was acclaimed a hero. It was good to get back again, good to witness the kindly treatment that was accorded my dear Victory, and when I learned that Delcarte and Taylor had been found at the mouth of the Rhine and were already back in Pan-America my joy was unalloyed.

And now we are going back, Victory and I, with the men and the munitions and power to reclaim England for her queen. Again I shall cross 30; but under what altered conditions!

A new epoch for Europe is inaugurated, with enlightened China on the east and enlightened Pan-America on the west -- the two great peace powers whom God has preserved to regenerate chastened and forgiven Europe. I have been through much -- I have suffered much; but I have won two great laurel wreaths beyond 30. One is the opportunity to rescue Europe from barbarism, the other is a little barbarian, and the greater of these is -- Victory.

THE MAN-EATER

THE MAN-EATER

PROLOGUE

A native woman working in the little cultivated patch just outside the palisade which surrounded the mission was the first to see them. Her scream penetrated to the living room of the little thatched bungalow where the Reverend Sangamon Morton sat before a table, an open tin box before him and a sheaf of preferred stock certificates in his hands.

The Reverend Morton had heard such screams before. Sometimes they meant nothing. Again they might mean the presence of an inquisitive and savage jungle visitor of the order of carnivora. But the one thing always uppermost in his mind -- the one great, abiding terror of their lives there in the midst of the savage African jungle -- was now, as always, the first and natural explanation of the woman's screams to leap to his mind. The Wakandas had come at last!

The missionary leaped to his feet, thrust the papers into a long manila envelope, placed them in the tin box and closed the cover as he hastened across the room to the wide fireplace. Here he kneeled and removed a flag stone from the hearth, slipped the box quickly into the aperture revealed beneath, rose, snatched a rifle from its hook over the mantle and rushed out into the compound. The whole thing had taken but a fraction of the time required to tell it.

In another room of the bungalow Mary Morton, the missionary's wife, and Ruth, his daughter, had heard the scream, and they, too, ran out into the compound. The Reverend Sangamon Morton found them there when he arrived, and calling to them to return to the bungalow, sped on toward the palisade gate, through which were now streaming the score of women and children who had been working in the garden.

Some native men were also hastening toward the gate from their various duties about the mission, converted heathen armed with ancient Enfields. The woman who had first screamed and whose shrill cry of terror had aroused the peaceful little community now fell to her knees before the Reverend Morton.

"Oh, sabe me, massa!" she cried. "Sabe me from de Wakandas! De Wakandas hab came!"

Morton brushed past her and hurried to the gate. He would have a look at the enemy first. The Reverend Morton was not a man to be easily stampeded. He had answered to false alarms in the past, and though he never permitted the cry of "Wolf!" to find him unready for the inevitable time when it should prove a true cry he was prone to scepticism until he should have the substantiating testimony of his own eyes.

Now, as he passed through the gate, his first glance at the approaching "enemy" brought a sigh of relief to his lips. Coming out of the jungle were strange black men, it was true -- warriors armed with spears, and even guns -- but with them marched two white men, and at the sight of the pith helmets and the smoke from two briar pipes a broad smile touched the lips of the Reverend Sangamon Morton.

The smile expanded into a good-natured laugh as he advanced to welcome the strangers and explain to them the panic into which their unheralded appearance had thrown his little community.

And so came Jefferson Scott, Jr., and his boon companion, Robert Gordon, to the little American Methodist mission in the heart of the African jungle. And there one of them, young Scott, found a wife in the missionary's daughter, Ruth. Robert Gordon remained for a month after the missionary had performed the simple ceremony that made his daughter Mrs. Jefferson Scott, Jr. Gordon was best man at the wedding, and with Mrs. Morton witnessed the marriage certificate.

The two young Americans had come to Africa to hunt big

game. Jefferson Scott, Jr., remained to cast his lot with his wife's people in their unselfish work among the natives. Gordon bade them goodbye at last to return to his home in New York, and the evening before his departure the Reverend Mr. Morton called him into the living room, removed the flagstone from the hearth, and, reaching in, opened the tin box and withdrew a large manila envelope.

"I wish, Mr. Gordon," he said, "that you would deliver this into the keeping of Jefferson's father. It contains practically the entire fortune which I inherited from my father and for which I have no use here, but which, in the event of anything befalling me, would be of inestimable value to Mrs. Morton and Ruth. It is not safe here. The Wakandas, if rumor is to be credited, are preparing to revolt against the Belgian authorities, and if they do we shall have to leave here and cross nearly half the continent of Africa to safety.

"Under such circumstances these valuable papers would but add to my anxiety and worries, and so I ask you to take them to Mr. Scott for safety until my mission here is fulfilled and we all return to America."

And so Robert Gordon bade them farewell and started upon his journey to America, the manila envelope safe in his inside pocket.

A year later a little girl was born to Ruth Morton Scott -- a little girl whom they christened Virginia, after the commonwealth of which her father was a native son.

When Virginia was a year old it came -- the hideous thing that was often uppermost in the minds of all that little band isolated in the heart of the savage jungle. The Wakandas revolted.

Lieutenant De Boes heard the challenge of a sentry at the gate. Languidly he looked in the direction of the sounds and inwardly anathematized whatever fool might be moving about in such insufferable heat. Presently he saw one of his noncommissioned officers approaching with a naked savage. The stranger was sweatstreaked and panting. His eyes were wide in terror. The corporal brought him before the officer, saluting. Lieutenant De Boes noted excitement in his soldier's expression.

"What now?" he asked, returning the salute.

"The Wakandas are upon the warpath," reported the subordinate. "This fellow says that they killed nearly all within the village and then started for the mission where the Americans are."

Lieutenant De Boes sat up quickly and, leaning forward toward the news-bringer, fired question after question at him. When he had satisfied himself that the man did not lie he leaped to his feet. All thoughts of heat or lassitude were gone. He gave a quiet sharp order to the corporal, and as that soldier ran across the parade ground to the beehive barracks De Boes ran indoors and donned his marching togs and his side arms.

Thirty minutes later a little company of fifty blacks in command of a single Belgian lieutenant filed through the factory gate and took up their march against a warlike tribe which numbered perhaps a thousand spears.

Once again came the terrified shriek of a native to the ears of the dwellers within the mission. Once again the men within ran toward the gates -- ready but doubting. Jefferson Scott, Jr. was first among them, for he was younger and could run faster than his father-in-law. And this time the wolf had come.

The Wakandas were at the gates by the time the two white men had reached them. The Reverend Sangamon Morton fell, pierced through the breast by a heavy war spear before ever he could fire a shot in defense of his loved ones.

Scott, reinforced by the handful of men converts who lived within the mission enclosure, repelled the first charge, his heavy express rifle and deadly accuracy sending the blacks back toward the jungle, where they leaped and shouted until they worked themselves into a sufficient hysteria to warrant another assault. Time and again the ebon horde swooped down upon the gates. Time and again the handful of defenders drove them back. Yet it was without hope that Jefferson Scott, Jr. fought. He knew what must be the inevitable outcome. Already his own ammunition was exhausted and there was but little more good powder available for the *Enfields*.

They might hold out another day, but what good would that accomplish? It would be but to defer the final frightful moment. If they could but get word to the Belgian officer and his little command over on the Uluki. Scott questioned his companions as to the feasibility of getting a runner through to the factory. It was impossible, they said, as the whole country between the mission and the Belgians would be overrun by Wakandas by this time. Not one would volunteer to attempt the journey. They had fought bravely at his side, but none dared venture among the Wakandas, the very mention of whose name filled them with unreasonable terror.

But it was the only hope that Scott had. He must get word to the factory. If his blacks were afraid to bear it he must do so himself. His only hesitancy in the matter was the thought of leaving his young wife and baby daughter to the sole protection of the native converts. During a lull in the fighting he returned to the bungalow and placed the matter squarely before his wife and her mother.

"You must go, Jefferson," said the older woman. "I can take your place at the gates. The men love me, I know, and will fight for me and Ruth as bravely as though you remained. I will remain beside them and give them the moral support they need, and if there is a spare musket I can use that, too."

And so it was that as soon as night had fallen Jefferson Scott, Jr. slipped into the jungle upon his useless mission -- useless, because a native had already carried the warning to De Boes.

Scott never reached the factory, nor did he ever return to the mission. Only the Wakandas know what his fate was.

De Boes and his soldiers arrived at the mission early in the morning after an all-night march. They came upon the rear of the Wakandas just as the savages made their last and successful charge. A score or more of the howling demons had scaled the gates and were among the defenders as the rifles of the Belgian's black soldiers volleyed into their rear. The Wakandas, taken wholly by surprise, broke and fled.

Inside the mission defenses De Boes found a dozen dead, and among them the body of courageous Mary Morton, lying just within the gates. In the bungalow Ruth Scott stood with a rifle in her hands, before the cradle of her little daughter -- bereft in a single day of father, mother, and husband. The kindly and courteous Belgian helped her bury her dead, and sent out parties into the jungle in search of Scott, keeping them out until fear that he had been killed became a certainty. Then he conducted the mother and child back to the factory and from there arranged for their conveyance to the coast. Two months later Ruth Scott and little Virginia arrived at the Virginia homestead of the widowed and now childless Jefferson Scott -- the father of her dead husband.

When, a year before, Jefferson Scott had learned of his son's marriage, he had not been displeased, though the idea of the boy remaining in Africa was not altogether to his liking. Then had come Robert Gordon with enthusiastic descriptions of the new daughter-in-law and her parents, and Jefferson Scott began to long for the return of his son and the coming of his son's wife to brighten the sombre life of the old mansion.

Gordon had delivered a long manila envelope into the elder Scott's keeping. "Mr. Morton felt that it would be safer here than in Africa," he explained. "It contains a considerable fortune in stocks, if I understood him correctly."

Then, after a long year, had come the news of the Wakanda uprising and the death of his son and the Mortons. Immediately Jefferson Scott cabled funds to his daughter-in-law, together with instructions that she come at once to him. That same night he took the long manila envelope from his safe to examine the contents, that he might have the necessary legal steps taken to insure the proper transfer of the certificates to Ruth Scott's name.

The manila of the wrapper was of unusual thickness, giving an appearance of bulk to the package that was deceptive, for when he opened it Jefferson Scott discovered but a single paper within. As he withdrew this and examined it a puzzled smile touched his lips. For a moment he sat regarding the document in his hand, then he shook his head and returned it to the envelope.

He did not place it again in the safe, but carrying it upstairs opened an old fashioned wall cupboard, withdrew a tin box from it, placed the envelope in the tin box, and returned it to the cupboard.

Two months later he welcomed Ruth Morton Scott to his fireside, and from that moment until his death she was as an own daughter to him, sharing his love with her little Virginia, whom Jefferson Scott idolized.

And in the nineteen years that intervened it is doubtful if the manila envelope or its contents ever again entered the mind of the grandfather.

CHAPTER I

The closed door of the bedroom opened. A bent and white-haired old negro shuffled out, his face buried in a red bandanna and his shrunken shoulders heaving to the sobs he could not control. Down at the negroes' quarters the banjoes and the old melodeon were stilled. Even the little piccaninies sat with hushed voices and tearful mien. In the big front bedroom of the mansion two women knelt beside a bed, their faces buried in the coverlet, weeping. There were tears, too, in the eyes of the old doctor, and even stern old Judge Sperry blew his great beak of a nose with unnecessary vigor as he walked to the window and looked out across the broad acres of his lifetime friend. Jefferson Scott was dead.

That night Scott Taylor, the son of Jefferson Scott's dead sister, arrived from New York. Virginia Scott had met him several times in the past, when a child, he had visited his uncle. She knew but little of his past life, other than that Jefferson Scott had paid on two occasions to keep him out of jail and that of recent years the old man had refused to have any intercourse whatever with his nephew.

Taylor was a couple of years her senior, a rather good looking man, notwithstanding the marks of dissipation that marred his features. He was college bred, suave and distinctly at ease in any company. Had she known less of him Virginia Scott might easily have esteemed him highly, but, knowing what she did, she felt only disgust for him. His coming at this time she looked upon as little less than brazen effrontery, for he had been forbidden the house by Jefferson Scott several years before, nor since then had he once communicated with his uncle. That he had returned now in hope of legacy she knew as well as though he had candidly announced the fact, and it was with difficulty that she accorded him even the scantest courtesy in her greeting.

Judge Sperry, who was searching among Jefferson Scott's papers in the library when Taylor arrived, took one look at him over the tops of his glasses, a look that passed slowly from his face down to his boots, ignoring his proffered hand and returned to his search without a further acknowledgement of the younger man's existence.

Taylor flushed, shrugged his shoulders and turned back to Virginia, but Virginia had left the room. He fidgeted about, his ease of manner a trifle jarred, for a moment or two, and then recovering his poise, addressed Judge Sperry.

"Did my uncle leave a will?" he asked.

"He made a will, sir," snapped the Judge, "about a year ago, sir, in which you were not mentioned, sir. He has made no other, that I know of. If I were you, sir, I should return to New York. There is nothing here for you."

Taylor half smiled.

"I take it you are looking for the will," he said. "Well, I'll just stick around until you find it. If you don't find it I inherit half the property -- whether you want me to or not."

Judge Sperry vouchsafed no reply, and presently Taylor left the room, wandered out across the grounds and down the road toward the little village, where, if there were no acquaintances, there was at least something to drink.

Later in the evening, fortified by several Kentucky bourbons, he returned, nor could Virginia's mother bring herself to refuse him the ordinary hospitalities of that old Virginian home, and so he remained, following the body of his uncle to the grave with the other members of the family, the friends and the servants.

And after the funeral he stayed on, watching with as eager eyes as the rest the futile search for the last will and testament of Jefferson Scott, but with hopes diametrically at variance with theirs. Naturally he saw much of Virginia, though not as much as he should have liked to see. He found that the little girl he had known years before had grown into a beautiful young woman -- and while it angered him to realize the contempt in which she held him, he was not so wanting in egotism but that he believed he might win his way eventually into her good graces. For this reason he never reverted to the subject of the will. He did his best to impress upon Virginia and her mother that his one object in remaining thus away from his business was in the hope that he might prove of some service to them now that he upon whom they both had leaned for advice and protection had been taken away from them. Mrs. Scott was beginning to tolerate him and Virginia to feel sorry for him, yet both could not but look forward with feelings of relief to the meeting of the administrators which was to be held in the library of the Scott house the following morning. They felt that the action then taken would decide their status legally and render the further presence of Scott Taylor unnecessary. That it had been Jefferson Scott's intention that Virginia should inherit his entire estate they both knew, and were equally positive that the administrators would adopt every legal means to carry out the grandfather's expressed wish. Judge Sperry had explained Taylor's legal rights in the event that no will should be discovered, nor was Virginia at all desirous of attempting to reduce the amount that might be legally his.

It was the evening before the meeting. Taylor had gone to town in the afternoon. Mrs. Scott already had retired and Virginia sat reading in the library when Scott Taylor entered. As the girl greeted him civilly her eyes took in his flushed face and unsteady carriage and she saw that he had been drinking more than usually. Then she let her eyes fall again to her book.

Taylor crossed the room and stood where he could watch her profile. For several moments he did not speak, then he came closer and took a chair directly in front of her. The effect of her beauty upon his drink-excited passions caused him to throw diplomacy and caution to the winds.

"Look here, Virginia," he said, leaning forward toward her unsteadily.

The girl looked up in polite questioning, but there was a warning light in her eye that a more sober man than Scott Taylor would have discerned and heeded.

"Yes?" The rising inflection was accompanied by a raising of the arched brows.

"Why not be friends, Virginia?" Taylor continued. "We're both of us due for a share of the old man's property. It amounts to a big bunch of coin, but it's mostly in farm lands. It ought not to be cut up. We ought to keep it intact. I got a scheme." He edged his chair closer until their knees all but touched. "We're about the same age. I'm not such a bad sort when you know me, and you're a peach. I always knew it, and this time I've discovered something else -- I love you." He was leaning so far forward now that his face was close to hers.

The girl's eyes were wide in astonishment and disgust. She rose slowly and drew herself up to her full height.

"I would not, for the world," she said, "intentionally wound any man who came to me with an avowal of honest love; but I do not believe that you love me, and, further, the manner of your coming to me is an insult."

Taylor had risen and was facing her. If possible she was even more beautiful in anger than in repose. His self-control vanished before the scorn in her eyes and in her voice.

"You can learn to love me," he muttered, and seized her in his arms. Virginia struggled, but he crushed her closer to him until his lips were above hers. With an effort almost superhuman the girl succeeded in covering Taylor's face with her open palm and pushing him from her. Unsteady from drink, the man staggered back against the chair he had left, toppled over it and fell in a heap upon the floor.

When, after an effort, he managed to crawl to his feet, Virginia had disappeared. Taylor sank to the edge of a chair, his face contorted with rage and humiliation. He was not so intoxicated but that he now realized the fool he had made of himself and the ridiculous figure he must have cut reeling drunkenly over the chair. His rage, instead of being directed against himself as it should have been, was all for Virginia. He would make her pay! He would have his revenge. She should be left penniless, if there was any way, straight or crooked, to accomplish it. And in this pleasant mood Scott Taylor made his unsteady way to bed.

It was late when Taylor awoke the following morning. Already the administrators had gathered with Mrs. Scott and Virginia in the library. It was several minutes before the man could recall to memory the events of the previous evening. As they filtered slowly through his befogged brain a slow flush of anger crept over his face. Then he recalled the meeting that had been scheduled for today. He glanced at his watch. It was already past time. Springing up he dressed hastily, and left his room. Half way down the stairs he heard voices coming from the library below. He paused to listen. Judge Sperry was speaking.

"Jefferson Scott never intended that that young scalawag should have one cent's worth of his property," he was saying. "He told me upon several occasions that he would not have his money dissipated in riotous living, and by gad, gentlemen, if I have anything to say about it Jefferson Scott's wishes shall be observed, and he pounded the black walnut table with a heavy fist.

"I think," spoke up another voice, "that when the simple proofs necessary to establish legally Miss Virginia's relationship to General Scott have been produced it will be a comparatively simple matter to arrange the thing as he would have wished it."

"Simple proofs necessary to establish legally Miss Virginia's relationship to General Scott!" The words ran through Scott Taylor's brain almost meaninglessly at first, and then slowly a great light broke upon him, his eyes went wide and his lip curled in an ironical smile.

A moment later he entered the library. His manner was easy and confident. He sneered just a little as Virginia deliberately turned her shoulder toward him. A vast silence fell upon the company as he joined them. He was the first to break it.

"I am glad," he said, "that we can now straighten out a few matters that have been causing several of you not a little annoyance." He glanced defiantly at Judge Sperry. "Jefferson Scott, my uncle, died intestate. Under the circumstances, and the law, I inherit -- I am the sole heir."

Mrs. Scott and the administrators looked at the young man in surprise -- Virginia kept her back toward him. For several seconds there was unbroken silence -- the bald effrontery of Taylor's statement had taken even Judge Sperry's breath away -- but not for long.

"Sole heir?" shouted the old man presently. "Sole heir? Sole nothing! You don't deserve a penny of your uncle's estate, and you don't get a penny of it, if I can prevent it."

"But you can't prevent it, my friend." Taylor assured him coolly. "You can't prevent it because, as I just said, I am the sole heir."

"I presume," bellowed the Judge, "that you have more rights here than General Scott's granddaughter?"

"He had no legitimate granddaughter," replied Taylor, the sneering laugh on his lips speaking more truly the purport of his insinuation than even the plain words he had used.

"What? You young scoundrel!" cried Judge Sperry, springing to his feet and taking a step toward Taylor.

"Don't get excited," said Taylor. "Of course it's unfortunate that it became necessary to touch upon this matter, but I gave Miss Virginia an opportunity to compromise last night, which she refused, and so there is nothing else for me to do but insist upon my rights. It's a very simple matter to rectify if I am not mistaken. All that Mrs. Scott need do is produce her marriage certificate, or the records of the local authorities where her wedding took place. And now, until she can establish the right of her daughter to make any legal claim whatsoever upon the estate of my uncle, I shall have to ask you all to vacate the premises and leave me in possession of what is mine and no one else's."

The administrators turned toward Mrs. Scott. She shook her head sadly.

"You all know, of course, as well as he does, that his charges are as false as they are infamous," she said. "I was married in the heart of Central Africa. Whatever records there were of the ceremony have long since been destroyed, I fear; and I fear also that it may be a difficult thing to legally prove my marriage. Robert Gordon of New York was one of the witnesses. If he still lives I presume an affidavit from him would be sufficient?" She glanced at Judge Sperry.

"It would," he assured her, "and in the mean time I intend to kick this miserable little puppy into the road." And he advanced upon Taylor.

It was Mrs. Scott who stepped in front of the Judge.

"No, my dear friend," she said, "we must not do that. He had, possibly, legal if not moral right upon his side, for until I can prove the legality of my marriage he is in the eyes of the law the sole heir. And in the meantime Virginia and I shall make our preparations and leave here as quickly as possible."

"You will do nothing of the sort," exploded the Judge. "You will stay right here. If you leave it will be a tacit admission of the truth of a lie. I won't hear of your leaving, not for a moment. If any one leaves, this rascally blackleg will be the one to go."

"No," spoke up Virginia. "I shall not leave. The Judge is right."

"As you will," said Taylor. "I can't kick a couple women out of my home if they insist on remaining."

"You'd better not," growled the Judge.

It was not until afternoon that Mrs. Scott found an opportunity to pen a note to Robert Gordon. She had not seen her husband's old friend since that day twenty-one years before that she had waved him farewell from the veranda of the bungalow within the palisade of her mission home. He had stopped in London on his way to America, met and married an English girl, and thereafter for long years had spent much time in England or in travel. It had not been until after the death of his wife that he had returned to New York permanently.

As Mrs. Scott finished the letter an automobile whirled up the driveway and came to a stop before the mansion. Women's voices floated in to her and to Virginia to whom she had been reading the completed letter. The latter walked over to the open doors, where she glanced out, and then, turning to her mother with an "Oh, it's Mrs. Clayton and Charlotte!" ran out to greet visitors.

Mrs. Scott, as thoroughly imbued with Southern hospitality as a native daughter, dropped her letter upon the desk and followed Virginia to the porch, where she found her friends insisting that she and Virginia accompany them on a drive to the village. As it was too warm for wraps neither mother nor daughter returned to the house, and only too glad of an interruption to the sorrows and worries that had recently overwhelmed them, entered the machine of the Clayton's and a moment later were whirling down the road in a cloud of dust.

Scott Taylor, who had been strolling about the plantation, returned to the house shortly after they had left and entering through the French windows of the library, chanced to note the open letter lying on the desk. It required no subjugation of ethical scruples upon his part to pick the letter up and read it.

The letter ran:

"My dear Mr. Gordon:

"My husband's father, Jefferson Scott, has just passed away, and as certain legal requirements necessitate a proof of my marriage to Jefferson I am writing to ask that you mail an affidavit to Judge Sperry, of this village, to the effect that you witnessed the ceremony.

"My marriage certificate is, I imagine, still in the tin box beneath the hearth of the mission bungalow where father always kept his valuables, but as even it may have been destroyed during the second uprising of the Wakandas I imagine that we shall have to depend entirely upon your affidavit. I understand that the savages left no stone standing upon another, and that every stick or timber was burned.

That was eighteen years ago -- a year after the massacre in which Jefferson, father and mother were slain, and so it is rather doubtful if anything remains of the certificate.

"I am particularly anxious to legally establish the authenticity of my marriage, not so much because of the property which my daughter Virginia will inherit thereby, as from the fact that another heir has questioned my daughter's legitimacy.

"I write thus plainly to you because of the love I know that you and Jefferson felt for one another, as well as to impress upon you my urgent need of this affidavit, which you alone can furnish.

Very sincerely,

RUTH MORTON SCOTT
Scottsville, Va.
July 10, 19__."

"H'm," commented Mr. Scott Taylor, with a laugh. "Well, I can let this letter go forward with perfect safety, as I happen to know that Robert Gordon, Esq., died two years ago."

CHAPTER II

Mr. Dick Gordon of New York, rich, indolent and bored, tossed his morning paper aside, yawned, rose from the breakfast table and strolled wearily into the living room of his bachelor apartments. His man, who was busying himself about the room, looked up at his master questioningly.

"I am wondering, Murphy," announced that young man, "what the devil we are going to do to assasinate time today."

"Well, sir," replied Murphy, "you know you sort o' promised Mr. Jones as how you'd make up a four-flush at the Country Club this morning, sir."

"Foursome, Murphy, foursome!" laughed Gordon, and then, shooting a sharp glance at his servant: "I believe you were handing me one that time, you old fraud."

But the solemn-visaged Murphy shook his head in humble and horrified denial.

"All right, Murphy: get my things out. I suppose I might as well do that as anything," resignedly.

Languidly, Mr. Dick Gordon donned his golf togs and stood at last correctly clothed and with the faithful Murphy at his heels bearing his caddie bag. He crossed the living room toward the door of the apartment, halted half way and turned upon his servant.

"Golf's an awful bore, Murphy," he said. Let's not play today."

"But Mr. Jones, sir!" exclaimed Murphy.

"Oh, Jones's foursomes always start at the nineteenth

hole and never make the first. They'll not miss me."

His eyes fell upon a tennis racket, and lighted with a new interest.

"Say, Murphy, we haven't played tennis in a coon's age," he exclaimed. "Go put those clubs away. I'm going to play tennis."

"With yourself, sir," questioned Murphy. "I never saw no one playing tennis at the club, sir, of a morning."

"I guess you're right, Murphy, and anyway I don't want to play tennis. Tiresome game, tennis."

"Yes, sir."

"Ha! I have it! Great morning for a ride. Hustle, you old snail, and fetch my things. Telephone Billy and tell him to bring Redcoat around. Get a move on!"

By the time Murphy had attended to the various duties assigned him and returned from the telephone he found his young master sitting on the edge of a chair with one boot on and the other half so, staring hard at the floor, a weary expression on his face.

"Can I help you, sir?" asked Murphy.

"Yes, you can help me take off this boot. It's too hot to ride, and besides I don't want to ride anyway. What the devil did you suggest riding for, eh?"

"Yes, sir."

"I wish that you would say no, sir, for a change, Murphy. You're getting to be a terrific bore in your old age. Go and tell Billy to never mind Redcoat."

"Yes, sir," replied Murphy, but he did not go.

"You'd better hurry, Murphy, and catch him before he leaves the stables," suggested Gordon after a moment, in which he had divested himself of his riding breeches and started to pull on the trousers of a street suit.

"It won't be necessary, sir," said Murphy. "I didn't telephone for Redcoat in the first place, sir. I knew as how you would change your mind, sir, and thought it wouldn't be worth while calling up, sir."

Gordon cocked his head on one side and surveyed his servant from head to foot for a long moment. "Yes, sir," he said, at last.

Clothed again he wandered back into the living room, wishing that there was something in the world to hold his interest for a moment. The photograph of a handsome woman caught his eye. He picked it up and looked at it for several seconds.

"She photographs well," he murmured, "and that is about all one can say for her. I'll bet an X-ray of her brain would-n't show three convolutions."

Then he passed to another, the picture of a young debu-tante at whose feet were half the eligible males of New York Society -- and all the ineligible. He tossed the photographs aside in disgust. One by one he examined others. All wearied him. Everything wearied him.

"I wish," he remarked, turning toward Murphy, "that there was something or some one on earth that could raise my temperature over half a degree."

"Yes, sir, said Murphy. "That must be the mail man, sir," as an electric bell rang in the rear of the apartment and Murphy turned toward the door.

A moment later he re-entered with a bundle of letters in his hand, laying them on Gordon's desk. The young man picked up the top envelope and opened it.

"Mrs. R__ requests the pleasure --" he read, half aloud, and dropped the invitation listlessly upon the desk to pick up and open the next. "The Blank Club announces -- "The Blank Club is always announcing tiresome things," he sighed, and dropped the communication into the waste basket. "Mrs. F. Benton J__ and Miss J__ will be at home__ which is a dang sight more than Mr. F. Benton J__ can ever say," com-mented Mr. Gordon, gathering up the next, which proved to be another invitation. One after another the young man opened the envelopes, nor did any succeed in erasing the bored ex-pression from his countenance. The last he glanced at with a faint tinge of curiosity before opening. The feminine hand writing was unfamiliar, which was nothing unusual, but the postmark it was that drew his interest -- Scottsville, Vir-ginia.

"Now, who the devil do I know in Scottsville, Virginia?" he asked himself as he drew his paper knife through the flap of the envelope. "Oh, it's addressed to Dad!" he exclaimed, suddenly noting his father's name upon the envelope. "Dear old Dad," sighed the young man; "I never lacked bully good company when you were alive, and I didn't know then what it meant to be bored. I wonder if you know how I miss you."

He turned first to the signature at the close of the letter. "Ruth Morton Scott," he read. "H'm, I've heard Dad speak of you, and Jefferson Scott, Jr., your husband, and the tragedy at the mission. Lord, what an awful place that must have been for a young girl! It was bad enough three years ago when Dad and I camped among its ruins; but twenty years ago the country must have been awful for white women."

As Dick Gordon read the letter through slowly his face reflected for the first time in days a real interest. Toward the close he muttered something that sounded like "Damned cad," and then he carefully re-read the letter. After the second reading he sat upon the edge of his desk, the letter still in the hand that had dropped to his knee, and stared fixedly and unseeingly at the barbaric patterns of the Navajo rug at his feet. For ten minutes he sat thus; then he sprang up, animation reflected upon his face and determination in his every movement. Weariness and lassitude had been swept away as by magic. Seating himself at the desk he drew writing materials from a drawer and for ten minutes more was busily engaged in framing a letter. This done he rang for Murphy.

"Skip out and post this, you old tortoise," he shouted, "and then go and book passage for the two of us on the first boat that sails direct or makes good connections for Mombasa -- do you know where it is?

"Yes, sir; Africa, sir," replied the imperturbable Murphy, in as matter of fact a tone as though White Plains was to have been their destination.

Mr. Dick Gordon always had been an impulsive young man, his saving characteristic being an innate fineness of character that directed his impulses into good channels, if not always wisely chosen ones. His letter to Mrs. Scott had been written upon the impulse of the moment -- an impulse to serve his father's friend coupled with a longing for adventure and action -- for a change from the monotony of his useless existence.

The following day, as Scott Taylor, mounted upon General Scott's favorite saddle horse, rode leisurely about "my plantation," as he now described the Scott estate, he chanced to meet the little wagon of the Rural Free Delivery carrier coming from town.

"Anything for The Oaks?" he asked, reining in.

The man handed him a packet of letters and papers, clucked to his bony old horse and drove on. Taylor ran through the letters. There was one that interested him -- it bore the name and address of Richard Gordon on the flap. This he thrust into his inside pocket. Then he rode up the driveway, turned his horse over to a negro, and entered the library. It was empty, and laying the balance of the mail upon the table he made his way to his own room. Here he quickly opened and read Gordon's letter to Mrs. Scott. His eyes narrowed and his brows contracted with the reading of the last paragraph: "Father has been dead two years; but I know all about the location of the mission, as I visited it three years ago while lion hunting with him. As I am just about to leave for Africa again I shall make it a point to recover the papers you wish."

Taylor crumpled the letter angrily in his hand. "The fool!" he muttered, "what does he want to butt in for?"

Then came a knock upon the door and Taylor hastily crammed the letter into the pocket of his coat.

"Come in!" he snapped, and an old negress entered with fresh towels and bed linen. As she moved in her slow and deliberate way about her duties Taylor sat with puckered brows and narrowed lids gazing through the window. It was not until the woman had left the room that he arose. Now he seemed to have reached a decision that demanded rapid action. He snatched off his coat, throwing it across the bed, where it dropped over the side to the floor beyond. His trousers he flung on the floor; his shirt, collar and tie upon the center table, and in fifteen minutes he was dressed in fresh linen and another suit and cramming his belongings into his bag.

Running downstairs and out to the stables, he shouted to a hostler to harness the team and take him to the station. Mrs. Scott and Virginia had the car out, so he was forced to content himself with the slower method of transportation. Forty-five minutes later he boarded a northbound train for New York, and late that night rang the bell of an apartment in West One Hundred and Forty-Fifth Street.

A bleached blonde in a green kimono opened the door in response to his ring.

"Why, hello, kid!" she cried when the dim light in the hallway revealed his features to her. "You're just in time for a snifter. Where you been keepin' yourself? Jim and me were talkin' about you not five minutes ago. Come on in; the gang's all here," and she grasped him by the lapel of his coat, drew him into the hall and slammed the door.

"I've been doing the rural," replied Taylor with a laugh; "and, take it from me, it's mighty good to be back again where there are some live ones."

He preceded the girl into the dining room of the little apartment, where two men, seated at the dining table with a deck of cards, a bottle of Scotch, a syphon and three glasses rose as he entered and greeted him with a noisy welcome.

"Well, well! Little ol' kid back again!" cried one.

"Hello, Jim! Hello, Bill!" cried Taylor, grasping their outstretched hands. "You sure look good to me."

"Get another glass, Blanche," Jim called to the girl. "Sit in, kid, and we'll have a little round o' roodle -- dollar limit -- whatd'yu say?"

"Piker game," sneered Taylor, with a grin. "I'm dealing in millions, just now. Throw your cards in the goboon and listen to me, if you want to make a hundred thou apiece." He paused to note the effect of his remark.

"Quick, Blanche!" cried Jim. "Get the poor devil a drink. Can't you see he's dying of thirst and gone bug?"

Taylor grinned. "I'm sure dying of thirst alright," he admitted, "but I'm not bug. Now listen -- here's how, thanks! -- you guys are broke. You always have been and always will be till you stop piking. Once in a while you pull down a couple of simoleons and then sweat blood for a week or so for fear you'll be pinched and get a couple of years on the Island. I've got a real proposition here; but it's a man's job, though there isn't any chance of a comeback because we'll pull it off where there's no lamp posts and no law."

He paused and eyed his companions.

"Spiel!" said Bill.

Taylor narrated the events that had taken place during the past week.

"And now," he concluded, "if this Buttinsky Gordon brings back that marriage certificate I can kiss all my chances goodbye, for there isn't a court in that neck of the woods that would give me a look in with that Scott chicken if she had a ghost of a case."

"And you want us to?" Jim paused.

"You guessed it the first time," said Taylor. "I want you to help me follow Gordon, take that paper away from him -- croak him."

For a moment the four sat in silence.

"Why do you have to croak him?" asked the girl.

"So he can't come back and swear that he seen the certificate," said Bill. "That 'ud be just as good as the certificate itself in any court, against the kid."

"There isn't the least chance of our getting in wrong, either," explained Taylor, "because we can lay it all onto the natives or to an accident and there won't be anybody to disprove it -- if we are suspected; but the chances are that we can pull it off without anyone being the wiser."

"And what did you say we got out of it?" asked Bill.

"A hundred thou apiece the day I get the property in my hands," replied Taylor. "If you could get hold of the certificate first it would be fine and dandy, but we've got to follow Gordon to Central Africa to find where it is, and by that time he'll have it. So the only chance we have is to pass him the K. O. and take it away from him. I'll sure breath easier after I've seen that piece of paper go up in smoke."

James Kelley and William Gootch were, colloquially, short sports. They had rolled many a souse and separated more than a single rube from his bank roll by such archaic means as wire tapping and fixed mills, but so far they never had risen to the heights of murder. The idea found them tremulous but receptive. Their doubts were based more upon the material than the ethical. Could they get away with it without danger of detection. Ah, that was the question -- the only question.

"Well?" said Taylor, after a long pause, during which the other two had drained their glasses while the girl sat revolving hers upon the table cloth between her fingers.

"I'm game," announced Kelley, dodging the girl's eyes and looking sideways at Gootch.

"So'm I!" declared the latter.

And so it happened that when Mr. Dick Gordon walked up the gang plank of the liner that was to bear him as far as Liverpool in his journey to Africa, three men, leaning over a rail on an upper deck, watched him with interested eyes.

"That's him," said Taylor, "the tall one, just in front of the solemn looking party that resembles a Methodist minister crossed in love -- only he ain't. He's Gordon's man."

As neither Gordon nor Murphy were acquainted even by sight or repute with any of the precious three, the latter made no attempt to avoid them during the trip. It was Taylor's intention to scrape an acquaintance with Gordon after they had changed ships at Liverpool, when he would then know for certain Gordon's destination, and could casually announce that he and his companions were bound for that very point on a hunting expedition.

All went well with his plans until after they had sailed from Liverpool for Mombasa, when the depravity which was inherent in Kelley and Gootch resulted in an unpleasantness which immediately terminated all friendly relations between Gordon and the three. Taylor had succeeded in drawing Gordon into conversation soon after sailing from Liverpool, when he casually remarked that he and his friends were bound for the country about Victoria Nyanza in search of lions.

"Is that so?" exclaimed Gordon. "I am going into the neighborhood of Albert Edward Nyanza myself, and shall take the route from Mabido around the north end of Victoria Nyanza." And a common interest established, the two became better acquainted.

Then Taylor introduced his two friends and later on Kelley suggested cards. Taylor tried to find an opportunity to warn his accomplices against the crookedness which he knew was second nature with them. He would have preferred to let Gordon win, but the estimable Messieurs Kelley and Gootch, considering a bird in the hand worth two in the jungle, swooped down upon the opportunity thus afforded them to fleece their prey. The result was that after half an hour of play Gordon rose from the table, a rather unpleasant light in his eyes, cashed in his remaining checks and quit the game.

"Why, what's the matter, old man?" queried Taylor, inwardly cursing Gootch and Kelley.

"I wouldn't force an explanation if I were you," replied Gordon coldly. "The captain might overhear."

Taylor flushed and Gordon walked away, which was the end of the acquaintance upon which Taylor had based such excellent plans.

"You boobs are wonders," sneered Taylor. "You must have made all of fifty dollars apiece out of it -- and ruined every chance we had to travel right to the mission in Gordon's company," and he turned disgustedly away and sought his cabin.

CHAPTER 

Sophronia was blithely humming Dixie as she went about her work on the second floor of the Scott house. Occasionally she broke the monotony by engaging in heated discussions with herself.

"Yassem," she said, shaking her head, "Ah never done laik dat Mistah Scott Taylor. He may be po' Miss Do'thy's boy; but he's po' white trash, jes' de same. Yass'm. An' look yere," as she pushed the bed out from the wall to ply her broom beneath. "Jes' look yere! Dere he's gone and lef' his coat. Shif' less, das what he is -- a throwin' his coat around laik dat," and she seized the garment with a vigorous shake.

Throwing the coat across her arm, the negress carried it down to the library, where Mrs. Scott and Virginia were sitting.

"Heah dat Mistah Scott Taylor's coat," she announced, laying it on the table. "What Ah done goin' do wif it -- give it to dat good-fer-nothin' nigger Samu-el?"

"No, Sophronia," said Mrs. Scott, "we'll have to send it to him," and she picked up the garment to wrap it for mailing. As she folded it a crumpled sheet of note paper fell from a side pocket. Virginia picked it up to replace it in the coat, when, by chance, she saw her mother's name upon the top of the sheet.

"Why," she exclaimed, "this is yours, mother," and she spread the note out, smoothing it upon the table top. "It's a letter to you. How in the world did it happen to be in Scott's coat?"

Mrs. Scott took the note and read it; then she handed it to her daughter. When Virginia had completed it she looked up at her mother, her face clouded and angry.

"Why, the scoundrel!" she exclaimed. "He actually has been intercepting your mail." Then she glanced again at the date line and her eyes opened wide. "Mother!" she ejaculated. "This letter must have come the very day Scott left in such a hurry. It must have been because of this letter that he did leave. What can it mean?"

Mrs. Scott shook her head.

"I know," announced Virginia. "He has gone to prevent Mr. Gordon from recovering the certificate or else to follow him and obtain possession of it himself. There could be no other explanation of his hurried departure, immediately after the receipt of this letter."

"It does look that way, Virginia; but what can we do?"

"We can wire Mr. Gordon at once."

"What can we say that will not appear silly in a telegram, unless we actually accuse Scott of criminal designs," argued Mrs. Scott, "and we cannot do that, for we have only conjecture to base a charge upon."

"I can go to New York and talk with Mr. Gordon," said Virginia, "and that is just what I shall do."

"But, my dear -- " Mrs. Scott started to expostulate.

"But I am," said Virginia determinedly, and she did.

To her dismay she found Mr. Richard Gordon's apartment locked and apparently untenanted, for there was no response to her repeated ring of the bell. Then she inquired at another apartment across the hall. Here a house man informed her that Mr. Gordon's man had told him that he and Mr. Gordon were leaving for Africa -- he even recalled the name of the liner upon which they had sailed for Liverpool.

What was she to do? Well, the first thing was to assure herself as to whether Scott Taylor had also sailed for Africa, and if not to arrange to have him watched until she could get word to Mr. Richard Gordon. The taxi that had brought her to Gordon's apartment was waiting at the curb. Descending to it, she gave the driver instructions to take her to the office of a certain steamship company -- she would examine the passenger list and thus discover whether Taylor had sailed on the same boat with Gordon; but after examining the list and finding Taylor's name not among those of the passengers it suddenly occured to her that the man would doubtless have assumed a name if his intentions were ulterior. Now she was in as bad a plight as formerly. She racked her brain for a solution to her problem. It would do no good to wire Gordon, for he would not know Taylor if he saw him, and anyway it was possible that Taylor had not followed him and that she would only be making herself appear silly by sending Gordon a melodramatic wireless.

"I only wish," she muttered to herself, "that I knew whether or not Scott Taylor has followed him to Africa. How can I find out?"

And then came a natural solution of her problem -- to search for Scott Taylor himself in New York. Her first thought was of a city directory, and here she found a Scott Taylor with an address on West 145th Street, and a moment later her taxi was whirling her uptown in that direction.

It was with considerable trepidation that Virginia Scott mounted the steps and rang the bell beneath the speaking tube. She feared Taylor and knew that she was doing a risky thing in thus placing herself even temporarily in his power; but loyalty and gratitude toward Richard Gordon, a stranger who had put his life, maybe, in jeopardy to serve her and her mother, insisted that she accept the risk, and so when the latch of the front door clicked and a voice, ignoring the speaking tube, called down from above for her to come up, she bravely entered the dark stairway and marched upward, to what she had no idea. She had been glad to note that the voice from above had been that of a woman. It made her feel more at her ease; but when she reached the topmost step and found a slovenly young woman with bleached hair and a green kimono awaiting her, her heart sank.

"Does Mr. Scott Taylor live here?" she asked.

"Yes, but he ain't at home. What do you want -- anything I can do for you?"

"Has he left the city?" asked Virginia.

The girl's eyes narrowed, and Virginia noted it, but she thought, too, that she saw a trace of fear in them. She was convinced that this woman could tell her all she wished to know, but how was she to get the information from her?

"May I come in a moment and rest?" she asked. "It's rather a long climb up here from the street," and she smiled -- one of those delightful smiles that even a woman admires in another woman.

"Sure!" said the girl. "Come right in. Don't mind how things look. I'm here alone now and takin' it easy. You have to keep things straightened around here when the men folks are home, or they're always growlin'."

So the men folks were away!

"What a cute little place you have here," said Virginia. "You are Mrs. Taylor?"

The girl flushed just a trifle. "No," she replied. "My man's name is Kelley. Mr. Taylor boards with us when he's in town."

And afterward when she addressed her as Mrs. Kelley, Virginia could not but note an odd expression around the corners of the girl's mouth.

"Is Mr. Taylor out of town now?" asked Virginia.

The girl looked her straight in the eyes for a moment before she replied.

"Say, look here," she demanded at last. "What's your game? Who are you, anyhow and what's your idea in doin' all this rubberin' after Kid Taylor?"

For a moment Virginia did not know what answer to make, and then, impulsively, she decided to tell this girl a part of her conjectures at least, in the hope that either sympathy for Gordon or fear of the consequences upon Taylor would enlist her services in Virginia's behalf. There was that in the girl's face which convinced Virginia that beneath the soiled green kimono and evidences of dissipation in the old-young face there lay a kind heart and a generous disposition. And so she told her.

Her story was not all news to Blanche. She had heard most of it from Taylor's lips. When Virginia had finished the girl sat glowering sullenly at the floor for several seconds. At last she looked up.

"I don't know," she said, "what strings Kid Taylor has on me. He ain't never done nothing except to egg Jim on first to one job and then to another that Taylor didn't have the nerve to pull off himself. Jim's been to the Island once already for a job that Taylor worked up an' then sat right here drinkin' high-balls an' tryin' to flozzie up to me while Jim and Bill were out gettin' pinched.

"An' now -- " she paused, a startled look coming into her eyes. "An' now he's framed up a murder for them, 'cause he ain't got the nerve to do it himself."

"You mean," cried Virginia, "that they have really followed Mr. Gordon to Africa to murder him?"

Blanche nodded, affirmatively. Then she leaned forward toward her caller.

"I've told you," she said, "because I thought you might find a way to stop them before they did it. I don't want Jim sent to the chair. He's always been good to me. But for Gawd's sake don't let them know I told you. Bill 'ud kill me, an' Jim 'ud quit me, I'd care more about that than the other. You won't tell, will you?"

"No," said Virginia, "I won't. Now, tell me, they sailed on the same boat as Mr. Gordon?"

"Yes, Jim and Bill and Taylor, an' they were goin' to follow Gordon until he got the paper, then croak him an' take it away an' say it was an accident or something."

Virginia Scott rose from the chair upon which she had been sitting. Outwardly she was calm and collected, but inwardly her thoughts were in a confused and hysterical jumble in which horror predominated. What was she to do? How helpless she was to avert the grim tragedy. She thought of cabling Gordon, but when she suggested the plan to Blanche the girl pointed out that it was too late -- Gordon must already have left the end of the railroad and be well upon his way into the interior.

For a moment Virginia stood in silence. Then she held out her hand to the young woman.

"I thank you," she said. "You have done right to tell me all that you have. Goodbye!"

"What are you going to do?" asked Blanche.

"I don't know yet," replied Virginia. "I want to think -- maybe a solution will come."

And as she was driving back to her hotel the solution did come -- in the crystallization of a determination to take the saving of Richard Gordon into her own hands. It was for her that he was risking his life. She would be a coward to do one whit less than her plain duty. There was no one upon whom she could call to do this thing for her, since she realized that whoever attempted it must risk his life in pitting himself against Taylor and his confederates -- desperate men who already had planned upon one murder in the furtherance of their dishonorable purpose.

She thought of writing her mother first; but deliberation assured her that her parent would do everything in her power to prevent the carrying out of a scheme which Virginia herself knew to be little short of madness -- and yet she could think of no other way. No, she would wait until it was too late to recall her before she let her mother know her purpose.

So instead of returning at once to her hotel, Virginia drove to the offices of a transatlantic steamship company, where she made inquiries as to sailings and connections for Mombasa, Africa. To her delight she discovered that by sailing the following morning, she could make direct connections at Liverpool. Once committed to her plan she permitted no doubts to weaken her determination, but booked her passage immediately and returned uptown to make purchases and obtain currency and a letter of credit through a banker friend of her grandfather.

The morning that she sailed she posted a long letter to her mother in which she explained her plans fully, and frankly stated that she had intentionally left her mother in ignorance of them until now for fear she would find the means to prevent their consumation.

"I know that, to say the least," she wrote, "the thing that I am going to do is most unconventional and I realize also that it is not unfraught with dangers; but I cannot see a total stranger sacrifice his life in our service without a willingness to make an equal sacrifice, if necessary, in his."

And when her mother read the letter, though her heart was heavy with fear and sorrow, she felt that her daughter had done no more than the honor of the Scotts demanded.

To Virginia the long journey seemed an eternity, but at last it came to an end and she found herself negotiating with an agent at Mabido for native porters and guards and the considerable outfit necessary to African travel. From this man she learned that Gordon had left for the interior a month before, but he had not heard of a man by the name of Taylor, though there had been, he said, another party of three Americans who had followed Gordon by about a week. These had been bound for Victoria Nyanza to hunt, and the agent smiled as he recalled their evident unfamiliarity with all things pertaining to their avocation.

Virginia asked him to describe these men, and in the description of one she recognized Taylor, and rightly guessed that the others were Kelley and Gootch. So three men, one of them an unprincipled scoundrel, had gone out into the savage, lawless wilds on the trail of Richard Gordon! Virginia went cold as the fear swept her that she was too late.

Further questioning of the agent revealed the fact that while Gordon and the other three had arrived simultaneously they had had no intercourse, and that Gordon had obtained considerable start on the others because of his familiarity with customs of African travel and the utter ignorance of the others of the first essentials of their requirements.

This hope sustained her; that Gordon with his superior knowledge and experience had been able to outdistance the others, and that she, by traveling light and carefully selecting her path, might overtake them before they overtook Gordon or met him upon his return.

With this idea in mind Virginia hastened her preparations,

and once on the march urged her safari on to utmost speed. Almost from the start she discovered that her head man, while apparently loyal to her, had but meagre control of the men of the safari, who were inclined to be insubordinate and quarrelsome. The result was that to her other burdens was added constant apprehension from this source, since it not only threatened her own welfare but the success of her mission as well.

It was upon the tenth day that the first really flagrant breach of discipline occurred -- one which the headman could not handle or the girl permit to pass unnoticed. The men had long been grumbling at the forced marching which had fallen to their lot since the very beginning, notwithstanding the fact that they had been employed with the distinct understanding that such was to be the nature of their duty. Today, after the mid-day rest, the porters were unusually slow in shouldering their packs, and there was much muttering and grumbling as the headman went among them trying to enforce his commands by means of all manner of terrible threats. Some of the men had risen sullenly and adjusted their burdens, others still sat upon the ground eyeing the headman, but making no move to obey him. Virginia was at a little distance waiting for the safari to set out. She was a witness to all which transpired. She saw a hulking black Hercules slowly raise his pack in laggard response to the commands of the excited headman.

Just what words passed between them she could not know, but suddenly the porter hurled his load to the ground, shouting to the others who had already assumed their burdens. One by one these followed his example, at the same time shouting taunts and insults at the frantic, dancing, futile headman. The armed members of the party -- the native escort -- leaned on their rifles and grinned at the discomfiture of the headman.

Virginia's heart sank as she witnessed this open break. It was mutiny, pure and simple, and her headman was quite evidently wholly incapable of coping with it. That it would quickly spread to the armed guard she was sure, for their attitude proclaimed that their sympathies were with the porters. Something must be done, and done at once, nor was there another than herself to do it.

The headman and the large porter were wrangling in high pitched voices. The other porters had closed in about the two, for it was evident that they would soon come to blows. The attitude of all the bearers was angry and sullen. The members of the safari stilled grinned -- this was the only reassuring symptom of the whole dangerous affair. They had not yet openly espoused the cause of the mutineers.

Virginia came to a decision quickly. She crossed the space between herself and the porters at a rapid walk, shouldering her way between the watchers until she stood between the headman and the bellicose porter. At sight of her they stopped their wrangling for a moment. Virginia turned to the headman.

"Tell this boy," she said, "that I say he must pick up his pack at once."

The headman interpreted her order to the mutineer. The latter only laughed derisively, making no move to obey. Very deliberately Virginia drew her revolver from its holster at her hip. She levelled it at the pit of the porter's stomach, and with a finger of her left hand pointed at the pack on the ground. She said nothing. She knew that she had committed herself to a policy which might necessitate the fulfillment of the threat which the leveled weapon implied, and she was ready to adhere to the policy to the bitter end.

The fate of her expedition hung upon the outcome of this clash between her porters and her representative, the headman; and upon the fate of the expedition hung, possibly, the very life of a stranger who had placed himself in jeopardy to serve her. There was no alternative -- she must, she would compel subordination.

The porter made no move to assume his burden, but he ceased to laugh. Instead, his little eyes narrowed, his heavy lower jaw and pendulous lower lip drooped sullenly. He reminded the girl suddenly of a huge brute about to spring upon its prey, and she tightened the pressure of her finger upon the trigger of her revolver.

"Tell him," she instructed the headman, "that punishment for mutiny is death. That if he does not pick up his pack at once I shall shoot him, just as I would shoot a hyena that menaced my safety."

The headman did as he was bid. The porter looked at the encircling faces of his friends for encouragement. He thought that he found it there and then an evil spirit whispered to him that the white woman would not dare shoot and he took a step toward her threateningly.

It was his last step, for the instant that he took it Virginia fired, not at his stomach, but at his heart -- and he crumpled forward to tumble at her feet. Without a second glance at him she wheeled upon the other porters.

"Pick up your packs and march!" she commanded, and those who could not understand her words at least did not misinterpret the menace of her levelled weapon. One by one, and with greater alacrity than they had evinced since the first day out, they shouldered their burdens, and a moment later were filing along the trail. The safari still grinned, for which Virginia was devoutly thankful.

From then on she became her own headman, using that dignitary principally as an interpreter, nor for many days was there again the slightest show of insubordination -- that came later, with results so disastrous that -- but why anticipate disaster?

CHAPTER IV

Far to the west Richard Gordon had penetrated the jungle to the site of the ruined mission. He had scraped around the woods which overgrew the razed walls of the bungalow, and at last he had come upon the flagging of the old hearth. Stone after stone he pried from its place until beneath one he at last came upon a tiny vault, and a moment later his groping fingers touched a rusted tin box that crumpled beneath them. Feeling carefully amid the debris, Gordon finally withdrew a long manila envelope which had withstood the ravages of time. It was still sealed, nor did he break it open, for it was all the box contained other than a few loose pieces of jewelry and therefore must contain the paper he sought.

Dick Gordon was elated by the success of his adventure. He had feared that even the old hearth might have disappeared and the paper with it, for he had no means of knowing how complete had been the Wakandas' demolition of the mission, as upon his former visit he had seen no sign of the old chimney and fireplace.

Early the following morning he set out upon the return journey toward the coast, confident that no further obstacles other than those ordinary to African travel lay between him and the delivery of the packet safely into the hands of Mrs. Scott.

How could he guess that to the east of him three American crooks, bent upon nothing less than his death, barred his way to the coast.

That they were making short marches and slow ones was of little moment to the three. They soon had tired of the hardships of African travel, and finally gave up the hope of overtaking Gordon before he reached the mission. To waylay him upon his return would answer their purpose quite as well, and so when they came at last to a village through which Gordon must pass upon his return to the coast it required little discussion of the question to decide them to await him there.

In view of generous gifts the native chief welcomed them to his hospitality. He set aside a commodious hut for the three whites. They unstoppered numerous bottles of Irish whiskey and the blacks brewed their native beer. The visit was a long-drawn Bacchanalian revel which the whites found more to their tastes than long, tiresome marches and the vicissitudes of ever changing camps.

But one day the peace of the community was rudely startled. A lion seized upon an unwary woman working in a little patch of cultivated ground outside the village. Her screams brought out the warriors and the whites; but the lion dragged his prey into the jungle, her screaming ceased, nor was she ever seen again.

The natives were terrified. They besought the whites to help them -- to go forth with their guns and slay the man-eater; but though they hunted for two days no trace of the marauder could they find. Then the blacks dug a pit and baited it with a live goat, and lest the lion escape even this they set a watch upon the pit that the whites might be called when the lion approached.

Nor did they have long to wait. Scarce had they secreted themselves when a huge lion stepped majestically from the brush. Raising his massive head he sniffed the air. His lower jaw rose and fell. The slaver drivelled from his jowls. Deep in his throat rumbled a low thunder, and presently at his side appeared a sleek lioness.

For a moment they stood thus, their yellow eyes sometimes boring straight ahead as though to pierce the thickets behind which the trembling natives crouched, or again moving slowly up and down the trail. Presently the lion's head went up in a quick movement of arrested attention. Instantly he froze to rigid immobility. His sensitive nostrils dilated and contracted, the tip of his tail moved. Aside from these he might have been chiselled from living gold, so magnificent he was.

Up wind, in a little clearing, two antelope browsed. Now and again the graceful male raised his horned head to sniff the air; his great wondering eyes scanning the surrounding jungle. Then he would lower his muzzle again and resume his feeding, yet ears and nose were always upon the alert.

The Judas breeze, kissing the soft coats of the antelope as it passed, bore down to the nostrils of the lions the evidence of the near presence of flesh -- of tender, juicy, succulent, red flesh. The king turned his royal head once toward his consort. A sound that was half sigh breathed from his great throat. Was it a message -- a command? Who may say? The lioness settled herself into a comfortable position in the long grass and her lord moved silently away, up wind toward the unconscious antelope.

A moment later an excited native detached himself from the watchers and sped away toward the village to notify the whites that the lions had come. Taylor, Kelley and Gootch caught up their rifles and followed the guide back toward the pit. At their heels was half the male population of the village, armed with short, heavy spears; but the chief, who had hunted lions with white men many times before, sent them all back with the exception of three who carried the whites' extra guns. There had been enough before to have frightened all the lions out of the country.

Even so, the white men themselves, clumsy in this unaccustomed work, made noise enough to bring the lioness to her feet as they crawled into the bushes beside the watchers. When finally they saw her she was standing head on gazing nervously toward their hiding place. It was evident that she was uneasy, and the old chief knew that in an instant she would bolt. What had held her so long in the face of the noise of the awkward white men he could not guess.

"Shoot!" he whispered. "Quick!"

Already the lioness was wheeling to depart when the three rifles spoke. Only one bullet struck the target, but that one was enough to transform the timid jungle creature into a mad engine of rage and destruction. Turning like a cat and growling horribly, the lioness charged without an instant's warning straight down upon the cover that hid her foes.

It was the first time in their lives that any one of the white men had seen a charging lioness, and it was too much for the dope shattered nerves of Kelley and Gootch. Flinging away their rifles, they turned and ran like scared rabbitts, their gun bearers and the watchers near them surprised into panic at the unwonted sight of terror-struck white men emulating their example.

Only Taylor, his gun bearer and the chief held their ground. Taylor was frightened -- few men are not in the face of a charging lion, especially if it be their first; but the blood of the Scotts flowed in his veins, and whatever else he might be, he was not a physical coward.

In the moment that ensued he took careful aim and fired again, and this time the lioness stopped -- dead. Taylor drew a deep sigh of relief. Great beads of perspiration stood upon his forehead. He wiped them away, and as he attempted to arise he noticed that his knees were weak and trembling. It wouldn't do for the chief to see that, so he sat down again and rolled a cigarette.

By the time the frightened ones had been recalled he was able to control his muscles. Gootch and Kelley came with their tails between their legs, like whipped curs.

"You guys missed your call," laughed Taylor. "You ought to have been lion tamers."

The twain grinned sheepishly.

"I'll see that hell-cat face in my dreams for the rest of my natural life," said Kelley.

Gootch shrugged with a shudder.

"Me for Broadway and the Tammany tiger -- it doesn't make such awful faces," he said.

"Well, let's go back to the village and have a drink on my

first lion," suggested Taylor, and the three departed, leaving the natives to rig a sling and carry the body of the lioness in.

When the lion left his mate he made his way stealthily in the direction of his quarry. Now and again he stopped to raise his head and sniff the air, or with up-pricked ears to listen.

Ahead of him, the buck, uneasy, though he had as yet located no enemy, moved slowly off, followed by his doe. Craftily the lion trailed them by scent. Presently he came within sight of them but they were on the move and the ground was not such as to favor a charge. So he stalked them -- cautiously, warily, silently -- the personification of majesty, of power, of stealth. He stalked them for a long time, until they halted again to browse upon the edge of a little plain, and then his majesty, wearied and impatient, ventured a charge from too great a distance.

Like a bolt he broke from the concealing jungle. With a speed that is only a lion's when it charges he sped toward them -- and still all unconscious they fed on. It was the doe who first looked up, and then two streaks of bay brown fled before the tawny, yellow flash. It was soon over. A dozen or more bounds convinced the great cat that he had lost, and with an angry roar he halted to glare for a moment after his disappearing feast, and then to turn, still rumbling, back into the forest toward his mate.

He came, after a time, to the spot where he had left her, but she was not there. He called to her, but she did not answer. Then he sniffed about. The scent of man was still heavy in the air, and the acrid odor of powder clung to the grasses and the branches, and -- what was that, blood? The smell of blood? The lion crossed and recrossed the trail. He walked about sniffing, and at last he came upon the spot where his mate had died. A great roar broke from his mighty lungs. He smelled about the trampled grasses. Blacks! And what is this, the scent spoor of whites? The blacks were familiar denizens of the jungle. He thought little of them one way or another. Sometimes he ate them for they were stupid creatures easily overcome: but the whites! He had had experience of them before -- of them and their acrid smoke and their painful bullets. His forearm had been creased by one and the scar still plainly showed.

The whites! How he hated them! Down went his nose to the trail. Which way had they gone? He would follow and avenge. Straight along the crooked jungle pathway led the spoor. Rumbling in his throat the lion followed, all engrossed in hate and rage, so that he did not see the trap until it was too late. Suddenly there was a giving of the trail beneath his feet. A snapping of small branches.

He clawed and tried to leap to safety, but in vain. The earth sank from beneath him, and snarling and beating with his armed feet he dropped into the blackness of the pit that had been dug for him. Nor, for all his great strength and cunning could he escape.

It was mid-afternoon, following a long march, that Virginia and her safari came upon a village where the headman had told her they would be well received and could doubtless trade for fowl and goats and vegetables. The prospect was alluring, for during the past week her hunters had been vouchsafed the poorest luck. Goat and chicken would taste good. Virginia's mouth watered. The mouths of her boys watered too; but not so much for goat and chicken as for the native beer for which this village was justly famous.

The chief was away when the visitors arrived, but his wife and son did honors in his stead. They, as well as the balance of the villagers, evinced the greatest curiosity. But few of them ever had seen a white woman before, and they clustered about her, feeling her flesh and garments, laughing uproariously at each new discovery, but according her every mark of friendship. At last, with difficulty, Virginia succeeded in arranging through her headman for a hut to which she might retire; but even here the women and children followed her, squatting about watching her every move. The interior of the hut was filthy, and the girl had been in it but a short time when she decided to summon her headman and have her tent and camp pitched outside the village.

When she went to find him, for she could not make any of the women understand her wants, she discovered him, with others of her safari, indulging freely in beer. Already they had consumed large quantities, and, with an unlimited supply in view, were loath to leave the immediate vicinity of the brew for the sake of pitching camps for her or for anyone else.

As she stood arguing with them through the headman she was suddenly aware of the approach of newcomers from the jungle. A little party of men were entering the village gates, and her heart gave a great leap of joy as she saw a white man among them. She had started forward impulsively toward him, half believing that it might be Richard Gordon, when she saw two other whites behind him, and recognized one of them immediately as Taylor. Her heart sank as she realized the predicament in which she had unwittingly placed herself. Taylor, seeing her here, would not need to be told to know what had brought her, and now, just when she most needed the loyalty of her boys, they were on the high road to inebriation.

She turned toward them quickly, however, placing herself behind them, out of sight of the advancing whites.

"Quick!" she whispered to the headman. "You must get the boys together at once. We will continue the march. Those men who have just entered the village are my enemies. Tell the boys of the safari to get their guns -- we may need them; but I must get out of this village at once."

The headman transmitted her commands to the porters and the safari, but they elicited only grumbling murmurs at first, and, when she urged her authority upon them, they openly refused to move from where they were. They said that they had marched far that day -- they could go no further -- they would not go further, and one who had consumed more beer than his fellows announced that he would take no more orders from a woman. And just then Scott Taylor came abreast the party and when his eyes fell upon Virginia Scott they went wide in incredulity and wonder.

"Virginia!" he exclaimed. "Where did you come from?

What on earth are you doing here?" And then as though he had guessed the answer his eyes narrowed and a lowering scowl clouded his face. "You've been following me, have you? Spying on me, eh? You think you can put one over on me, do you? Well, you've got another think coming, young lady."

Virginia Scott looked coldly at the speaker, utter contempt in the curve of her lip and the expression of her level eyes.

"Yes, I followed you, Scott," she replied. "I know you all too well, you see, not to have guessed something of the ulterior motive which prompted you to come to Africa immediately upon the heels of Mr. Gordon. We found his letter to mother, you see, in your coat pocket, the coat that you accidentally dropped behind your bed before you left. If you will take my advice, Scott, you will take yourself and your precious friends here back to the coast and out of Africa as fast as you can go."

Taylor had been thinking rapidly as the girl spoke, yet he was at a loss what step to take next. If she knew that he had followed Gordon to Africa then her mother knew it too, and whatever harm might befall Gordon here would be laid at his door even though he found the means to quiet Virginia. The means to quiet Virginia! The thought kept running through his head over and over again. The means to quiet Virginia! He gave his head a little shake as he let his eyes rest on the girl's face again. She was very beautiful -- even more beautiful in her khaki and tan than she had been in the soft summer dresses and clear white complexion of the Virginia days.

"Will you take the chance and go?" she asked presently. "I promise that I will say no word of this that will harm you. Each of us is half Scott -- I would not willingly harm my own blood, nor will I see you penniless when the estate comes into my hands."

The mention of the estate brought Taylor up with a start. It also brought a gleam into the eyes of Kelley and Gootch, who had been interested listeners to the conversation. Kelley leaned toward Taylor.

"If you go back, Kid," he asked, "who's goin' to pay me an' Bill the hundred thou apiece?"

"I'm not going back, you fool," snapped Taylor. "I've come too damned far to go back now."

"What are you going to do, Scott?" Virginia asked the question in an even voice. She well knew the moment was fraught with hideous possibilities for her.

"The first thing I'm going to do," growled Taylor, "is to put you where you can be watched, and where you won't get another chance to go and blab all you know or think to Mr. Butinski Gordon."

He stepped quickly to the girl's side as he spoke, and, though she reached for her revolver his hand was too quick for her and the weapon was wrenched from her grasp before she could use it, as use it she most certainly should, had she the opportunity. Taylor seized her wrist and he stood there holding her, scowling down into her face. Virginia returned the scowl, and spoke a single word, loud enough for the other whites to hear.

"Coward!" That single word was filled with loathing and contempt supreme. It stung the man as would no torrent of invective. It stung and roused all the brute within him.

With an oath he jerked the girl roughly after him as he turned and crossed the village street. Straight toward the hut occupied by himself and his two associates he dragged her, and at his heels came Kelley and Gootch.

"Get a rope," snapped Taylor when they were inside. "We'll truss this vixen until we can plan what's best for her. And anyway we haven't had that drink yet on my first lion."

Gootch found a rope and together the three men bound the girl securely. Then they went out of the hut, taking a bottle of whiskey with them.

After they had left Virginia exerted every effort to free herself of her bonds; but strain as she would she could not slip them an inch. The afternoon wore on. She could hear loud talk and laughter of the drinking whites and blacks, and she trembled as she thought what the return of those three, flushed with drink, might mean to her.

And night fell and still she lay a prey to grim terror and the physical tortures of her bonds and the unclean mats upon which they had thrown her.

CHAPTER V

Swinging along at the head of his safari, Dick Gordon puffed upon his blackened briar and hummed a gay tune of the roof gardens. The black boys at his heels laughed and chattered and sang. They were a merry party, for Gordon had a way with him that kept men singing at their work until they forgot that it was work. He could get more miles out of a safari than many a hardened and hard, old explorer, for he treated his boys like children, humoring or punishing as seemed best, but never permitting an injustice, never nursing an irritation, and never letting them forget that he was master. From headman to meanest porter they loved him, respected him, each thought that he would wade through blood for the big, singing bwana; but they were soon to find that it was easier to think than to wade when the chances were even that the blood might be their own.

They were nearing a native village where beer flowed like water, and Gordon, having had one previous experience of the place and the effects that it had upon his men for two consecutive marches, had decided to camp short of the village and pass it on the fly next morning. They had come almost to the spot he had selected for their camp, when the roar of a lion, almost at his feet brought Gordon to a sudden stop at the verge of a pit cunningly hid in the trail. A hole a few paces further on showed where the lion had disappeared and why he was roaring thus up out of the bowels of the earth.

Gordon approached and peered into the excavation. There

below him crouched a huge, black maned lion. At Gordon's elbow was his gun bearer. To turn and grasp the ready rifle was the work of but a moment, but when he had raised the weapon to his shoulder and levelled it upon the beast below him something brought him to a sudden stop. His men were gathered about the pit now throwing taunts and insults at the beast.

"Poor devil," thought Gordon. "It's a shame to pot you like this without a chance for your life -- " He paused and then -- "I'm damned if I'll do it."

Young Mr. Gordon was, as you may have guessed, a creature of impulse. He was wont to act first and think later, which is a mighty fine way to do the right thing if one is inherently right at heart, and doesn't chance to be laboring under the insidious toxin of anger. Then, too, Dick Gordon loved animals, and particularly he loved the great fierce cats of the jungle. To him there was no more inspiring sight than that of a mighty lion, and as he looked at the one below him, even in the dim light of the pit, he realized that never before had his eyes rested upon so magnificent a creature as this great, black-maned prisoner. He lowered his rifle and turned toward his headman.

"Let's have a little fun," he said. "It's not sport to shoot a lion in a pit. I never have, and I never shall. We'll let this old boy out where he'll have a run for his money and then I can take a little pride in his skin when I get it home."

The headman grinned. He was something of a sport himself, but not when it came to lions.

"How you get him out, bwana?" he asked.

Gordon examined the pit. Its roof was constructed of several stout saplings crossed with lesser branches and brush. To drag a couple of the larger logs until their ends dropped into the pit would be the work of but a moment, then the lion could clamber out if he were not injured, and there was nothing in his appearance or manner to indicate that he was not entirely whole.

Gordon explained his plan to the headman and gave his orders for the porters to lay aside their loads and drag the poles far enough to let their ends drop into the pit. The men grinned and shrugged, and looked for handy trees, for they knew that a maddened lion is lightning unchained. Gingerly they laid hold of the saplings and commenced to haul upon them, but when the ends had come to the pit's verge and were about to drop down and liberate the lion they paused , still grinning, though sheepishly, and begged to be excused, as it were. The headman explained to Gordon that the lion would be sure to get one of the men at least and he thought that it would be a useless waste of life when they already had the lion safely imprisoned and nothing gained by liberating him.

Gordon shrugged good naturedly. "You Li'le A'thas can take to the trees," he said, "and hurry up about it. I'm going to let loose this man-eating son of Belial," and he grasped the end of one of the logs and proceeded to pull.

The blacks, seeing his act, tarried not for even a free translation of his words, but scampered to right and left, clambering to the safety of the lower branches with the agility of monkeys. Only Gordon's gun bearer remained at his post. The young man, seeing him, directed the boy to place the rifle a few paces to his right where he could take it up and fire should it be necessary.

"Lean it against that tree over there," he directed. "After I drop the logs down I can reach it before the lion can climb out, if he is inclined to be nasty instead of grateful."

The boy, glad enough to be relieved of his duty, though he would have remained at his post in the face of a dozen lions had Gordon not dismissed him, did as he was bid, himself taking refuge in the tree at the base of which he leaned the rifle, cocked and ready to his master's hand.

Gordon measured the distance between the pit and the tree with his eyes, and calculated that even though the lion charged after climbing from his prison it would take him a moment or two to reach level ground and with that advantage Gordon could easily reach his rifle and bring the beast down before it was upon him.

The element of risk in the adventure appealed to the young

New Yorker. He would be pitting his own skill and prowess against the skill and prowess of the lion. The animal would have an almost even break with him, for if Gordon failed to stop him with his first shot the victory would be to the great cat. This was sport! Gordon felt a thrill of excitement tingling along his nerves as he drew slowly upon the end of one of the logs.

Below him the lion stood motionless glaring up into his face, and uttering occasional low growls. As he worked Gordon glanced often at the great beast, admiring his splendid stature, his great mane and his massive head. The lion was wondering if this creature was one of those who had slain his mate. What was he doing? Why was he pulling the cover from his prison? Why had the loud noise and the acrid odor that accompanied these white skinned humans not yet assailed his ears and nostrils? The lion was puzzled. He cocked his head upon one side, watching intently -- so intently that he forgot to growl.

Gordon dragged the end of one of the logs until it just hung upon the rim of the pit, then he drew its fellow to the same position. A single, quick, heavy pull upon the two together should precipitate the ends into the bottom of the trap.

Dick Gordon glanced behind him once more that he might finally fix in his mind the exact location of his rifle, then he surged back with a firm grip upon the logs, the dirt at the opposite end of the pit crumbled from the edge and the two logs dropped their further extremities side by side to the bottom.

At the same instant Gordon turned and ran for his rifle. The lion leaped nimbly to one side to avoid the falling logs, instantly grasped their significance to him and with an agile leap was upon them and at the edge of the pit by the time Gordon had covered half the distance to the tree where his gun leaned, ready to his hand.

Seeing the man fleeing the lion gave a single terrific roar and burst into the full speed of the charge. The natives in the trees screamed loudly to Gordon, the man turned his head, thinking the lion must be already upon him, and in the little instant that his eyes were taken from his path, his foot caught in the protruding root of a creeper and he was down.

But for this he might have reached his weapon and put in one good shot. Even now he had to scramble to his feet and race on; but even as he half rose a great body struck him from behind and hurled him back to earth -- a great, tawny, hairy body that towered above him grim and terrible.

A thousand thoughts raced through Dick Gordon's mind in the brief instant the lion stood over him. He thought of his revolver and his knife in their holsters at his side -- as a last resort he would use them. He had heard of men being in positions similar to his own and escaping unharmed -- of the lions leaving them for some unaccountable reason without inflicting even a scratch upon them. Gordon determined to wait until the lion took the offensive. He lay very quietly, just as he had fallen, half upon his side. One great forepaw was opposite his face, for the lion straddled him. Gordon even noted the ugly, jagged scar upon the inside of the forearm. The boys in the trees were shouting and hurling branches at the huge beast. The animal paid no more attention to them than as though they had been so many little monkeys. He lowered his mighty head and sniffed the body of his prey. Gordon could feel the muzzle touching his back lightly, and the hot breath upon his neck and cheek. The lion puzzled. This was not one of those whom he sought. For several minutes that seemed an eternity to Gordon the beast stood above him. What was he thinking? Could it be that he was searching through his savage brain for an explanation of the man's act in releasing him from captivity? Who may say?

But this we do know, that with one great paw he turned Gordon over on his back, sniffed him from head to foot, looked straight into his face for a full minute and then turned and stalked majestically down the trail, leaving unharmed the puny creature whose career one closing of those mighty jaws would have terminated forever.

Scarce believing that he could credit his own senses, Gordon rose slowly to his feet and gazed after the lion. Behind him his boy slid from the tree, and, seizing Gordon's rifle, ran forward and thrust it into the man's hand. Thus awakened from the stupor of the shock he had received, Gordon mechanically threw the weapon to the hollow of his shoulder. Quickly the sights covered a spot in the middle of the beast's back just behind the shoulders, the trigger finger pressed slowly back. The blacks all silent now, awaiting in breathless expectancy the shot that was never fired.

For a moment Gordon stood thus like a statue. Then, with an impatient shake of his head he lowered the weapon.

"I can't do it," he muttered. "The beast could have killed me but didn't. If I killed him now I'd be less than a beast. I wonder why he left us? Could it have been gratitude? Shucks. Gratitude nothing! He wasn't hungry, or else the boys frightened him away," and at the latter thought Gordon could not repress a grin as he recalled the great carnivora's apparent utter contempt for the yelling natives.

And as he stood watching the leisurely departure of the king until he was hidden by a turn in the trail the belief that it might have been gratitude insisted upon intruding itself upon his thoughts.

"Anyway," he said half aloud, "it'll make a pretty story, even if it's not the true explanation."

His boys had all descended from their trees by this time and were grouped about him, chattering to one another, and loudly expatiating upon the wondrous feats of bravery they would have performed -- "if." Gordon broke in upon their afterclap.

"Come!" he said. "Take up your packs. We ought to be near the stream that passes beside the beer village -- we'll make camp as soon as we strike it."

A half hour later they found a suitable spot for their camp, and Gordon, protected by a mosquito net, stretched himself in his hammock to enjoy the luxuries of a pipe and a book before the evening meal should be prepared.

Exhausted from her struggles to free herself from her bonds, Virginia lay in dumb misery listening to the sounds of revel without. The blacks were dancing now. Their hideous yells reverberated through the forest. The dancing light from the great fire they had built to illuminate the scene of their orgy rose and fell fitfully across the open entrance of the hut in which the girl lay.

Her own men would be joining in the mad revel, she well knew. No use to appeal to them. Already they had shown the calibre of their loyalty. Only the headman had remained at all staunch in his fealty to her and he was a weak vessel even when sober.

Now that he was drunk, as he doubtless was, she could not appeal to him with any hope of a response.

Now and again she heard the voices of the white men, maudlin from drink. She shuddered as she contemplated their return to the hut. Again she struggled vainly with her bonds. Hope was well nigh extinguished, for what hope could there be for her among these wild savages, and cruel, relentless whites?

As the blacks danced and the whites drank with them, another creature than Virginia Scott heard the Bacchanalian noises of their drunken revel. A great, black-maned lion, grim and silent, prowled about the palisade, sniffing and listening. Now and again he would halt, with his head cocked upon one side and his ears uppricked. Then he would resume his tireless pacing. Round and round the outside of the enclosure he paced his stealthy beat.

Occasionally a low, a very low moan, escaped his lips -- a weird, blood-freezing moan that, happily for the peace of mind of the revelers, was drowned by their own hideous noises. What were his intentions? That he seemed searching for something or someone was evident. Once or twice he paused and lifting his head measured the distance to the top of the palisade. To the very gates had he followed the spoor of the white men who had slain his mate. For them he had come. Were they within? He could not catch their scent; but though he had circled the palisaded village several times his sensitive nostrils had discovered no spoor fresher than that which ended at the village gates. His brute sense told him that they must be within. Why did he hesitate? He was no coward; but neither was he any fool. He knew the powers and the purpose of guns and spears, and he knew too that once within the palisade with the man-people, while all were awake, he might be killed before he had accomplished the revenge upon which he was bent, and so he bided his time -- a fierce and terrible thing, padding noiselessly through the black night just beyond the palisade.

The night wore slowly on. Less and less became the sounds of revelry as one by one the blacks succumbed to the influence of their native beer and the white man's whiskey. Presently Taylor rose unsteadily and made his way toward his hut, staggering little, for it was his boast that he could carry his load like a gentleman.

Virginia, wide eyed and sleepless, saw him approaching. In the extremity of her fear she rolled to the far side of the hut to lie there silent and motionless in the hope that he had forgotten her prescence and would not notice her. Taylor sober might be appealed to in the morning. There must be a fibre of chivalry somewhere in the soul of any man in whose veins flowed the honored blood of the Scotts; but Taylor drunk would be adamant to any influence of his passions.

From the darkness of her corner Virginia saw how slightly he staggered and her hope renewed. He might not be so badly intoxicated as she had feared; but as he lurched through the low doorway her heart sank, for he called her name aloud in a thick voice that belied the steadiness of his carriage.

She did not reply, and he crossed the hut, stooping and feeling for her with his hands. Presently he touched her, and an "ah!" of satisfaction broke from his lips.

"'Lo, sweetie," he mumbled.

Virginia did not answer, feigning sleep instead. He grasped her by the shoulder and shook her.

"Wake up, kid!" he shouted. "I'll show you I'm not shush a bad sort. 'S crooks out there wanted me to croak you; but I'm a gelmun; I won't croak you; if you treat me right."

He dragged her to a sitting posture and put his arms about her. She could not push him away or fight him off, for her arms were pinioned behind her.

"Scott!" she cried. "Think what you are doing! I am your own cousin."

"Firsh cousin once removed," he corrected.

"Please, Scott!" she pleaded. "Please leave me alone."

For reply he kissed her.

"You beast!" she cried.

"No beast," he assured her. "To show what a good fellow I am I'm goin' to take these ropes off you," and he commenced to fumble with the knots.

Virginia saw a ray of hope now in his drunkenness. Sober, his reason would have warned him against releasing her; but drunk he had all the foolish assurance of drunkenness. The knots baffling him, he drew his hunting knife and cut the cords.

"Now," he said, "you can show me how mush you love me," and again he seized her and strained her to him. At his hip swung a revolver. Virginia had coveted it from the first. Now it was the work of but a moment to snatch it from its holster and press it against the man's stomach.

"Take your hands off me," she said, "or I'll pull the trigger," and she poked the muzzle against his ribs.

Taylor knew in an instant what she had accomplished and it sobered him. Slowly his hand crept down to seize hers where it held the weapon close against him.

"Put up your hands," she warned him, "and put them up quickly. I shall take no chances, Scott, and I give you my word that I'd breath freer if you were dead."

The man raised his hands above his head and Virginia sprang to her feet.

"Now stay where you are," she commanded. "Don't come out of this hut before morning. If you do, or make any attempt to stay or recapture me, I shall certainly make it my sole point in life to kill you before I am retaken."

Slowly she backed across the floor toward the doorway. She would arouse her men and at the point of Scott's revolver force them to accompany her from the village. She was desperate, for she knew that worse than death was the best that she could hope for from Scott Taylor.

It was with a sigh of relief that she passed the low portal and found herself in the pure air of the moonbathed tropical night. A prayer of thanksgiving was on her lips; but it was never breathed, for scarce had she emerged from the interior of the hut than she was roughly seized from behind and the revolver wrenched from her grasp.

CHAPTER VI

As Virginia turned to struggle with her captors she saw that they were Taylor's twc accomplices, and now Taylor, released from the menace of the revolver, rushed from the hut to the assistance of his fellows. It required the combined strength of the three to subdue the girl, who was fighting with the strength of desperation for life, and more than life.

But at last they overcame her and dragged her back into the hut. Here they shoved her to the far side, and, panting from their exertions, stood glowering at her. Taylor was wiping blood from his hand. Virginia Scott, in the extremity of her need, had been transformed in the moment of battle to a primordial she-thing, and as her first human ancestor might have done, had fought with tooth and nails against her assailants. Kelley, too, had felt her strong, white teeth sink into his flesh and Gootch bore a long scratch from temple to chin.

"The ---- ----," exclaimed the latter. "We'd orter of croaked her in the first place."

Taylor was eyeing the girl through narrowed lids. All the beast that was in him shone from his evil eyes. He turned and whispered quickly to Kelley and Gootch.

"Are we in on it?" asked the former.

Taylor nodded. "I don't care," he said.

"And then we give her the k.o. and put her away behin' the hut," supplemented Gootch. "The groun' 's soft an' the diggin'll be easy."

"I told you that's wot you'd orter of done in the first place," grumbled Kelley. "It'll leave you the only heir an' there won't be nobody to squeal about Gordon w'en he don't show up no more."

"Go to it," growled Taylor; "there can't be any cat bite me up without paying for it."

The two crooks advanced toward the girl and seized her. Taylor waited to one side. Slowly they forced her to the floor of the hut and held her there, though she fought with all the strength remaining to her.

And outside the palisade the black maned prowler sniffed and listened. Now a little, vagrant breeze eddied through the stagnant night. It swirled across the village compound, and it bore upon its wings to the nostrils of the carnivora the fresh scent of the white men. With a low growl the great beast crouched and sprang. Lightly as a feather he topped the palisade and dropped noiselessly within.

For a moment he stood motionless, peering about. There was no one in sight. With long, easy strides, his supple muscles rolling in the moonlight beneath his smooth hide, the destroyer crossed to the nearest hut and sniffed at the chinks in the thatched wall. Then he moved to another and another, searching for the prey he wanted. And all unconscious of this grisly presence the blacks within slept on in blissful ignorance of the hideous menace roaming at will through their village.

In the white men's hut the three brutes struggled with the battling girl. Their victory was not to be the easy thing they had bargained on, and as they fought to subdue her their positions changed from time to time. Once she caught Gootch's thumb between her teeth, nor released her hold until she had almost severed it from his hand.

Cursing and moaning, the crook withdrew from the battle for a moment to sit with his back toward the door nursing his hurt. Kelley and Taylor were still endeavoring to overpower their quarry without killing her. Their faces were toward the door. Suddenly Virginia felt their grasps relax and saw their eyes, wide in horror, directed across her shoulder. She turned to discover what had so quickly diverted their attention from her, and she gasped at the sight that met her eyes. Framed in the doorway was the massive head of a huge lion. Gootch had not seen the beast. He was rolling to and fro drunkenly, holding on to his injured thumb.

Without a word Taylor and Kelley turned and commenced clawing frantically at the frail thatching of the hut's rear wall. In a moment they had torn an opening large enough to permit their bodies to pass through, and were gone into the night beyond. At the same instant the lion gave voice to a terrific roar, and Virginia dodged through the rent that Taylor and Kelley had made and sprawled to the ground outside. She saw the two scoundrels fleeing toward the right, and instinctively she turned toward the left. She had taken but a few steps when there fell upon her ears the most bloodcurdling scream of mortal agony and terror that ever had smote upon them in her life. She had not imagined that the human voice could compass such freezing fear as that which shrieked out its high pitched wail upon the silent jungle night.

The cry compelled her to turn her head back in the direction of the hut she had quitted, and there, in the full light of the equatorial moon, she witnessed that which will be seared upon her memory to her dying day.

She saw Gootch, half through the opening that had given escape to Kelley, Taylor and herself, clutching frantically at the turf at the sides of the torn hut wall. His features were distorted by agony and horror supreme.

He shrieked aloud to the friends who had deserted him and to the God that he long since had deserted, and ever, slowly and horribly, he was being drawn back into the interior of the hut by an unseen power. All too well Virginia guessed the giant force, the hideous bestial force, that was dragging the terrified man backward to his doom within the dark interior of the hut; yet, fascinated, she could but stand and watch the grim and terrible tragedy.

Slowly the body disappeared, and then the shoulders. Only the head was left and the hands, the latter still clutching futilely for a hold upon the frail wall. The face white and distorted by fear and suffering. And then the head was drawn back out of sight, the hands gave up the last hold; there was a frightful wail from within the gloomy interior, a wail which mingled with a savage, thunderous roar -- and then silence.

The cries of Gootch aroused the natives. Warriors were pouring from every hut -- the whole village was aroused. Virginia turned and resumed her flight. Straight toward the gates she ran. To unbar them was the work of but a moment. Beyond was the terrible jungle; the grim, cruel, mysterious jungle; but behind was a fate more terrible than any the jungle could offer. Without another backward glance the girl pushed the portals wide and scurried into the darkness of the forbidding forest.

The blacks, attracted to the hut occupied by the white men by Gootch's screams, waited a few paces from the entrance and shouted to their guests to ascertain the cause of the commotion. The lion within, warned by their voices, turned from his prey and stuck his great head out through the doorway. At sight of him the blacks howled in mingled terror and defiance. They waved their spears and shouted, hoping to frighten the beast from his hiding place.

Annoyed and rendered nervous by their din, the carnivore roared back his challenge, and amid a shower of hurtling spears dashed from the hut. For a moment he stood bewildered while the blacks retreated, and then he turned and trotted toward the palisade. Seeing him retreat the natives gathered courage and pursued. He skirted close in the shadow of the wall for a short distance, coming presently upon the gates which Virginia had left open. There he paused for an instant to turn a snarling face toward his pursuers, a face which brought them to a sudden halt, and then, wheeling, darted through the gateway and was gone.

Stumbling through the jungle night, Virginia Scott was occupied by but a single thought -- to place as much distance between herself and Scott Taylor as she could. In what direction she was going, to what nameless fate she did not consider. For the first half hour hers was the flight of panic -- unreasoning, mad, hysterical. And surely she had been through enough that day to shake steadier nerves and more experienced heads than hers.

Thorns and underbrush clutched at her short skirt and khaki jacket, tearing them; scratched her hands, her arms and face; tangled themselves between her feet and tripped her. Again and again she fell, only to scramble to her feet once more and plunge on deeper and deeper into the unknown. The myriad jungle noises fell for a time on deaf ears -- the movement of padded feet, the brush of bodies against vine and bush, the fluttering of weird wings registered not at all upon her fear-numbed brain.

And then, above all other sounds, broke one that blasted its way to her perceptive faculties. Thunderous, ominous, earth-shaking, terrible, it shattered her preoccupation and awoke her to a sense of the nearness of other dangers than that from which she was fleeing.

It was the roar of a lion. To her tense nerves it sounded close behind her. The girl paused, stark and rigid, listening. She stood with her clenched hands tight against her bosom. Her breath came in little gasps. She could feel her heart beating against her ribs -- she could hear it; above all the noises of the jungle it sounded like a traitorous tattoo, beating out a call to the prowlers of the night, guiding them to their prey.

For a moment she stood thus, until out of the blackness from which she had come she thought she heard the stealthy pad of great feet. With a shudder and a little gasp she turned to flee from this new menace. On she stumbled, bruised, bleeding, hopeless. For how long she could not know. Time had ceased to exist in the meanwhile, and man made units of seconds, minutes, or hours -- each heart beat measured an eternity. She had been fleeing thus through the blackness of tortured terror since time began -- she would continue thus to flee, hopeless, until the last trump, and then the thing behind her would spring, frightful talons would fasten themselves in her soft flesh, giant fangs would sink deep in neck or shoulder. It would be the end. The end! The thought brought her to a sudden stop. The end! It was inevitable.

Why flee the inevitable?

She leaned against the bole of a tree, panting like a winded doe that, after a brave battle for liberty, finds itself spent and awaits resignedly the coming of the hounds.

She waited, listening for sounds of the coming of the beast of prey she felt sure was upon her trail. She listened, but she heard no sound to indicate that the beast was close at hand. However, she did not attempt to delude herself into a feeling of false security. She well knew the uncanny soundlessness of the passing of the giant cats when they chose silence.

But what was that? A body, black against the blackness of the jungle, had moved among the trees to her right. She strained her eyes in the direction of the shadowy form. Yes! There it was, and another and another. Suddenly two spots of fire glowed dimly from the point upon which her gaze was concentrated. Close beside them appeared two other spots.

Virginia shrank back against the tree, horrified. A little prayer rose from her silent lips. God! They were coming closer. Stealthily, noiselessly, they were creeping upon her. The rough back of the tree behind her gave to the frenzied force of her clutching fingers. A piece broke off, coming away in her hand. Such a little thing may sometimes prove the most momentous of a lifetime. To Virginia it brought a lightning train of thoughts that opened an avenue of hope in her hopeless breast. The tree! Why had she not thought of it before?

They were coming closer now --would there be time? She turned and measured the girth of the bole with her arms. It was not a large tree -- in that lay still greater hope. A sudden snarling broke from the things creeping upon her, and at the same instant she leaped as high as she could, embraced the stem of the tree and scrambled rapidly aloft.

There was a rush below her, a chorus of angry growls, and something brushed her foot. She heard the click of jaws snapping together below her, and then she drew herself to the comparative safety of a lower limb.

With reaction came a faintness and a giddy dizziness that

threatened to plunge her from her sanctuary, but she clung desperately, and after a moment gained control of herself. Then, painfully and wearily, she crawled a little higher among the branches until she found a spot where she could recline in greater safety and comfort.

Here she lay sleepless through the balance of the night -- a few hours which seemed endless to her -- while the jungle surged back and forth below, around, and above her, and the jungle noises, fearsome and uncanny, rose and fell, a devil's discord jangling on raw nerves.

Through those long hours Virginia sought, by planning, some ray of hope for the future, but each essay in this direction brought her to a dead stop against the black wall of fact. She was alone, unarmed, and lost in the jungle. She was surrounded by savage beasts and savage men by any one of which she would be considered natural prey.

To retrace the long journey from the coast, even though she knew the trail, would be impossible, and equally impossible would be the task of going ahead in search of Richard Gordon, whom she knew to be somewhere to the west of her. The more she weighed her chances for existence against the forces of destruction pitted against her, the more hopeless appeared her situation. Even the coming dawn, ordinarily a time of renewing hope, brought no added buoyancy to her jaded spirits -- only a dogged determination to fight on to the inevitable end, and then to die bravely with a consciousness of having fought a good fight, as became a granddaughter of Jefferson Scott.

As daylight dispelled the darkness about her and objects that had assumed grotesque and menacing proportions by night receded and shrank to the common places of day Virginia's eyes sought the ground below for a glimpse of the creatures whose menace had driven her to the safety of branches before; but, search as she would, she could discover no sign of dangerous beast, and at last, realizing that she could not remain in the tree forever, she dropped to the ground and resumed her flight. Noting the direction of the sun she turned her face toward the west, deciding at least that her only hope of salvation lay in Richard Gordon and influenced equally, too, by the obligation she felt strong upon her to find and warn him of the menace which lay in wait upon his homeward trail.

That she would find him she had little hope; but at least she would have the poor satisfaction of clinging to duty to the last, however futile her attempt to fulfil that duty.

She had not gone a great distance when she became aware of the uncanny sensation that she was being followed. Turning, she looked back into the jungle behind her; but saw nothing. Yet again, the moment she had resumed her way, she could have sworn that she heard something moving through the vegetation at her heels. How long this continued she could not have told; but at length it so preyed upon her nerves that she was once more reduced to a state of panicky terror equal to that which had claimed her the preceding night.

If she could have seen the thing that dogged her footsteps, even to know that it was some fierce and terrible creature of destruction, her nervous suffering would have been less; but to feel its eyes upon her and yet not to see it, to hear its padded footsteps and to see twigs disturbed was horrible.

A dozen times she was on the point of clambering into a tree; but hunger and thirst which had already assailed her told her in no uncertain terms that there must be no tarrying except in the last extreme of danger. While she had strength she must go on and on, for if she did not find food and drink she soon would have no strength to go.

Twenty times she must have turned to search out the prowler that stalked her, yet she had had no slightest glimpse of him, when she broke, quite unexpectedly, into a small clearing. Straight across this she made her way, and toward the center turned again to cast a nervous glance rearward, and then she saw the thing upon her track -- a mangy, hideous hyena.

Virginia knew that men looked down upon this repulsive beast, calling him a harmless coward; but she knew too many a man had fallen prey to the enormous strength and ferocity of these same creatures. She knew their cunning and their cruelty, and that, like all other hunted beasts they were as perfectly aware when man was unarmed as was man himself.

She had heard tales of their courage too; of their attacking lions and dragging his kill from beneath the very nose of the king of beasts. And so she did not deceive herself, as have others to their sorrow, as to the cowardice or the harmlessness of this, nature's most loathsome creature. Fifty yards ahead was a low tree growing solitary in the clearing. She quickened her pace, and turning her head, saw, to her horror, that the hyena had broken into a trot and was coming straight for her. Even so, she could reach the tree; she was quite near it now. The hyena was not charging, just trotting slowly toward her. Evidently he was too sure of his prey to feel any necessity for exerting himself.

Virginia reached the tree in ample time to climb to safety, and it was with a little prayer of relief that she looked up for a hand hold upon a lower branch -- a prayer that froze upon her lips and turned to a scream of horror, startled from overwrought nerves, as she saw a great snake coiled in the branches above her head.

CHAPTER VII

When daylight broke upon the village from which Virginia had escaped it found Taylor and Kelley, shaken but sobered, preparing to set out in search of Virginia. In the jungle outside the palisade they had buried the torn remnants of what had once been Gootch, and then they gathered their men together and set forth upon the trail of the girl.

Spreading out in a great circle, two or three together, they beat the jungle in all directions. Chance led the two whites with a handful of men toward the west, and a shred of torn khaki clinging to a thorn bush put one of the natives upon her trail. After that it was easy and the party made rapid progress in the wake of the fleeing girl.

And to the west another camp was astir. Breakfast was served and disposed of, and Dick Gordon, humming "It's nice to get up in the morning," shouldered a light sporting rifle, and with his gun bearer at his heels with his express set out along the coastal trail of his safari.

The day was beautiful, Gordon was happy. Broadway held more pitfalls than the jungle. His was but a happy care free jaunt to the coast. He was already commencing to feel sorry that his quest was over and his outing past its zenith. Back to the humdrum of civilization! He shrugged disgustedly. Not an untoward occurance upon the entire trip. The monotony of New York had followed him into the wilds of Africa. He had been born, evidently, to the commonplace. Adventure shunned him.

And then, directly ahead and so close that it sounded shrill upon his ears, rose the scream of a terrified woman. Gordon leaped forward at a rapid run. In a dozen paces he broke from the jungle into a small clearing to a sight which surprised him no less than would the presence of a Numidian lion loose upon Fifth Avenue.

He saw first a dishevelled white girl clothed in torn khaki, her hair loosened and fallen about her shoulders. In her hand was a broken branch and snarling about her was a huge hyena, closing in ready to charge.

Before either the girl or the beast realized that a new factor had been precipitated into their encounter, Gordon had thrown his rifle to his shoulder and fired just as the hyena charged. With a yelp of agony the hideous creature tumbled over and over almost to the girl's feet, and as it came to rest two more bullets pinged into its carcass, finishing it forever.

Gordon had run forward, stopping only momentarily to fire, and an instant after his last shot he stood before the girl looking down at her with astonishment and incredulity written large upon his countenance. She looked up at him in equal astonishment. He saw her reel, and dropping his rifle, steadied her with his arm.

"In the name of all that is holy," he said, "who are you, and what are you doing here alone in the jungle?"

"You are Mr. Gordon?"

He nodded. "Yes, my name is Gordon; but how the -- how in the world did you know that and who are you?"

"I am Virginia Scott," she replied. She was still trembling and unstrung. It was with difficulty that she composed herself sufficiently to answer him coherently.

Gordon's eyes went wide at the disclosure of her identity.

"Miss Scott!" he exclaimed. "What brought you here? Didn't your mother get my letter telling her that I would bring her the papers from the old mission?"

"Yes," she explained, "but another saw your letter first -- Scott Taylor, my mother's cousin, and he set out after you to -- to -- oh, it is terrible, Mr. Gordon -- he has followed you to kill you."

"He was the other heir?"

Virginia nodded.

"And you have taken these frightful chances to warn me?" he asked.

"There was no other way," she replied.

He questioned her further, and bit by bit wrung from her the whole terrible story of the ordeals through which she had passed.

"And she has done all this for the sake of a stranger," he thought. "What a girl!"

He had been watching her closely as she talked, and he found it difficult to take his eyes from her face. It was a very beautiful face. Even the grime and the dirt and the scratches could not conceal that fact. "You have done a very wonderful thing, Miss Scott," he said. "A very brave, and wonderful, and foolish thing. I thank God that I found you in time. I shudder to think what your fate would have been had chance not led us together at the right moment."

As they talked another party came to the edge of the clearing upon its eastern verge -- came and halted at the sight disclosed before their eyes. It was Taylor, Kelley and their blacks. They had heard the shot and hurried forward, but cautiously; as they were sure that Virginia was not armed.

When Taylor saw the girl and Gordon together he saw the end of all his plans -- unless -- . His eyes narrowed as the suggestion forced itself upon him. Here were these two who stood alone between him and fortune. Two shots would put them from his path forever. Should either ever reach civilization again Scott Taylor would become an outcast. The story of his villainy would make him a marked man in the haunts he best loved. Never again could he return to Broadway.

Gordon's back was toward him. The girl's eyes were hidden from him by the man's broad shoulders. Taylor stepped from behind the tree that had concealed him. He took careful aim at his first victim -- the man. And at that moment Gordon shifted his position, and Virginia's horrified eyes took in the menace at his back.

It was too late to warn him. There was but a single chance to save him. There was no sign in her expression that she had discovered Taylor. He was readjusting his aim to the changed position of his target, and he was taking his time about it, too, for he could not afford to bungle or miss.

At Gordon's belt swung his revolver. Virginia was so close she could touch him by crooking an elbow. She did not have to take a step closer, and it was the work of but a second to whip the revolver from its holster, swing it up on Scott Taylor and pull the trigger. At the report Gordon wheeled in surprise toward the direction the girl had fired. He saw a white man drop a rifle and stagger out of sight behind a tree, and then the girl grasped him by the arm and drew him behind the tree beneath the branches of which they had met.

"It was Taylor," she whispered. "He had levelled his rifle at you. He would have shot you in the back, the cur."

"I thought," said Dick Gordon in a wondering voice, "that I owed you about all that a man could owe to a fellow-being; but now you have still further added to my debt."

"You owe me nothing; the obligation is still all upon the side of my mother and myself," replied Virginia. "But if you want to add a thousand-fold to that obligation I can tell you how you can do it."

"How," asked Gordon eagerly.

"By getting me and yourself out of this hideous country and back to America as quickly as it can be done."

"Good," cried Gordon. "We'll start in just a minute, but first I'm going after that human mephitis and put him where he won't shoot any more at a man's back or bother women," and calling to his men, who were now coming up, he started across the clearing in pursuit of Taylor.

That worthy, however, eluded them. Wounded in the forearm, he had scurried into the jungle, half supported, half dragged by Kelley, who, while feeling no loyalty toward his leader, shrank with terror from the thought of being left alone to the mercies of the blacks in the center of Africa.

The reward he had about given up with the sight of Gordon and the girl together, for with Gootch dead and Taylor wounded, it seemed practically hopeless to expect to prevent Gordon and Virginia returning to America. Kelley knew that he couldn't do it alone, nor would he try. He could knife a man in the back with ease, but a look at Gordon had assured him that it would not be profitable employment to attempt to get near enough to that athletic and competent looking young man to reach him with a knife. No, Kelley was through, in so far as further attempts at crime in his present surroundings were concerned.

"Get 'em back in the good ol' U.S.," he urged Taylor, "an' I'll agree to help you; but Africa -- never again!" and he raised his right hand solemnly above his head.

Taylor smiled ironically. "Yes! Get 'em back in the good old U.S.," he mimicked. "They'll go back of themselves fast enough, you boob, without any help from us, and they'll make little old U.S. so damned hot that it won't hold us. If that cat hadn't pinked me I'd stop 'em before ever they reached the coast, but," and he winced with pain, "I'm all in for a while; but by God, I'll follow them to the States and get them there; there can't anybody put anything over on me like this. They can't rob me of what's mine by right even if it isn't mine by law, and I'll show 'em."

Virginia was for giving the native village of her adventures a wide berth, but Gordon assured her that they must pass it on the trail to the coast, and that he was rather anxious to do so and interview the chief. The tone of voice in which he stated his determination filled Virginia with alarm and also made him promise that he would do nothing to arouse the wrath of the village.

But pass the village they did, and much to their surprise the first people they saw emerging from the gates to meet them were several white men. They proved to be a party of wild animal collectors coming down from an excursion toward the north. In sturdy cages they bore several young lions, a few leopards, hyenas and other specimens of the fauna of the district through which they had passed. Now they were on their way to the coast, but the stories they had heard of the wonderful black maned lion that had terrorized the village and killed a white man there the night before had determined them to stop long enough to attempt to capture the splendid beast.

Gordon and Virginia tarried with them but a few minutes, then continued their way to the coast, which they reached without incident after what was, to Gordon at least, the pleasantest journey of his life. Had it not been for the anxiety which he knew the girl's mother must be suffering on account of her mad escapade he would have found means to prolong the journey many days.

CHAPTER VIII

At the coast they found that they would have to wait a week for a steamer, and having cabled Mrs. Scott that Virginia was safe under his care, Gordon felt at liberty to rejoice that they had made reasonably good connections. It might have been worse -- chance might have brought them to the coast only a day ahead of a steamer.

Gordon, unspoiled by wealth and attentions and scheming mamas, lacked sufficient egotism to think that Virginia Scott might be attracted to him as he was to her. There had been other girls who he had known desired him, but these he had not cared for. Very soon after he had met Virginia he had realized that here at last, in the wilds of Africa, he had found the one girl, the only girl, and straight-away he had set her upon a pedestal and worshipped silently from afar.

To think that this deity might stoop to love a mortal did not occur to him, and, strange to say, he was content to love her without declaring his love -- but that was while he had her alone and all to himself. How it would be when she returned to the haunts of eligible men did not occur to him.

Very adroitly -- at least he thought it was adroitly accomplished -- he discovered from her own lips that she was not engaged, and thereafter his bliss knew no bounds. It had been difficult for Virginia to repress a smile during the ponderous strategy with which he maneuvered the information from her, and also it had been her first intimation that Richard Gordon might care for her. It troubled her, too, not a little, for Virginia Scott was not a young lady to throw her heart lightly into the keeping of the first good looking man who coveted it. That she liked Gordon immensely she would have readily admitted; but she had given no thought to a deeper interest nor but for the suggestion the young man blunderingly put into her head might such a thought have occurred to her -- at least not so soon.

But the idea, implanted, became food for considerable speculation, with the result that she now often discovered herself appraising Gordon in a most critical manner. "As though," she mused, "he were a six cylinder limousine, and I wanted to be sure that I like the upholstery -- which I do, but there's something wrong with his sparking device," and Virginia laughes softly to herself.

"What's the joke?" asked Gordon, sitting beside her on the hotel veranda.

"Oh, nothing -- just thinking," replied Virginia, evasively; but she turned her face away to hide a guilty flush, and as she did so her eyes alighted upon the head of a long column marching into the town.

"Oh, look!" she exclaimed, glad of any pretext to change the line of thought. "Who do you suppose it can be?"

Gordon looked in the direction she indicated, rose and walked to the end of the veranda, and then called back over his shoulder.

"They're the collectors. I wonder if they got their man-eater?"

Virginia was at his side now, and at her suggestion the two walked down the street to meet the incoming caravan. The collectors were delighted to see them again, and in response to Gordon's inquiry pointed to a stout cage in the middle of the long line.

"There he is," said one of them, "and he's a devil."

Gordon and the girl dropped back to have a look at the latest capture, finding a huge, black-maned lion crouching in the narrow confines of his prison. His yellow eyes glared balefully out upon them, his tail moved restlessly in angry jerks, and his bristling muzzle was wrinkled into a perpetual snarl that bared long, ugly looking fangs.

"He does look like a devil, doesn't he?" remarked Gordon.

A crowd was gathering about the cage now, and as one approached more closely than his majesty thought proper he leaped to his feet and dashed madly against the bars. Roaring loudly and clawing viciously in an attempt to reach the presumptuous mortal -- who shrank back in terror, much to the amusement of the other onlookers.

"What a beauty!" exclaimed Virginia.

Gordon was looking very closely at the lion, and instead of replying moved forward nearer the cage. The lion growled savagely, hurling himself against the bars, and then Gordon stepped quite close to him. The beast stopped suddenly and eyed the man in silence. A look, almost of human recognition, changed the expression of his face. He growled, but no longer angrily -- a growl of friendly greeting Gordon could have sworn.

"I thought as much," said the man, turning toward Virginia and one of the collectors at his back. "See that jagged scar on the inside of the forearm there?" he asked.

The collector nodded.

"This is the fellow I liberated from the pit," continued Gordon, "and he remembers me."

"Well, I shouldn't bank too strongly on his gratitude if I were you," warned the collector.

"No, I don't intend to," laughed Gordon.

Two days later Virginia Scott and Richard Gordon took passage upon a northbound steamer, and among the other passengers and cargo were the collectors and their wild beasts.

For several days after receiving his wound Taylor was down with fever; but the moment he could travel he and Kelley set off on their return to the coast, the former bent now upon carrying his felonious designs to a successful conclusion even if he had to rob and murder Gordon in the heart of New York. The man was desperate. His expedition had cost him all the money that he could beg, borrow or steal. He owed Kelley not alone the promised reward but several hundred dollars in cash that the latter had advanced toward the financing of the work. He must have money -- he must have a lot of it -- and he was determined to get it. Never in his life had Scott Taylor been so dangerous an enemy; and in this state of mind he and Kelley caught the steamer following that upon which Virginia and Gordon had sailed.

Gordon whiled away the hours of the voyage, when he could not be in Virginia's company, before the cage of the great lion. No one else could approach the beast, with the possible exception of Virginia Scott, whom the animal seemed to tolerate so long as Gordon was near. Toward all others the tawny man-eater evinced the most frightful rage; but when Gordon approached he became docile as a kitten, permitting the American to reach inside the bars and scratch his massive, wrinkled face,

At Liverpool Gordon bade farewell to his savage, jungle friend, for he and Virginia were to take a fast liner for New York, the collector following upon a slower vessel.

"Goodbye, old man," said Gordon in parting, stroking the mighty muzzle. "The chances are we'll never see each other again; but I'll never forget you -- especially as I most vividly recall you as you stood over me there in the jungle debating the question of your savage jungle ethics, while gratitude and appetite battled within your breast -- and see that you don't forget me; though you will, of course, within a month."

The lion rumbled in his throat and rubbed his head luxuriously against the bars as close to the man as he could get, and thus Gordon left him.

Within a few days the huge beast was sold to a travelling American circus, where he was presently exhibited to wondering crowds, "Ben, King of Beasts, the Man-Eating Lion from the Wilds of Central Africa." He roared and ramped and struggled for liberty for days, but at last he seemed to realize the futility of his efforts, and subsided into a sullen quiet which rendered his keepers even more apprehensive than had his open rebellion.

"He's a ugly one," commented the big Irishman, whose

special charge Ben was; "an' deep, too. He'll get some 'un yet. Yeh can't never trust these forest critters; they're all alike, only Ben he's worse."

CHAPTER IX

Mrs. Scott had met Virginia and Gordon at the dock, where, in the excitement and rejoicing of the reunion of the mother and daughter, the manila envelope and its contents were forgotten until long after Gordon had seen the two safely aboard their train for home.

Before parting with him both had urged that he visit them at an early date, and gladly indeed had Gordon promised to do so. It was not until their train had pulled out of the station that Virginia recalled the paper for which Gordon had made the long journey and risked his life.

"He must have forgotten it, too," she said; "but he'll probably discover it and mail it to you today."

Mr. Richard Gordon did not, however, discover the manila envelope for many days thereafter. It had crossed the Atlantic in one of his bags in the special care of the loyal Murphy, and that gentleman had removed it, with other papers, as was his custom, to a certain drawer in Gordon's desk where "unfinished business" reposed, awaiting the leisurely pleasure of Mr. Gordon.

But that young gentleman found upon his arrival in New York a matter of far greater interest than unanswered letters and unpaid bills. It was an urgent demand from an old school friend that he accompany the former a-motoring into Canada on a fishing expedition.

He had met this friend in the grill of one of his clubs the day he landed in New York, and fifteen minutes later had promised to leave with him early the following morning.

Mrs. Scott and Virginia waited a reasonable time, and then, hearing nothing from Gordon, the girl wrote him, and as fate would have it her letter reached New York the very day that witnessed the return of Taylor and Kelley, and the latter, sent to ascertain the whereabouts of Gordon, preceded the postman into the apartment building where Gordon's bachelor home was located by a few paces.

Turning to see who was behind him, Kelley had an inspiration born of former practice and long years of taking anything that he could get his hands on, provided it belonged to another.

"If there's anything for my friend Gordon," he said to the mail carrier, "I'll save you a trip up as I'm going up to see him now."

Unsuspicious, the carrier shuffled off a half dozen pieces of mail matter and handed them to Kelley, who resumed his way to the elevator, stuffed the letters in his pocket and a moment later rang the bell of Gordon's door. Murphy answered the summons and, thanks to a slight disguise, failed to recognize the card sharp of the trip out.

"No, sir, Mr. Gordon is not in," he replied to Kelley's inquiry. "He has gone out of town for a couple of weeks. What name, sir?"

"Oh, he doesn't know me," replied Kelley. "I'll call again after he comes home. It's just a little business matter," and he turned and departed.

Back in the flat on West One Hundred and Forty-fifth Street, Kelley handed the mail to Taylor. One by one the envelopes were steamed open and the contents read. Only the letter from Virginia was of interest or value to the conspirators.

"He's still for the paper," announced Taylor when he had finished reading Virginia's note, "and he'll go down there with it. That's the place to get him and the paper at the same time. I know the lay of the land there. We'll duck for Scottsville and lay for Mr. Butinski Gordon. Seal up those letters, Kelley, and put 'em into Gordon's mail box."

Two weeks later Dick Gordon sat once more before his desk in his apartment and attacked the accumulated correspondence in the "unfinished business" drawer at his right hand.

"Well, I'll be -- what do you know about that?" he exclaimed, as he read Virginia's letter, and then he rummaged through the mass of envelopes before him, drawing a great sigh of relief as his search finally uncovered the long manila envelope.

"Hey, Murphy!" he called. "Ring up and find out when the first train through Scottsville, Virginia, leaves."

The following day he alighted at the station of the sleepy little town, engaged a negro to drive him to The Oaks, and was presently making his dusty way in the direction of the stately Scott household.

Two minutes after he had driven off Kelley rushed breathlessly into the barroom of the tavern where Taylor was engaged in a game of cards with a marooned traveling man. Leaning close to Taylor's ear Kelley whispered; "He's come!"

"Where is he?" asked Taylor.

"Driven off toward The Oaks," replied Kelley.

"All right -- he'll keep 'til night," and Taylor resumed the pleasurable task of separating the traveling man from his expense money.

At The Oaks Gordon discovered that Mrs. Scott and Virginia were visiting friends at a nearby town.

"Dey'll be back to-morrer, Mistah Gordon," said the old colored butler, "an' Ah knows dey'll be mighty prolashus to see you-all. Dey's been expectin' you for a right smaht. Yo come right along of me, an' I'll show you yore room -- you mos' suttiny gotter stay till Miss Ruth an' Miss 'Ginia returns."

"It's might good of you," said Gordon, "and I'll do it. Let me see, you are Washington, are you not? I've heard Miss Virginia speak of you."

"Yassah, I'm Washington Scott, sah," replied the old fellow, beaming with pride and pleasure to learn that he had been the subject of 'Quality's conversation. "Yassah, Marssa Jefferson Scott's great gran' daddy bought my great gran' daddy 'bout fouah hundred yeahs ago and we been in de fambly eber since. Ah been de Gen'l's body servant evah since Ah ben a li'le shaver."

"Your people have sure been with the Scotts for some time, Washington," commented Gordon, with a smile, as he followed the old man up the grand staircase to the second floor.

Gordon's room lay at the far end of a long hall, overlooking the roof of the veranda, and a pleasant, wooded lawn at the side of the house.

The young man passed the balance of the day wandering about the grounds, chatting with the negroes, and longing for the coming of the morrow that would bring Virginia Scott. In the evening he sat upon a settee beneath a tree on the front lawn, smoking and listening to the banjoes and the singing of the negroes in their quarters down the road.

Bordering the fence grew thick shrubbery which hid the road, as it also hid from his eyes the two silent figures that crept stealthily in its shadow.

As they watched him Gordon arose, tossed his cigar aside and turned toward the house. From across the bottom lands two miles away came faintly the rumble of a train. Suddenly a shrill whistle from an engine screamed through the quiet night, almost immediately afterward followed by a dull, booming sound that seemed to shake the earth. Gordon paused and listened.

"If that wasn't a wreck," he mused, "it at least sounded mightily like it, but it probably wasn't at that. Noises always seem exaggerated at night."

For a moment Gordon stood listening, then he turned toward the house again, entered it and ascended to his room. The two figures in the shrubbery circled the grounds until they reached a point where they could see his windows. There they waited until a light appearing proclaimed that Gordon had gone to his room.

"We'll loaf around until he's asleep," whispered one of

the prowlers.

Fifteen minutes later the light in Gordon's chamber was extinguished.

"He's turned in," whispered the other prowler.

"We'll stick for a quarter of an hour longer," said the first, "an' give him a chance to get to sleep."

For a while both were silent. The quiet of the soft summer night was broken only by the cicadas, the subdued croaking of frogs in the bottoms, and strains of Southern melody from the negro quarters.

"Don't them coons never go to bed," growled Kelley querulously.

Taylor made no response. He was fidgeting uneasily. He wished the job well over. Time and again he fingered the automatic in the side pocket of his coat. Once he drew the weapon out and for the dozenth time that day removed the cartridge clip and counted the shells. "Nine of 'em and one in the chamber," he commented. "That's ten -- oh! -- " The clip had slipped from his nervous fingers and fallen to the ground. Hastily he snatched it up and slipped it back in the grip of the weapon.

"Come on!" he whispered to Kelley. "We'll sneak in up to his door and listen there -- this waitin' gets my goat."

"Mine, too," said Kelley, and the two slunk from tree to tree until they were well in the shadows of the house. Then they circled to the veranda steps, mounted and paused beside the French doors opening into the library. Taylor was in advance. He was about to enter when a telephone bell broke the silence of the interior with a brazen clanging, bursting upon their startled ears with all the terrific volume of a pounding fire gong. The two men drew back hurriedly, slinking into the deeper shadows at the end of the porch and crouching behind a swinging porch seat.

Presently a light shone in the library -- waveringly at first, and then brighter and steadier as the old butler entered with a lamp and set it upon the table. The telephone bell was still ringing intermittently. Taylor and Kelley strained their ears to catch his words, but could not.

He was talking to Virginia Scott. "We decided to come to-night instead of tomorrow," she said. "There was a wreck about half a mile from the station which delayed us -- we had to walk in from where the accident occurred. Send Jackson to town with the machine for us at once."

"Yes, Miss 'Ginia, Ah send him punctiliously," replied the old man.

A moment later he was routing Jackson out of bed and posting him off to the village. Taylor and Kelley remained in hiding, for the old butler waited out upon the veranda until he had seen the car turn into the pike and disappear in the direction of Scottsville. Then he turned slowly and entered the house, plodding upward to his room that he might dress to properly receive his returning mistress. He took the lamp with him, leaving the library lighted only by the moon which now streamed a silver shaft through the doors and windows.

When they were sure that he had gone Taylor and Kelley crept from their hiding place and entered the library, leaving the French doors wide open. At the foot of the stairs they paused, listening. Some one was moving about on the floor above. It was the butler. Fearing that he was returning to the first floor the conspirators dodged into the music room, the doorway of which was close to the bottom of the stairs.

Ben, King of Beasts, objected strenuously to being loaded upon a flat car. Although the process consisted merely of rolling his wheeled cage up an incline onto the car, he objected to every change of location which necessitated the closer proximity of hated man, and the disturbing of his royal reveries.

But loaded he was, and then came the hateful jolting and pounding of the rumbling train, the screech of whistles, the grinding of brakes, and all the other noises of a switching circus train in a railroad yard. It seemed an eternity before the long train pulled out of the village and the nerve racking discords gave place to the rhythmic rumble of the open right of way, which finally lulled the irritable beast to slumber -- a slumber that was rudely awakened by a piercing shriek of the engine's whistle, followed almost immediately by a terrific crash, and the pounding of the derailed flat over the ties for a hundred yards until at last it toppled into the ditch, hurling its cargo of terrified beasts through a barbed wire fence into a field beyond.

Ben's cage rolled over and over, one end of the top snapping a telegraph pole off short a few feet above the ground. After it had come to rest beyond the tangled wire of the demolished fence the lion lay half dazed for several minutes. Then he rose gingerly, as though expecting to discover that all his bones had been broken. He shook his giant head and rumbled out a low roar. His cage was lying on its side. What was that? Ben cocked his head upon one side and gazed incredulously at a gaping rent in front of him. The roof had been torn away by impact with the telegraph pole -- there was a great hole, barless, through which two lions might have walked abreast.

Ben approached the opening and looked out. Before him stretched an open meadowland. He raised his nose and sniffed. A little tremor of joy ran through his great frame.

For an instant he stood there, listening. He heard the shouts of approaching men mingled with the screams and roars of terrified beasts about him. Lightly he sprang through the opening in the broken cage. He was free! Men were running toward him from the rear of the train. They had not seen him yet. For an instant he hesitated as though minded to remain and wreak vengeance on the human race; then a glimpse of distant woods and the lure of the open was too much for him. In long, easy bounds he loped away across the meadowland. A shallow swale running upland from the railroad appealed to his primeval instinct for cover. It hid him effectually from the sight of the men now crowding about the derailed flat.

Dropping into a swinging stride, he moved straight upwind. All about him was the scent of cattle. He licked his chops and whined. A barbed wire fence presently barred his way. This was something new! He sniffed inquiringly at it; then he curled his lips disdainfully at the puny strands that the foolish man-creatures had thought to imprison him with, for he believed that this was a new sort of cage constructed especially to hold him.

He raised a mighty forepaw and smote it. The sharp barbs pierced his flesh, eliciting an angry growl. He raised his eyes to measure the height of the barrier. It was low, pitifully low. Still growling, Ben bounded over it. The wind now brought down to his nostrils the strong scent of sheep and cows and swine, filling him with lust for the hot blood, the dripping flesh of the warm, new kill.

Further on a Virginia rail fence loomed before him. He took it without a pause and an instant later stood in the dust of a white turnpike. Across the road was a hedge and from beyond the hedge came the mingled odors of man and herbivora. The lion lowered his head and walked through the hedge. He found himself upon a well kept lawn, dotted here and there with shrubs and trees. At the far side of the lawn rose a large white structure, gleaming in the moonlight.

Majestically the imperial beast moved across the close cropped sward -- a golden lion on a velvet rug of green. A settee lay in his path. It was something new, and all new things were to be investigated. He sniffed at it, and on the instant his whole manner changed. A nervous tremor of excitement ran through his supple body. His tail twitched and trembled. His eyes glowed brighter. A low whine broke from his savage lips.

Down went his nose to the grass. The spoor was fresh and plain -- it was the spoor of his one man-friend. Ben followed it across the lawn to the foot of the veranda steps. Here he paused, looking dubiously up at the man-made structure. It might be another trap built for his capture; but no, the man-friend was there, and it must be safe.

The lion mounted the steps, still sniffing with lowered nose. Upon the veranda a new spoor lay fresher over that of the other -- a spoor that set his tail to lashing angrily and put a hideous light into his yellow eyes -- wicked and implacable now. 'The scent led through open doors into the interior. The beast thrust his head within and surveyed the room. He saw no one, but plainly he caught the scent of those whose scent he first had learned where it mingled with the blood of his slain mate.

Treading softly, he entered the room, the thick rug beneath padded feet giving forth no sound. In the center of the library he halted. A flood of moonlight pouring through the open doorway fell full upon him, revealing him in all his majesty of savage strength and alertness.

For all he moved now he might have been a mounted specimen standing there upon the Oriental rug beneath his feet, for he was listening. A slight sound had come to those sensitive ears from out of the darkness of the music room. His yellow eyes bored straight ahead through the open doorway before him.

Taylor, hearing no further sounds from above, whispered to Kelley to follow him. Cautiously he moved toward the doorway leading into the library at the foot of the stairs. As he peered out his eyes suddenly went wide, his lower jaw fell, his knees trembled, for, standing motionless in the center of the library, he saw a huge lion.

For an instant the man was paralyzed with terror; and then the lion, giving voice to a single quick, short growl, charged. Taylor dodged back into the music room, too terrified to scream. Directly behind him was Kelley. In his mad panic of fear Taylor hurled his accomplice backward to the floor. Then he scrambled beneath a grand piano just as the lion leaped into the room. The first object that the beast's eyes encountered was the prostrate form of Kelley. For an instant the beast's attention was occupied, and Taylor took the slender advantage that was his to scurry from the room and race madly up the staircase to the second floor.

He ran straight for the closed door at the far end of the hall, the door leading into Richard Gordon's room. He scarce reached it when the lion, abandoning the grisly thing upon the music room floor, bounded from the room and up the stairway in pursuit.

CHAPTER X

Washington Scott, in the act of dressing for the return of his mistress, heard strange sounds that filtered upward from the first floor to his room upon the third. Seizing his lamp he made his way slowly downward upon his old and shaky legs. He was in the act of turning the knob of the door at the foot of the stairway that opened into the second floor balcony when he heard footsteps rushing frantically past.

Cautiously he opened the door and peered out in time to see a man dodge into Gordon's room and close the door. So quickly had the figure disappeared that the old butler had not recognized the intruder, but he was sure that it was not Mr. Gordon. He would investigate. Stumping laboriously into the hall, he turned in the direction of Gordon's room. He was just opposite the old fashioned wardrobe built into the wall near Gordon's door when the rush of strange footfalls ascending the stairway caused him to turn his eyes in that direction.

"Gord a'mighty," shrieked the old man, as his eyes fell upon the hideous visage of the wide-jawed carnivore.

It was too late to retreat to the stairway down which he had just come. He had heard the lock turn in Gordon's door. There was only the old-fashioned cupboard in the wall beside him. Not in fifty years had Washington Scott moved with such celerity as he evinced in the next quarter second. With a wrench he tore the door open -- like a youthful hurdler he vaulted into the dark closet, slamming the door to after him.

Within was a crash of broken flooring and then silence.

The lion rushed past the old man's hiding place without even pausing to investigate. He was after bigger game than a decrepit old darky.

As Taylor dashed into his room, Gordon, awakened by the noise, sprang from his bed. Taylor, knowing that the time for stealth was past and that the whole house would be aroused in an instant, drew his revolver from the side pocket of his coat and fired point blank at Gordon as the latter rose in his bed. The bullet passed through Gordon's pajama coat and pinged into the wall behind him.

Then Taylor, with a mental "nine more," pulled the trigger again. There was no responding report and Gordon was upon him. Frantically Taylor pressed the weapon to his victim's body and pulled the trigger -- futilely. In returning the clip to the automatic when it had fallen to the ground from his nervous fingers earlier in the evening he had reversed it, so that the cartridges were pointed to the rear, jamming the mechanism after the first shot had exploded the cartridge already in the chamber.

Once in Gordon's grasp, Taylor realized how hopelessly he was outclassed. The clean life of his antagonist found Taylor helpless in the other's power. Yet the man fought on desperately, for he knew that a long prison term awaited him should he be made captive now.

Around and around the room the two men struggled. Taylor beat madly at Gordon's face, but the latter sought the other's throat, striking only occasionally, and then only when a blow could be well delivered and effective.

In the hall beyond the lion had halted before the door to sniff and listen. From within came the sounds of combat and the scent of friend and foe. The great beast opened his wide jaws and roared out a thunderous challenge -- a challenge that sent Washington Scott cowering in terror to the furthermost recesses of the little closet and brought Gordon to a momentary pause of wonder in the battle he was waging for his life in the guest chamber of the Scott mansion.

But Richard Gordon had not time to give then to an investigation of the terrifying roar just without his room. He wondered, but he fought on, slowly but surely overcoming the weakening Taylor.

The lion pushed against the door with his forepaw. It did not open. He clawed at the panels, madly, thunderously. No frail wood could long withstand that mighty force. Splinters were torn away. The two men within the room heard, and one was terrified and the other wondering.

Gordon was pushing Taylor back against a table, further and further, when the latter, in a sudden and momentary burst of energy, struggled up and fought his conqueror back a step or two. Beneath their feet lay a rug, rumpled and twisted as they had passed back and forth across it. Gordon's feet caught in it as Taylor surged against him, and he fell heavily backward, striking his head against the edge of a chair.

Taylor could scarce credit the good fortune that had saved him at the eleventh hour. Gordon lay unconscious beneath him. The lion was battering the door to pieces just beyond. Behind him was an open window leading onto the roof of the veranda. Taylor half started to make a break for escape from the lion when the object of his mission rushed to his mind.

He had risked too much to abandon all now when success, such as it was, lay in his grasp. Hastily he sprang to his feet and ran to the chair where Gordon's clothes lay. As he snatched up a garment and began to run hastily through it a panel crashed in beneath the lion's powerful blows and Taylor saw the gleaming, yellow eyes glaring at him through the aperture.

With a gasp of terror the man ran his hand inside the coat, his fingers came in contact with a long manila envelope, and he knew that he had won. Stuffing the prize into his own pocket, he turned and scrambled through the window to the roof of the veranda, ran to the edge and lying upon his stomach lowered himself quickly until he hung by his hands. Then he let go and dropped to a soft landing in a clump of bushes beneath.

Almost simultaneously the last of the door fell in beneath Ben's battering, and the lion sprang into the room. For just an instant he lowered his muzzle to the face of the prostrate Gordon, sniffed, whined, and then caught Taylor's spoor and followed it through the window onto the roof.

Gordon, but momentarily stunned, sat up just in time to see the hind quarters of the lion disappearing through the window. Leaping to his feet he followed and looked out. He saw the great beast approach the spot where Taylor had dropped to the ground. For a moment the lion stood there measuring the distance -- it was too great a leap for so heavy a beast except as a last resort.

Turning quickly away, the animal trotted to the far end of the roof. Below this there was a low shed and a moment later the carnivore was slinking through the shrubbery of the Scott grounds hot upon the trail of the fleeing Taylor.

Gordon, convinced that the lion had followed Taylor, though filled with wonder not only that a savage, jungle beast should be roaming at large in peaceful Virginia, but as well that the brute should have passed him by without harming him, ran from his room, calling the servants.

The old butler, hearing his voice, answered him in trembling tones from his hiding place.

"Mistah Go'don!" he cried. "Where is he? Am he went?"

Gordon paused. The voice came apparently from the closet beside him.

"Where are you?" he asked.

"Ah's heah -- in dese heah clos'es hamper. Ah's stuck fast. If he am went please come an' hep me outen heah."

"He's 'went' all right," replied Gordon, opening the door of the closet, to find that Washington had broken through the bottom and was so tightly wedged that it required the combined efforts of them both to liberate him. Other house servants were timorously creeping down the stairs by this time, but when they found that a wild beast was prowling somewhere about, most of them promptly retreated to their rooms, where they fell to praying. A few remained to follow Gordon back to his room. A sudden fear had crept over the young man.

Taylor could have followed him for but one purpose. Had he been successful, after all, in his quest? Gordon found his coat lying on the floor, and a hasty examination revealed the fact that the precious document had been removed from it. Snatching an old fashioned muzzle loader from one of the servants, Gordon hastened down the stairs and out onto the lawn. A sullen roar down in the direction of the negroes' quarters guided him in the direction the lion had taken, and which was, Gordon felt sure, the same as that in which Taylor had fled.

The moment that Taylor had extricated himself from the bushes he ran around to the front of the house and down past the negroes' shacks, passing out onto the turnpike below them and following that in the direction of Scottsville. He did not know that the lion had followed him, imagining that the beast had remained to maul and possibly to devour Gordon. The thought, while it induced a shudder, was far from unwelcome, since it compassed the elimination of Gordon, and so, as far as Taylor knew, the only witness to his presence in the Scott home.

Behind him a silent shadow moved along his trail. In long, undulating strides the great cat stalked its prey. Taylor had passed behind the cabins of the negroes, for several of the blacks were still sitting before their doorsteps strumming on their instruments or gossiping among themselves; but the lion had caught a glimpse of the quarry, and so no longer must follow a scent. He had seen Taylor vault the fence into the turnpike, and without increasing his gait he moved straight toward him. His way led past the darkies. They had been discussing the strange sound that had come from the big house.

Broken and muffled from having issued from the interior of the house, Ben's single roar had come down to them, half drowned by the nearer noise of their banjoes. One had thought that it might have been the wail of a sick cow, another had attributed it to "Marse Jeffe-son Scott's ghos'."

"It soun' to me like one a dem lines Ah done seen at de

cucus las' fall," ventured a tall, lanky black.

"Wow!" exclaimed a woman. "Don' you talk no lines aroun' heah or Ah cain't sleep a wink tonight for thinkin' 'bout 'em."

"Sho, honey," exclaimed the first speaker. "Yo don' need worry none 'bout no lines whiles Ah'm 'roun'. Ah eats 'em alive, Ah does. Dey ain' nuffing to be afeared of. Why, Ah seen a white man go right in a cage wif ten of 'em, an' he takes a big whip an' he lashes dem lines jes same 's if dey was mules. Jes laik dis," and the darkey seized his banjo by the neck and struck out ferociously at imaginary lions.

Swinging around to chastise one directly behind him, his eyes fell upon the huge head and glittering eyes of Ben, just protruding from about the corner of the cabin a few paces away. For one brief, horrified, instant the black man stood petrified with terror. His mouth flew agape, his eyes started from his head, and then, with a blood curdling shriek, he dove head foremost for the doorway of the cabin.

The sudden cessation of his valiant lion taming had attracted the attention of the others to the direction his eyes had taken. They, too, saw Ben but an instant after their fellow had discovered him.

Their screams mingled with his, as did their arms and legs and bodies, as the half dozen negroes launched themselves simultaneously for the same small doorway. Scrambling, clawing, screaming, fighting, they battled for the safety of the interior until they became so tightly wedged in the narrow aperture that they could make no further progress.

Ben, surprised into a sudden stop at the first sight of them, now approached majestically, for his way led by their threshhold. He paused a moment to sniff at the wildly kicking legs of the tangled mass. The discord of their fear-laden voices must have grated upon his nerves, for, with his mouth close to them, he gave vent to a single, mighty roar, and then passed on.

The blacks, paralysed by terror, became rigid and silent as death; nor did they move again until long after the great beast had passed out of sight.

Along the road from Scottsville purred the big Scott car, bearing Mrs. Scott and Virginia from the station to The Oaks. A quarter of a mile below the negroes' quarters the car came to a stop.

"What's the matter, Jackson?" asked Virginia.

"Ah dunno, Miss," replied the chauffeur, getting down from his seat and raising one side of the bonnet. For a moment he fussed about between the engine and the control board, trying first the starter and then the horn.

"Ah guess we-all blowed a fuse," he announced presently.

"Have you others, or must we walk the rest of the way?" inquired Mrs. Scott.

"Oh, yasam, Ah got some right year," and he raised the cushion from the driver's seat and thrust his hand into the box beneath. For a moment he fumbled about in search of an extra fuse plug.

"Who's that coming down the road?" asked Virginia.

Mrs. Scott and the chauffeur both looked up. They saw a man, running now, directly in the middle of the road and coming in the direction of the machine. An instant later, another figure bounded into sight behind the man. Mechanically the chauffeur, while he watched the approaching man, had clipped the new fuse plug into place -- the car was ready to run again, but at sight of the lion the black lost his head completely, uttered a wild yell of dismay, and bolted for the opposite side of the road, vaulted the fence and disappeared.

Mrs. Scott and her daughter sat as though turned to stone as they watched the frantic efforts of the man to outdistance the grim beast now rapidly closing up to him.

Directly in the full glare of the headlights, not a dozen paces from the car, the lion overtook his prey. With a savage roar and a mighty leap he sprang full upon Taylor's back, hurling him to the ground.

Virginia Scott gasped in dismay. In the man's hand was a revolver, and as he fell he rolled upon his back and, placing the muzzle against the lion's breast, pulled the trigger; but again the jammed weapon failed to work, which was as well, for it would have but inflamed the rage of the maddened beast without incapacitating him.

For an instant the lion stood over his fallen enemy. He raised his head, glaring straight into the brilliant lights of the automobile. Fascinated with the horror of it, the two women watched. They saw Taylor struggling futilely now beneath the huge paw that rested upon his breast. The man's nerve was gone. He whimpered and screamed like a terrified puppy.

"God!" whispered Virginia. "It's Scott."

Her mother but shuddered and drew closer to her.

Aggravated by the struggles and the noise of his prey, Ben lowered his head. His distended jaws were close to Taylor's face, his yellow eyes glared into the fear-mad orbs of the man, from his deep chest there rumbled a thunderous roar, then his jaws closed like a huge steel trap, and Scott Taylor ceased to be.

Mrs. Scott gave a short, involuntary scream and buried her face in her hands. Attracted by the sound, the lion raised his dripping jaws and again eyed the glaring lights. Beyond them he could see nothing; but from beyond them had come the sound of a human cry.

Virginia watched the beast intently. Should she and her mother leave the machine and attempt to escape, or were they safer where they were? The lion could easily track them should he care to do so after they had left the car. On the other hand, the strange and unusual vehicle might be sufficient safeguard in itself to keep off a nervous jungle beast.

While she was pondering these questions Ben continued to gaze steadily toward them. Finally he lowered his head to his prey once more, sniffed at it a moment, then seized the body by the shoulder and dragged it a few paces to one side of the road. Here the lion was out of the direct glare of the headlights. Again he looked toward the car. Now he could see it. He cocked his head upon one side and rumbled in his throat. He did not like the looks of this strange thing. What was it? He would investigate.

Abandoning Taylor's body, he paced slowly forward toward the car. Mrs. Scott shrank closer to Virginia, too terrified by this time to scream. The girl kept her wits, but still was at a loss as to what move to make or as to whether she could make any that would be better than remaining rigidly quiet under the lion's investigation.

The beast was beside the car now. Leisurely, he placed a forepaw on the running board and raised himself until his giant head topped the side of the tonneau. Slowly he intruded his wrinkled muzzle until his nose brushed Virginia's skirt.

Mrs. Scott could bear the strain no longer. With a low moan she fainted. Now there was no escape for Virginia. The girl steeled herself to meet the end bravely.

The great cat was sniffing at her skirt and growling hideously.

CHAPTER XI

With the old musket in his hands Richard Gordon ran rapidly toward the negroes' quarters, from whence he had heard the lion's roar. Here he found the terrified blacks still fast in the doorway, making no move to extricate themselves. He shouted to them, asking which way the lion had gone. Hearing a white man's voice, the pile disentangled itself and presently one was sufficiently recovered from his terror to inform Gordon that they did not know which way the lion had gone, for the simple reason that, all having their eyes shut, they had not known that he had departed at all until they had heard Gordon's voice.

But from the window of an adjoining cabin, a frightened, nightcapped head was thrust timorously, and a trembling voice issuing from shaking lips vouchsafed the information that their owner had seen the lion leap the fence into the turnpike and disappear in the direction of town.

Without waiting to listen to the harrowing details which now broke from a half dozen pairs of lips, Gordon ran to the fence, vaulted it and started down the road at a rapid trot. He had gone but a short distance when the lion's roar again sounded, this time straight ahead and at no great distance.

The man, bent solely on overtaking Taylor and wresting the manila envelope from him, went warily now that he might avoid the lion, for he was too experienced a big game hunter to place any reliance on the archaic weapon he carried. It would do to bring Taylor to a stand, but for the lion it was scarce adequate, though in the day of its prime men had hunted the king of beasts with its counterpart -- and some of them had returned to narrate their exploits.

A turn in the road revealed the headlights of an automobile and set Gordon to wondering. A little closer and he saw a crumpled something lying at the side of the road. Gordon crept to the shadow of the bushes that lined the fence. The moon was bright, the shadows dense. He moved cautiously forward. The thing by the roadside was the body of a man. It must be Taylor's. But where was the lion?

Then he saw him, standing with his forefeet upon the running board of the machine and his head thrust inside the car. A sudden whimpering from the other side of the bushes where he crouched attracted Gordon's attention. It sounded like a man crying.

"Who is that?" whispered the young New Yorker.

"Oh, Lawd!" exclaimed a voice from beyond the foliage. "Is dat you, Mistah Go'don? Has de line aten 'em all up?"

"Eaten whom?" cried Gordon, half recognizing the voice of the Scott chauffeur.

"Mis' Scott and Miss Virginia -- deyse in de cah, an' he's eaten of 'em up."

With a cry that was half curse and half moan Dick Gordon sprang to his feet and without further attempt at stealth, bounded toward the automobile. As he ran he shouted aloud to attract the lion's attention. The beast withdrew his head from the tonneau and eyed the intruder. Gordon halted a dozen paces from him, still calling aloud in the hope of inducing the beast to leave the machine and come toward him.

With dignity the king of beasts lowered his forepaws to the ground and turned about to face the man.

"Are you there, Virginia," cried Gordon. "Are you unhurt?"

"I'm here," she replied. "He has not touched us yet; but you! Oh, Dick, be careful or he'll get you as he did Scott."

"Dick!" She had never used his first name before, and even now in the midst of danger -- in the face of death -- his heart leaped in glad response to the love and solicitude in her dear voice.

"Can you drive?" he cried.

"Yes, I can drive," she replied.

"Then climb over and drive," he commanded. "Drive anywhere, as fast as you can, but, for the love of heaven, get out of here."

"But you?"

"Never mind me, I'm armed," and he raised the futile old relic of Revolutionary days to his shoulder.

The girl, realizing that her mother's safety lay in her hands and that neither could help Gordon, clambered over into the driver's seat and started the engine. With the whir of the starter Ben wheeled about with a low snarl, but in the instant the girl drew the speed lever back into low, pressed down on the accelerator, let in the clutch, and the car shot forward.

Still the lion seemed in doubt. He took a few steps toward the car, which he could easily reach in a single bound. He paid no attention now to Gordon, and the latter, fearing that the beast might spring upon the passing car, burned his bridges behind him and did the one thing that occured to him to divert the brute's attention.

In the few moments that he had watched the animal he had become half convinced that the lion was his former friend of the jungle and the steamer. He could not be sure, but the magnificent proportions and the massive head were the same. Even so he could scarce hope that the savage beast, maddened by the taste of human blood and rendered nervous by all through which it had passed during the brief interval since it had entered the Scott home, would recall him or its former friendliness toward him.

But this was all apart from the main issue -- the saving of Virginia and her mother from those rending fangs. The man had held his musket levelled for a moment on the lion's shoulder, and then, with an exclamation of disgust, had tossed it aside. He would pit all against the chance that the lion was Ben, and so, shouting loudly, he ran straight for the grim beast.

Glancing behind him the lion saw the man approaching rapidly. He paused, and the car, shooting into second and high, sped beyond his reach. Then the lion turned to face Gordon, and Gordon, seeing that the occupants of the car were beyond harm, halted in his tracks.

For seconds that seemed hours to the man the two stood facing each other. It was the lion who moved first. He advanced slowly and deliberately. The moonlight flooded him. Gordon's eyes dropped to the great forearm, searching for the jagged scar that might at least give him some faint hope. Nor did he look in vain, for there, plain in the moonlight, was the serrated mark that told him that the beast was Ben.

Almost simultaneously with his discovery came a loud hail from the field below the road. The lion halted at the sound and both he and Gordon turned their eyes in the direction of the voice. They saw three men, armed with rifles. They were the circus owner and the two keepers. "Stand where you are," shouted the owner. "That beast is a devil. Don't move and we can get him before he charges."

At the same instant the three raised their guns and took aim at the splendid statue standing rigid in the moonlight.

It has been said that Mr. Richard Gordon was a creature of impulse, nor did his next act belie his reputation. Twice, Ben, King of Beasts, had spared his life. Tonight he had captured and punished the scoundrel, who would have killed Gordon but for the timely appearance of the lion. The man's debt to the beast was one that Richard Gordon could not, in honor, ignore.

With a cry of "Don't shoot!" he leaped toward the lion, placing himself between the animal and the rifles. He was so close that he could touch the tawny shoulder. Ben lowered his head and sniffed Gordon's clothing. A little whine escaped the savage lips. Gordon put forth his hand and laid it on the shaggy mane and the lion pressed close against his side, rubbing his head along the man's leg.

The astonished owner and keepers lowered their rifles and approached a trifle nearer, though still keeping a safe distance.

"For the love o'Mike," exclaimed one of them. "Whadya know about that!"

"Who in the name of Phineas T. Barnum are you, anyway?" asked the owner.

"I'm a friend of Ben's," Gordon laughed back, and then, briefly, he told them of his past acquaintance with the animal.

"Want to sell him?" he asked finally.

"He's a very valuable animal," commented the owner, shrewdly, sensing a profitable deal, but Gordon interrupted him.

"All right," he said. "I'll just let him go and you can come and get your valuable animal."

The owner laughed. "You got me, I guess," he said. "What'll you give me for him?"

"Just what you paid for him, plus transportation charges to the New York Zoo -- I'm going to present him to the city."

"It's a go," said the owner. "We couldn't never take him alive without your help."

"Throw me your ropes," commanded Gordon. "I'll put them on him and then we'll lead him up the road to the house of a friend of mine until you can get his cage over here."

Without difficulty he adjusted two ropes about Ben's neck, tossed an end of each to a keeper, patted the lion on the head, and turned his attention to the body of Taylor beside the road. His first thought was of the manila envelope and this he quickly found and transferred to his own pocket. Then he sought for signs of life, but a careful examination revealed the fact that Taylor was dead.

"Come along," he said, and taking his place at Ben's shoulder he led the way up the road to the Scott lawn.

At sight of the lion entering the grounds the servants who were gathered about the veranda steps fled to the interior of the house, leaving Mrs. Scott and Virginia alone. The girl saw with relief that Gordon was unharmed and that the lion had been secured, and running down the steps she hastened forward to meet the young man.

Taking both hands in hers as he stepped forward from the lion, she tried to thank him, but her voice choked and the words would not come. He pressed her hands tightly in his and led her onto the veranda, where Mrs. Scott awaited them.

"At last," he said, and handed her the manila envelope. She took it in nervous fingers as she thanked him for all that he had risked and done for her and here she mechanically tore the wrapper open. In the brilliant moonlight even fine print might easily have been read; and as she withdrew the contents of the envelope she gave a little exclamation of surprise as her eyes fell upon the sheaf of papers within.

"Why, what are these?" she exclaimed, running quickly through them.

Gordon and Virginia stepped to her side.

"Let us go into the library," said Mrs. Scott. "I do not find the marriage certificate here."

Together the three stepped into the house. Outside the keepers, each having taken a turn about a tree with his rope, waited for the return of the owner, who had gone back to the wreck for a team of horses and a wheeled cage for Ben. The lion, nervous now that Gordon had left him, growled continuously.

Inside, Virginia, Mrs. Scott and Gordon leaned over the long library table, upon which were spread the contents of manila envelope, under the strong light of a reading lamp. Carefully Gordon examined each paper.

"Why these are stock certificates of considerable value," he said. "There is no marriage certificate here. But our quest was not entirely in vain. These certificates, probably of no great value when they were purchased years ago, now represent a fortune. There are several industrials alone that are worth today more than a hundred times what they must have sold for when these were issued. They are in your father's name, Mrs. Scott."

"Yes, but the marriage certificate," responded the older woman. "What can have become of it? I so wanted it, after the unjust accusation of Scott Taylor."

Gordon shook his head.

"It is a mystery," he said. "I brought every article that remained in the strong box beneath the hearth. There was no evidence that another had been there before us -- had there he would have removed these also, and the few pieces of jewelry that were hidden there."

"Well," said Mrs. Scott, with a sigh, "of course now it is just a sentiment, I suppose, for whether Virginia is allowed the property of her grandfather or not she will be independently wealthy in possession of these stocks alone."

Just then a startled cry resounded through the house. It came from the music room behind them, and as they turned in that direction they beheld Washington Scott, ashy blue from fright, rush trembling into the library from the music room.

"Oh, Lordy, Miss Ruth!" he cried. "Der's a daid man in de music room -- wif his face all chawed off'n him. Oh, Lordy!"

Gordon stepped quickly to the door of the music room, and there on the floor revealed by the light from the library lamp that filtered into the room, lay a sight that caused him to turn and warn back Virginia, who was following close upon his heels.

"Ben has been here ahead of us," he explained. "This must be one of Taylor's companions -- Kelley probably, though his face is not recognizable now. Washington," he continued, turning to the shaking black, "bring me a sheet -- I'll cover this -- and then you might telephone to town for the Coroner and an undertaker."

When Washington had fulfilled his missions he clung closely about the family, evidently terrified at the thought of going to other parts of the house for fear he might stumble upon others of Ben's victims.

"Let's go upstairs and see where he broke down the door of your room, Dick," suggested Virginia, and together, Washington bringing up the rear, they all filed up the stairway. The splintered door filled the two women with amazement, so complete had been its destruction, and then Washington, wishing to share some of the glory of the adventure, called their attention to his hiding place.

"Ah done broke through de bottom," he giggled nervously.

Virginia, taking a lamp from the old servant's hand,

peered into the cupboard.

"Why, there's quite an opening beneath this," she remarked, and reflecting the lamp's rays downward with her palm she looked into the black hole beneath the splintered flooring. A moment later she had thrust her hand and arm deep into the aperture, and when she withdrew them she held a shiny, black box.

"What do you suppose this is doing here?" she asked.

"It must have been a secret hiding place of your grandfather's for valuables," suggested her mother.

"Let's have a look at the contents then," cried the girl, but the box would not open to her efforts.

She handed it to Gordon.

"See if you can open it," she said.

Gordon examined it for a moment.

"It's locked -- we'll have to pry it open," he said. "Get a screw driver, please, Washington, and we'll go down to the library again and investigate Miss Virginia's find."

By the time Washington had located a screw driver the others had gathered once more about the library table, the little black box the center of attraction. With the tool Gordon quickly pried the lid open, disclosing a number of papers within. These he handed immediately to Mrs. Scott, who ran through them quickly. "Why, here's your grandfather's missing will, Virginia," she cried, handing a legal appearing document to the girl.

"Sure enough," exclaimed the latter, glancing through it. "And it is just as Judge Sperry said, he has left everything to me, with the exception of the income from certain property which is to be yours, mother, during the balance of your life."

"What is in that manila envelope?" asked Gordon. "It bears a startling resemblance to one that I carried from Central Africa to Central Virginia."

Virginia picked up the envelope in question and opened it. Her voice rounded into a little "Oh!" of delighted surprise.

"Why, mother!" she cried. "Here it is right here. Here it has been all the time, right under our noses, and we never knew it and sent Dick almost to his death looking for it in Africa," and she handed the much sought for and elusive marriage certificate to her mother.

A hand long dead had placed it in that envelope, and in the hurry of Robert Gordon's departure from the mission had mistaken the manila envelope containing it for another identically like it which held the valuable stock certificates that Reverend Sangamon Morton had wished to send to his son-in-law's father for safe-keeping.

"My mission was not entirely fruitless, however," remarked Gordon, gazing smilingly into Virginia's eyes.

"Indeed it was not," cried Mrs. Scott, not catching the double meaning of his words. "Had it not been for you Ben would have died in the pit the natives dug for him. Washington would not have had to clamber into the cupboard to escape him, and the secret of the false bottom and the little box might have gone undiscovered for generations. In reality it is to you we owe the finding of the stock certificates -- and, candidly I am most interested in the marriage certificate; but then I am a sentimental old woman," and she laughed gently.

"I too am interested in a marriage certificate," remarked Gordon, and again he looked into Virginia's eyes, and again she looked away.

A few minutes later the young people strolled out onto the lawn together to have a look at Ben. The great lion whined a delighted welcome as he caught sight of Gordon. The girl he permitted to approach him, too. On either side of the massive head the two stood, their fingers twined in the black mane. Across the savage head their eyes met, and held.

"I love you," said Mr. Richard Gordon, for the keepers were drowsing at their posts.

Virginia cast a quick glance in their direction. Neither was looking. She leaned forward toward the man, and their lips met above the fierce and loyal head of Ben, King of Beasts.

And if you do not believe their story, just go to the Zoo the next time you are in New York, and look for a great, black maned lion with a scar upon one of his mighty fore-arms.

TO THE READER

If you enjoyed this book, you will be glad to know that there are many others just as well written, just as interesting, to be had in the Fiction House Press Library.

You will find the Fiction House Press Library online at

www.FictionHousePress.com

www.ingramcontent.com/pod-product-compliance
Lightning Source LLC
LaVergne TN
LVHW091051080826
845145LV00002B/708

9781647205850